# Murder Makes Waves

# Murder
# Makes
# Waves

## Anne George

AVON BOOKS  NEW YORK

For Jean and Joe
with thanks for The Little Mermaid,
King Tut, and The Top of the Mark.

AVON BOOKS
A division of
The Hearst Corporation
1350 Avenue of the Americas
New York, New York 10019

Copyright © 1997 by Anne George
Interior design by Kellan Peck
Visit our website at **http://AvonBooks.com**
ISBN: 0-380-97527-0

Library of Congress Cataloging in Publication Data:
George, Anne.
  Murder makes waves / Anne George.
    p.  cm.
  I. Title.
PS3557.E469M87   1997                                    96-45549
813'.54—dc21                                             CIP

First Avon Books Printing: August 1997

AVON TRADEMARK REG. U.S. PAT. OFF. AND IN OTHER COUNTRIES, MARCA REGISTRADA, HECHO EN U.S.A.

Printed in the U.S.A.

FIRST EDITION

QPM   10  9  8  7  6  5  4  3  2  1

3 6009 00016 2122

# Chapter

# 1

"**S**he looks good, doesn't she, Patricia Anne, in spite of being dead," my sister, Mary Alice, whispered.

"Shhh," I answered. But Sister is not easily shushed.

"Don't you hate it when they give dead people those fakey smiles? You know. Stuffing their cheeks like Marlon Brando. Couldn't say a word if they had to."

The lady in front of us turned around. "Shhh."

"Sorry," I murmured. And to Mary Alice, "Shhh" again, accompanied this time by a small nudge with my elbow.

The gray casket was blanketed in a simple arrangement of spring flowers and greenery. It loomed large in the small stone chapel. There was no music to comfort the mourners, though the stillness was broken by an occasional muffled sob. In the front row, the widower, his young face frozen, sat holding the hands of his two little girls.

And then a stir as Father Patrick O'Reilly entered through

1

a side door and took his place at the altar, directly above the casket. In the dim light, for no sun shone through the windows this day, his white robe seemed blue. He held out his arms in supplication.

"My friends, our sympathy is extended to the family of Sarah Lane Goodall. She was a very special presence on this earth and she will be missed. We welcome you to this service in her memory. May we pray."

Every head in the chapel was bowed. The little girls on the front row leaned closer to their father.

"Lord Jesus, our Redeemer, You willingly gave Yourself up to death so that all people might be saved and pass from death into a new life."

Beside me, Mary Alice began to sniffle.

"Listen to our prayers, look with love on Your people who mourn for their dead sister. Lord Jesus, You alone are holy and compassionate: forgive our sister her sins."

"She didn't do anything that bad!" Mary Alice whispered loudly.

"Shut up!" I whispered back.

"Do not let our sister be parted from You, but by Your glorious power give her light, joy, and peace in heaven where You live forever and ever. Amen."

Mary Alice sobbed loudly into a Kleenex. "It was just that one time and her husband wasn't paying her any attention. Ignoring her."

The woman in front of us turned around again. I thought she was going to tell Sister to hush again. Instead she said, "I'm glad the priest got there in time to hear her confession. Maybe she'll still make it into heaven."

"I wonder how much repenting it takes," Mary Alice said.

"Shhh," came from all directions.

Mary Alice looked over her shoulder. "Well, it's something some people need to know."

"Y'all shut up," I said to the two. "You're disturbing everybody in the theater." I handed the popcorn to Mary Alice. "Here."

On the screen, ghosts pushed their way between the mourners. For a moment I was confused, then I remembered they were characters who had died during the earlier part of the movie. Sort of like *Our Town*, I realized, minus the umbrellas.

The camera panned on the guilty man as he sneaked into the back of the church. His shifty eyes, slicked back hair, and bow tie were a dead giveaway.

"Looka there, Patricia Anne." Mary Alice poked me in the arm. "You'd think he'd be ashamed to show his face."

"He'll get his comeuppance," the woman in front assured us.

"Shhh," the people around us again demanded.

I'd had enough distractions. I spotted an aisle seat several rows back and moved while Father O'Reilly was intoning, "Hail! Holy Queen, Mother of mercy, our life, our sweetness, and our hope. To you do we cry, poor banished children of Eve."

Unfortunately, Mary Alice realized the seat beside her was empty. "Mouse?" she whispered my nickname loudly.

"Mouse!" the woman in front squealed.

"Mouse!" There was a lot of shuffling for belongings then a general exodus for the doors. In the commotion, I almost missed seeing the ghosts usher the villain from the chapel for his comeuppance, which, as far as I could tell, consisted of him being ushered to hell by some black goblins. A religiously eclectic movie, to say the least.

"Now that was some movie," Mary Alice said when the lights came on in the nearly empty theater, and she had come up the aisle to meet me. "I swear, though, I don't think I've ever seen so much talking—then all that coming and going. Somebody ought to complain to the manager."

"Let's go get some frozen yogurt," I suggested quickly. The theater manager's office was probably already filled with disgruntled patrons complaining about rodents.

"Okay. Chocolate and vanilla swirl, though. Last time you talked me into getting apricot that tasted like figs. Yuck. I can't even imagine how they got apricot yogurt to taste like figs."

"They were tropical apricots," I said. "Maybe they are supposed to taste like figs." I followed Mary Alice through the lobby and down the street, drafting like a race car. My sister is six feet tall and admits to weighing 250. I'm almost five-one and weigh 105. At some point in the sixty years we have been sisters, I latched on to the theory of aerodynamics, which simplifies my keeping up with her.

"Shouldn't make any difference. They're always doing apricots that way, though. Like they can't quite get them right. Remember that lipstick I bought a couple of weeks ago called Apricot Splendour? Turned out pink as a boiled shrimp in spite of the fancy way they put the $u$ in splendor. You want it? It's too light for me."

"Sure. Pass it along."

Mary Alice opened the door of Yogurt, Please, and cool air rushed out to greet us. It was the first week of June, but in Alabama, that's summer. The thermometer in front of the bank across the street read eighty-nine.

"Get us a table," she said. "I'll get the yogurt."

"This is my treat. You got the movie."

"Don't be silly. Will Alec will pay for this one."

We grinned at each other. Will Alec Sullivan was her first husband, the one with, I believe, all the Coca Cola stock. Sister has been married three times and widowed three times. All three husbands were rich, twenty-eight years older than she was, and adored her.

"Let him pay," I agreed.

I found a table at the back of the shop and sat down with the sense of unreality one has coming from a movie in the afternoon. I glanced at my watch. Three o'clock. My husband, Fred, wouldn't be home until six. I'd have plenty of time to stop by the Piggly Wiggly and pick up something. Maybe a barbecued chicken and a salad.

I was making a mental grocery list when Sister handed me my yogurt and pulled out the chair across from me.

"Week after next is my sixty-fourth birthday," she said. "I thought I ought to tell you."

I dipped my spoon into the yogurt. "Okay."

"Everybody thinks I'm going to be sixty-six."

"Including the Bureau of Statistics." I tasted the creamy confection. "Ummm."

"That means that next month instead of being sixty-one, you'll be fifty-nine. Won't that be nice?"

"No. It means I'll have to go back to teaching. I couldn't retire until I was sixty." I turned the plastic spoon upside down and licked it. "What's this about? You'll be sixty-six and I'll be sixty-one. So what?"

"So I've decided not to be sixty-six."

"Okay. Let me know when we get to be twins."

The ice cream chair squealed as Mary Alice sat down. "Don't be a smartass. I've decided I'm not going to be eighty years old when the twins start college."

I stirred the chocolate around in my yogurt and did some quick arithmetic. The twins, Fay and May, are Mary Alice's two-year-old granddaughters. "You won't be," I said happily. "You'll be eighty-two." I moved my legs quickly. Sister has always been a kicker.

"I have decided I'll be seventy. Or sixty-nine. That's a normal age for grandparents of college kids." She examined her plastic spoon. "You know, I've never figured out why they make these spoons so deep. You always have to stick your tongue way down in them or wait until the yogurt melts and sip it like soup. You're going to have the same problem, you know."

Since I've been Mary Alice's sister for so long, the jump in topic to the plastic spoon didn't confuse me at all. The problem she was talking about was that, with the exception of my son Alan, our kids were taking their own sweet time having kids of their own.

So I repeated the obvious lie. "Age is all in your mind."

"Get real." Sister stirred her yogurt thoughtfully.

I decided to change the subject. "Remember when we didn't know what yogurt was? Never even heard of it?"

"Granddaddy used to eat clabber with sugar and cinnamon on it. Same thing."

"Yogurt sounds better than clabber."

"No, it doesn't. Yogurt's an ugly name."

So much for that conversation. I glanced over at Sister and the light dawned.

"It's a man. You've met a younger man."

Sister smiled sheepishly.

"Who is he and how much younger?" I had to speak loudly because a group of teenagers, stylishly dressed in tatters, had come into the shop and were yelling out orders.

"His name is Berry West."

"Barry?"

"Berry. Like straw. And he's about sixty."

Sixty? I grinned.

"What?" Mary Alice said. "What are you grinning about?"

"I thought you were going to say forty-something. What's the problem?"

"I'm used to older men."

"That's the truth. How old is your boyfriend Buddy Johnson? Ninety? Has he recovered from your hot tub yet?"

"He's fine."

A young man in a Yogurt, Please maroon shirt with a yellow collar approached our table. "Hey, Mrs. Hollowell. How are you?"

Fortunately, the name Terry Bates was embroidered on his pocket, as well as the information that he was a Yogurt, Please assistant manager. Multiply 150 students each year by thirty years, and a teacher is grateful for anything that jogs the memory.

"Hey, Terry," I said. "How are you?"

"Fine, Mrs. Hollowell. It's good to see you."

"You, too, Terry." It was true. A younger Terry Bates was emerging from the mist of memory. Back row, second from the left. Quiet.

He put three dollars on the table. "This one's on me."

"Why, how nice, Terry. Thank you."

"Thank you, Mrs. Hollowell."

I watched him walk away, through the group of teenagers, back behind the counter. I love you, Terry. I love every one of you. Why did I quit teaching?

Mary Alice put the three bills in her purse. "You quit because you knew 'Beowulf' by heart."

Had I asked the question aloud? And had I really given that as my reason?

Then Sister said, "He's in real estate."

"Who is?"

"Berry West, Mouse. He's in real estate development. You

made me tell you his name, so don't you want to know about him?"

"Absolutely. Where did you meet him?"

"At a party at the museum. How come you and Fred never come to those parties?"

"We're not invited."

"Really? Well, anyway, this was a wine tasting party and you're allergic to alcohol so you didn't miss anything. But something just told me to wear my black dress without a back. You know how those little voices just come to me sometimes? This one said, 'Mary Alice, wear your black dress without a back.' "

I pushed my empty cup away. "Was it male or female?"

"Was what male or female?"

"The voice."

Mary Alice scowled at me. "Do you want to hear this or not? It's really very romantic."

"I want to hear it."

"Well, there I was at the museum in my black, backless dress talking to Gertrude Stacy and I heard this man's voice say, 'You have the loveliest back I've ever seen,' and I turned around and saw this handsome man—I mean an Adonis, Mouse—walking away, and I thought he might have been talking to someone else though Gertrude said no, it was me he was talking to. So in a few minutes, I'm getting one of those little quiches you can buy frozen at Sam's, and I hear, 'You have four dimples in your back.' And it was him. Berry. We're going out to dinner tonight."

"Four dimples in your back?"

Mary Alice beamed. "Isn't that romantic?"

Fortunately, no answer was expected.

"He's bound to know I'm older than he is, though." Sister put her empty cup in mine and crumpled up her napkin.

"So what?" I said. "You're an interesting woman to talk to and you look great. I love the color of your hair." This was a new role for me, building up Sister's confidence. Berry must be an unusual man.

"It's Marigold. You really ought to try it. Get rid of that gray."

"You're right. I should get rid of my gray." I'd gone too far. Sister flipped her yogurt spoon at me. Luckily, it was empty.

The crowd of teenagers left as loudly as they had arrived, torn shirts and jeans flapping.

"How come this Berry guy's available?" I asked in the sudden quiet.

"Pure luck. His wife died last year."

I looked at Sister to see if she was serious. She was.

"What?" she asked when I frowned. "What?"

"It wasn't very lucky for his wife."

"It might have been. You don't know."

There was no way to answer that. I pushed my chair back and announced that I had to go home.

"To fix Fred's supper?"

"Why not?"

Mary Alice followed me from the shop and across the street to the parking lot. "You two need a break from each other."

"Nope." I unlocked the door of my '87 Cutlass Cierra. Heat rolled out to meet me. "We're just catching on to this marriage thing."

"Dear Lord!"

"Call me in the morning. And thanks for the movie."

Sister nodded and headed toward her car, a new black Jaguar; I headed home happily to Fred.

*   *   *

Birmingham is a lovely city, never more lovely than in June when it becomes what people envision when the word *South* is mentioned. If spring is a riot of colors, early summer is a riot of smells. Gardenia bushes are so laden with blooms their branches brush the ground; magnolias are everywhere. Mix in the tea olive bushes and the honeysuckle vines on every fence and you have a heady mixture, one that makes a porch and a swing a thing of joy after dark.

Fred and I live in a neighborhood where most of the houses were built in the 1920s and 1930s, many of them with stucco exteriors. It's a quiet neighborhood with sidewalks and big trees, convenient to everything. It was, and still is, a good place to raise a family.

I left the Piggly Wiggly with a barbecued chicken and with some peaches, the first of the year, and headed down the shady streets. To my right, atop Red Mountain, the statue of Vulcan, the largest iron statue in the world, gleamed in the summer sun. Actually, Vulcan was mooning me, since he faces downtown Birmingham and I was in the valley behind him. His big iron rear end is such a familiar sight, that I usually don't notice it. Today, though, there were scaffolds hanging from the statue. Surely, I thought, they weren't going to actually extend the old boy's apron around to cover his prodigious backside as they had been talking about doing for years. Surely they were just patching some rusty places. I tried to remember if a petition had been tacked on the bulletin board recently at the local Quik-Mart to be signed by people offended by the big bare butt. That happens fairly frequently. But I didn't remember having seen one.

My neighbor, Mitzi Phizer, was in her yard dead-heading a huge gardenia bush. When I parked my car, I walked over to ask if she had heard anything about Vulcan. She hadn't.

"It's got to be repair work, though. They'd be crazy to cover him up. It would be like the folks in Copenhagen putting a bra on The Little Mermaid."

Comparing the statue of Vulcan to The Little Mermaid was quite a leap of artistic imagination, but I knew what Mitzi meant.

I grinned. "He just wouldn't be as much fun with clothes on, would he?"

"That's the way life is, Patricia Anne. I keep having to remind Arthur."

"Surely you jest."

We smiled at each other in the companionable way of friends who have lived next to each other for almost forty years. We had helped each other through births, deaths, miscarriages, in-laws, children, grandchildren.

Mitzi nodded toward my groceries. "The Piggly Wiggly's been slaving over a hot stove again, I see. That barbecue smells wonderful."

"Mary Alice and I went to a movie. She wanted to tell me she's decided not to be sixty-six on her birthday. She's decided to reverse the arrow of time."

"If aybody can do it, she can. Does she have a specific plan in mind?"

"Lying. Consider yourself forewarned."

Mitzi laughed. "You want some gardenias?"

I did. By the time Fred got home, the whole house smelled of gardenias and peach cobbler. Ah, summer!

Fred owns a small metal fabricating plant and loves it. I think he was hoping that one of our sons, Freddie or Alan, would join him in the business. Instead, both of them live in Atlanta where Alan works with a utility company and Freddie solves problems in a "think tank." Lord only knows what kind of problems he solves, but he makes a lot of money doing it. Our daughter, Haley, calls him "the thinker." Haley, at thirty-four, is our youngest. She's a surgeon's assistant in an open heart unit. She was widowed a couple of years ago when her husband, Tom Buchanan, was killed by a drunk driver, but has recently been seeing someone seriously. Freddie's still "thinking" about getting married, and Alan has a wonderful wife, Lisa, and two boys.

And all of this because of the man who had just come in the kitchen, the man who was hugging me and asking, "Is that cobbler?" Damn! Forty years and that hug still gets to me.

"Fresh peaches." I snuggled against him.

"My cup would runneth over if I had a couple of aspirin and a beer."

I leaned back quickly. "What's the matter?"

"Just a headache. The damn air conditioning broke down in the office again today. I'll grab a shower and I'll be fine." He reached in the refrigerator for a Lite. "Did you and Mary Alice go to the movie?"

"Yes. Get your shower and I'll tell you about it."

"I've got something to tell you, too." The serious expression on his face scared me. This was totally unlike the Fred who has spent forty years allaying my fears.

"Oh, God," I whispered. I could feel the blood draining from my face. He had a brain tumor, inoperable.

"A man called on me today from Universal Metals in Atlanta. Jake Rice, nice fellow. He offered me an interesting deal, one we need to talk about. I'll tell you about it as soon as I get cleaned up." Fred disappeared down the hall.

I pulled out a kitchen chair and sat down weakly. Damn it! All Fred had said was he had something to tell me, and I had him dead and buried. This would not do.

The timer on the oven buzzed and I got up and took the

cobbler out. Fred and I would sit at the table at the bay window and eat supper and he would tell me his news. Then while I straightened up the kitchen, he would read the paper or go out and walk around the yard and give our dog, Woofer, a treat. We'd watch the Atlanta Braves or some sitcoms. At ten, we'd watch the news and Fred would go to sleep before it was over. I would read a while longer before I turned out the light on my side of the bed. This was what we had done the night before, what we would do tomorrow. This was what every marriage of forty years should be: calm, happy, still a nice spark from a hug. A total fusion of two into one. Scary.

I reached for the phone; Mary Alice answered. "I need an adventure," I said.

"You got anything in mind?"

"No. I may need some help."

"Are we talking physically adventurous like white-water rafting or bungee jumping?"

"I don't know."

"Hmm. I'll think about it."

I was hanging up the phone when a refreshed-looking Fred reappeared.

"Mary Alice?" he asked.

I nodded. "Did you know she has four dimples in her back?"

"Is that all?" He picked up the paper, sat down at the table, and looked at the front page.

"Fred," I said, "do you ever feel like you need an adventure?"

He spread out the paper. "Not really, honey."

Which, of course, was one of the reasons I loved him. Sometimes things don't make a grain of sense.

# Chapter
# 2

"**A**nd this Universal Metals wants to buy Papa out?" It was the next morning, and our daughter, Haley, was sitting in the den with a glass of iced tea.

"It's not exactly a buyout," I explained as best I could. "It's a merger. Instead of being the sole owner of Metal Fab, he'll own a comparable share of Universal Metals. Metal Fab will become part of the larger company."

"Is that good?"

"Your papa seems to think so. He's going to Atlanta next week to talk to them more in depth and look at their operation. He's also going to visit a company in Chattanooga that became part of Universal about a year ago. He knows the man who owned it and says this man will be honest with him about whether he's satisfied."

Haley reached over and put her glass on the coffee table. She has recently had her strawberry blonde hair cut short and highlighted. I think it looks great, but she calls it her Little Orphan Annie look. "The thing about it," she said, "is that Papa won't know how to act without Metal Fab. I mean, think about it, Mama; he eats and sleeps that shop. Always has. Remember how upset he was when he was considering selling out?"

"Well, they've assured him he can stay on as manager as long as he wants. So maybe being a small part of a big company is the answer. He's sixty-four, you know. Or will be soon. He needs time for some fun."

"Mama, Papa's idea of fun is unlocking the door at Metal Fab every morning."

"I know," I agreed. "Financially it's a good deal, though."

We were both quiet for a moment. I had been putting Woofer in the backyard after our morning walk when Haley showed up, and I had started telling her Fred's news right away. Now I asked her, "How come you're not at work? Nobody's heart's plugged up?"

"The doctor's on vacation. I'm on call for emergencies. No regular schedule." She got up and walked toward the kitchen. "You want some more tea?"

"No thanks. How's Philip?" I could hear ice clunking out of the icemaker.

"He's fine," she called. Philip Nachman is a very nice man, the nephew of Sister's late second husband (also named Philip Nachman, which gets slightly confusing). Haley and Philip met at their mutual cousin's, Debbie Nachman's, wedding in March and have been inseparable ever since. Philip is a doctor, an ENT, (ears, nose, throat) which is great; he's also twenty years Haley's senior, which worries us.

Haley came back with more tea and sat down on the sofa. I had been so preoccupied with Fred's news, I hadn't paid much attention to her. Now I realized something was bothering her.

"You okay?" I asked.

"Philip and I seem to be at a crossroad."

"A serious one?"

"He doesn't want any more children. He says he's had as much getting up with sick babies and as much Little League as he can take." Haley's eyes filled with tears. "And I can understand that, sort of. Matthew's married, and Jenny's a senior in college, so Philip's free for the first time in twenty-five years." The tears spilled over. "But I want my own child. I want my own family." The family she should have had with her young husband Tom Buchanan; the future that a drunken driver had stolen from her with one swerve.

I moved to the sofa and held Haley while she cried. So much for being "free" when your children are grown.

"He knows how strongly you feel about this?"

Haley nodded, wiped her eyes, and straightened up. "He says he loves his two dearly, but they're grown and that's that."

"Oh, honey, I'm sorry.

Haley nodded and sighed. "I want Philip and I want a baby. I just don't think I can choose, Mama."

I had no easy answers for her.

As soon as she left, saying she was going to go shopping for an outfit, that maybe that would make her feel better, I dialed Sister's number and got the answering machine. "About the adventure," I said, "get busy with your thinking. Haley might want to join us."


"Men!" my friend Frances Zata said at lunch later that day. We were eating at The Oak Cupboard, which is a lovely restaurant if you don't mind foliage getting in your food.

Plants are everywhere in The Oak Cupboard, hanging from the ceilings and windows, cascading from planters between booths. Mary Alice has quit eating there since an encounter with a hanging basket of asparagus fern left her with a knot on her head. She says there's too much oxygen in the place for her; it makes her dizzy. As for me, I'm neutral. But Frances loves it. She says it's like eating in a rain forest. Cozy. I've never thought of rain forests as being cozy, but, like I say, I'm neutral. And the food is about as close as Birmingham gets to exotic cuisine. That's because Mrs. Peck, who has owned The Oak Cupboard as long as anyone can remember, considers the diner's plate her canvas. She's even had this philosophy printed on the front of the menu. What it means, I've decided, is that she believes she can get away with serving almost anything if the colors are pretty. Most of the time, it works. Especially when she gives the dish a French name and charges a fortune for it.

"God's truth," I said, agreeing with Frances's indictment of the whole male sex. I eyed a forkful of something red and orange with green polka dots on it. "This," I said to Frances, "looks a lot like what was in a jar of orange-cranberry relish I threw out yesterday that had been in the refrigerator since Christmas before last."

"It's some kind of carrot souffle," she said. "It's good."

"What are the green and red things?"

"Mint and some cherries cut up, or maybe cranberries. It could even be some of that red stuff they put in fruitcakes."

"That red pineapple stuff?"

"Just try it."

I stuck the fork in my mouth. The souffle was delicious.

"I told you," Frances said when she saw my pleased expression.

"Beats the school cafeteria to hell and back," I agreed.

Frances's fork stopped halfway to her mouth. For a moment, the carrot souffle hung in the air like a teeny orange sun. Then Frances lowered her fork to her plate. "Am I going to be sorry, Patricia Anne, in September?"

What she was talking about was the fact that she had just retired from Alexander High after a career of thirty years, the last fifteen as counselor. I had retired the year before from the same school where I had taught English for thirty years.

"The day after Labor Day, you'll be dancing a jig."

"You're lying, but thank you." Frances picked up her fork again. "You and I are both such old war horses, we'll chomp at the bit for the rest of our lives when we hear a school bell."

"True. But it's time to find out what's beyond those school walls."

"I know. But I'll miss the kids. Hell, I'll even miss the lunchroom food."

"Yes," I admitted, "you will."

Frances is one of the most elegant looking women I've ever known. She's sixty, just a few months younger than I am, but she looks, maybe, fifty, thanks to a discreet visit to a plastic surgeon in Atlanta a few years ago. I had gone with her and had been sorely tempted to have my eyes done. When school started and everyone told Frances how "rested" she looked, I wished I had given in to temptation. Now I thought that maybe that could be my adventure. Have everything lifted, tightened, lightened. Have my naturally curly hair straightened and tinted Marigold. Wear it back in a chignon like Frances.

"Looks like he would have known Haley would want a family, young as she is," Frances said, getting back to the subject "Men!"

"None of Mary Alice's three older husbands balked at her getting pregnant. In fact, they were all delighted." I forked up the last of the carrot souffle. "Of course that was Mary Alice, not Haley. She probably didn't give them a chance to balk."

Frances laughed. "How's she doing?"

"She's fine. She was in a swivet yesterday because she had a date with a man who wasn't ninety. She was nervous about going out with some man who is actually a few years younger than she is. Says she's going to start counting backward on her birthdays."

"Good for her. Is she still on the museum board?"

"And symphony board. And Arts Council. Even the Humane Society. She was on TV a couple of weeks ago. You know those spots where they show the baby animals and try to get people to adopt them? She had a kitten that clawed hell out of her. The curator at the museum adopted it. He said you had to appreciate an animal with courage like that."

A waiter removed our plates, checked to see if we wanted dessert, and brought us coffee. "Who's the new, younger man?" Frances asked.

"His name is Berry West. I don't know him."

Frances was stirring Sweet 'n Low in her coffee and looked up in surprise. "Oh, I do. His wife was a friend of my ex brother-in-law's ex sister-in-law. He designs those old-fashioned communities. You know, Patricia Anne, like Seaside and Blount Springs where you can walk to everything and you sit on the porch with your neighbors. Tin roofs. That kind of thing."

I didn't even try to figure out the relationship. "He designed Blount Springs and Seaside?"

"No, but that's the kind of thing he does." Frances picked

up her coffee and took a sip. "Berry West. How about that. Did Mary Alice have a good time on their date?"

"I haven't talked to her today."

"Oh." Frances put her cup down, sloshing the coffee slightly in the saucer. Most of her gestures are so graceful, I looked up in surprise. Her hands were shaking, and she pressed them against her cheeks.

"What's the matter?" I asked, alarmed at her sudden change of mood. "Are you sick?"

"Oh, Patricia Anne. I wasn't going to talk about this at lunch, but it's all I can think about. David's been transferred to London. He and Sharon were married last week at the courthouse and they're leaving for London Saturday. They'll be there at least three years."

"Oh, Frances, I'm so sorry," David is Frances's only child. She and his father were divorced and then the father was killed in an automobile accident when David was a child. Frances and her son have always been very close. David had even chosen to live at home and go to college at the University of Alabama at Birmingham rather than leave home. And now he had married a girl whom Frances didn't care for (she had confided that to me weeks before) and was going to live in a foreign country.

I reached over and took her hand. "You should have told me right away, not let me babble on about Haley and Mary Alice."

"It was good for me to hear you talk. I'm ashamed of my reaction, to tell you the truth." She shrugged. "My son has married a girl he loves, he's healthy, and he's got a good job with a promotion. What's sad about that?"

She was asking *me* what was sad about that? I hadn't even been able to take my kids to college, I was so upset at their

leaving home. I was grieved that two of them lived 150
miles away in Atlanta. And she was asking *me*? Bad choice.
I didn't answer. We drank our coffee in silence. Later on,
I left another message on Sister's phone that I had an idea
Frances Zata might also want to be included in the
adventure.

"I'm not your imagination," Sister grumbled. She was sitting on my back steps looking through the newspaper when
I got back from taking Woofer for a walk. "How come I'm
supposed to plan things for you? You're still blaming me
because we were in Sweden when Chernobyl blew up."

"I am not. I know it wasn't your fault."

"Gee, thanks." She folded a page of the paper and handed
it to me. "Look, Mouse. Here's a picture of Berry and I at
the museum reception."

"Me. Berry and me."

She snatched the paper back. "Do you want to see it?"

"Yes."

"Then quit correcting my grammar."

"For heaven's sake, Sister, you wouldn't say 'here's a picture of I.' "

"I might."

I snatched the newspaper back and looked at the picture.
In it Sister was standing between a man and a woman. All
three smiled at the camera and held up wine glasses. The
caption read, "Janet Rotten, Mary Alice Crane, and Berry
West enjoy the bubbly at the recent champagne reception at
the Birmingham Museum of Art." Sister was a foot taller
than either of the others. I was startled. This man was an
Adonis? This short, balding man was the one for whom she
was planning on turning time around? Not that I've got
anything against short people, God knows. At five-one I fit

right in. But this man's nose would fit into Mary Alice's cleavage when he hugged her.

"He's a little shorter than I am, but isn't he cute?" Sister asked.

"Cute," I said. I studied the picture. That's not the word I would have used. But then I felt guilty. He was probably a very nice man. It was just that Sister had built his looks up so. An Adonis! Enjoy the bubbly? I thought as I handed her the paper. "How come you're sitting out here in the heat?"

"I couldn't find the dog turd."

"Fred thought it was one of Woofer's and picked it up with a trowel and threw it over in the ivy. I'm not about to look for it; there's poison oak all in that ivy patch."

"Looks like it would have clinked on the trowel."

"Must not have."

"Why didn't you tell him the key was in it? That thing cost me eight dollars."

"I did. He forgot."

"Shows you how real it looked. Sure beat that fake rock you had by the steps. Where's the key now?"

"Under the pot of begonias over yonder. I've got my own, though." I got up from the steps. "Come on in and tell me about your date with Berry."

"It was great." Sister followed me into the kitchen. "He called and said to dress casually, that he had a surprise. And, Mouse," Sister pulled out a chair and sat down, "it was wonderful. He had By Request fix a lovely picnic basket, and we went to the Oak Mountain Amphitheater to see Michael Crawford. I'd been meaning to get tickets, but it was sold out when I called."

"How wonderful," I said, and I meant it.

"And he's funny, Michael Crawford is. I've always

thought of him as just singing. But he's a comedian, too. He had that audience right in his hand. It was great."

"Did he reach way out on 'The Music of the Night'?"

Mary Alice slightly cupped her hands and did a pretty good *Phantom of the Opera* reach.

"Oh, my." I got each of us a Coke from the refrigerator. "I would have loved to have seen that."

"You could have. All you have to do is buy two tickets and get Fred up off his butt."

"True. We're in a rut, aren't we?"

"Yep."

"Maybe things will be changing soon." I told Sister about the offer Fred had had for the business, that he would be going to Atlanta and Chattanooga the next week to find out all the details.

"Are you going with him?"

"Don't think so. He hasn't mentioned it."

"Why don't you go to Destin with me, then? They're having a writers' conference at Sunnyside I'm going to."

I took a sip of Coke. "You're deserting a man who takes you to see Michael Crawford and plies you with goodies from By Request?"

"Oh, he's going to be down there. Some friend of his is building a big development on Choctawhatchee Bay. He wants to go check it out."

"Hmmm." Twenty-five years ago, Sister bought a three bedroom condo in Destin, Florida, "The World's Luckiest Fishing Village" (so the sign at the bridge says). Located on the Panhandle between Panama City and Fort Walton Beach, Destin was, at that time, a few old beach houses on piers and a few stores on Highway 98 that sold mostly fishing supplies. We thought she had lost her mind. That high-rise condo stuck out like a sore thumb. For heaven's sake, we told her, there's not even a grocery store!

"It's a great investment," she assured us. "You need to get in on it."

We should have known what was going to happen. Highway 98 has six lanes, condos have bloomed like mushrooms, and elegant shops, restaurants, and, yes, grocery stores are right outside the big iron security gate that guards Sister's building and that looked so dumb by itself out on the beach not too long ago. It has been interesting, and in some ways sad (the little houses on piers are gone), to see so much change. It was bound to happen, though. The whitest beaches in the world are along this coast, and the water temperature is in the eighties until November.

"Haley and Frances might like to come, too," Sister said. "It won't be an adventure, but it should be fun."

"I'm sure they would if they can work it out. When are you going?"

"Monday, I guess. That's not carved in stone, though. We could stay as long as we wanted. Even take separate cars."

It sounded great to me. I could use some nice warm dips in the Gulf and some elegant meals. It would be fun if the four of us could go together, too.

"You want me to call them and see?" I asked. But I knew what their answers would be.

"Last time there were four of us women down there," Sister said, "all we did was eat, play bridge, and watch dirty movies. We had a great time."

"Whoa," I cautioned. "One of the women this time is my daughter."

"She was one of them last time, too." Sister smiled sweetly.

# Chapter

## 3

Frances and Haley both jumped at the chance to go to Destin.

"But I can't come until Tuesday," Frances said. "I've got a dentist's appointment Monday. A new crown I've got to get put on as soon as possible to start getting my money's worth."

"I'm already packed," Haley said.

As for Fred, he wasn't sure the girls' vacation was such a good idea. "How long will you be gone?" he wanted to know. "Who's going to water the plants and take care of Woofer?"

Lord, Mary Alice was right! Fred at I needed a few days apart.

"I'm leaving Monday, I'll be gone at least a week, and Mitzi will take care of Woofer while you're in Atlanta," I answered, stretching my arm out like The Phantom of the

Opera to get a can of Healthy Choice Split Pea and Ham soup from the pantry for supper.

But the truth is that we are apart so seldom that by Sunday night we were already missing each other. Our usual TV watching was punctuated with "I'll call you tomorrow night at ten" (Fred), and "Remember you'll be an hour ahead of us" (me). "Don't let Mary Alice drive too fast. She has a heavy foot" (Fred). "Don't drive too fast. You know how they're always working on the Atlanta interstates" (me). We finally went to bed early, exhausted at the thought of going in different directions the next morning.

"Y'all need to go to a marriage counselor," Mary Alice had told me once when I made the mistake of telling her how I felt when Fred and I were going to be apart for a few days. "That's not healthy."

The funny thing is that once we say goodbye, I have this great feeling of freedom. Go figure.

Mary Alice's black Jaguar pulled into our driveway about eight the next morning. Fred carried my suitcase and hang-up clothes out and I followed with a styrofoam cup of coffee. The plan was to go by and pick up Haley at her apartment.

"You want some coffee?" I asked Sister.

"Nope. Thought we'd stop in Clanton for a snack."

Fred put my clothes in the car; I kissed him goodbye and got in the front seat. He shut the door and *swack!* the seatbelt grabbed me. Coffee went everywhere; I screamed.

"What happened?" Fred opened the door and looked at the mess in amazement.

"It's okay," Sister said. "It'll wipe right up from these leather seats." She was worried about the seats? The seatbelt had caught my bent arm in just the right position to catapult hot coffee from my head to my feet, and she was worried about her car?

"Lord!" Fred said. "What did you do, honey?"

"Not a damn thing." I crawled out of the car.

"It's the automatic seatbelt," Mary Alice explained. "You can't forget to buckle up."

"Now you tell me. I've even got coffee in my hair. God, what a mess!" Such a mess, I had to shower, wash my hair, and change clothes. When I got back, the leather seats had been wiped off and Fred and Sister were talking about the other safety features in the car.

"Anything else going to surprise me?" I asked. My hair was wet and the shirt and pants I had rinsed out and left hanging over the shower rod might have permanent coffee stains.

Mary Alice assured me that there wasn't and that she hoped I would get in a better mood, that happy campers were a necessity for a happy trip. Before I could say anything, Fred closed the door, and this time the seatbelt didn't seem to grab me like it had before. So much for being forewarned.

"Y'all are late," Haley informed us as we pulled up to her apartment.

"Your mama's fault," Mary Alice said. "She decided to wash her hair after I got there. What's all that?" She pointed to the various sacks, bags, and suitcases that surrounded Haley. There were so many, it looked like she had been evicted.

"I never can decide what I'll need at the beach," Haley said.

"Well, you're playing it safe." Mary Alice opened the trunk of the car and we started piling stuff in.

"A cappuccino machine, dear?" she asked.

Haley nodded. "You never know."

Mary Alice rolled her eyes at me. I didn't say a word; I'd had enough trouble with coffee that morning.

By ten o'clock, we were hauling down I-65. We made our first pit stop forty miles south of Birmingham at the Shoney's at Clanton.

"I've died and gone to heaven," Haley said, coming back from the restroom. "Remember, Mama, how we went all the way across South Carolina begging Papa to stop at a bathroom? Tom was like that, too, never wanting to stop."

"You miss a lot of Confederate cemeteries that way," Sister said. "And caves. And folks selling quilts."

"You know what I want, Aunt Sister?" Haley reached for a sweetroll. "I want to stop in Georgiana and see the Hank Williams Museum."

"We'll do that," Sister promised. And we did. We also stopped at The House of Turkey, took a detour to see Hurricane Lake, and walked through a daylily nursery in Wing, Florida. We bought boiled peanuts in Red Level at a farmers' market and washed them down with Grapicos. And while we were doing all this, we had come down from the Appalachians, traversed the great fertile Black Belt below Montgomery, and entered the coastal plain. As we crossed the Mid-Bay Bridge across Choctawhatchee Bay, the sun was low in the sky, and ahead of us the Gulf of Mexico was a green mirror.

Haley sighed contentedly. "Eight hours to make a four-and-a-half-hour trip. Wonderful."

We entered the city limits of Destin and Mary Alice slowed down. The speed limit is thirty, which doesn't mean thirty-one. Sister's learned this the hard way. "Y'all want to eat first or go to the apartment?" she asked.

"Go to the apartment," Haley said. "Maybe we'll see the green flash." What she was talking about was the bright green flare that is visible some evenings as the last orange of the sun disappears into the Gulf. Even if it doesn't appear, and usually it doesn't, just watching the sun sink into the water is spectacular.

"We'll have to hurry then," Sister shaded her eyes with her hand and looked toward the western horizon. "The sun's going down fast."

We made it to the condo balcony just as the sun touched the water.

"Don't look right at it," I warned Haley.

"Look through your fingers," Mary Alice said, holding her hand before her face.

"What good does that do?" I asked.

Mary Alice leaned over the balcony railing. "Don't be silly. It cuts out half the rays."

I was still trying to figure out a response to this when the sun disappeared into the water. There was no green flash, but that was okay. The western sky was every color of pink and orange, and the crowd of sunset watchers gathered on the seawall below us applauded. We did, too.

"A good one," Haley announced.

"Mary Alice!" A man had broken away from the crowd and was standing below our balcony.

"Hey, Fairchild!" Sister called down.

"I saw your light come on!"

"What light through yonder window," I murmured to Haley.

"I'll bet he knew when she came in the gate," Haley murmured back. "I think it's the pheromones."

"Fairchild Weatherby wouldn't know a pheromone if it hit him over the head. I think Aunt Sister's are dried up, anyway."

"Y'all shut up," Sister said. Then to the figure below, "How are you, Fairchild?" It came out as Fay-uh-chile.

"She's talking Southern," I said. "We might as well go on and start unloading the car."

"Maybe if we wait a while, Fay-uh-chile will help us," Haley said.

"True." We went back into the living room and left Mary Alice flirting with Fairchild, who stood six floors below her. Not an easy thing to do.

"I love this place," Haley said, settling down on the sofa.

"I do, too," I agreed. In spite of being a luxury condo facing the Gulf of Mexico, the apartment was not done in the "beachy" style much favored on the Florida Panhandle. No interior decorator had placed little shell soap dishes in the bathrooms or furnished the living room and dining room with white rattan furniture and lucite tables. Instead, there was a deep beige sofa to sink into, one that had once been in Sister's den in Birmingham. One that had been recovered many times because it was, simply, the most comfortable sofa in the world. The diningroom table was an oak one I had found at an estate sale. Three of the chairs matched. Each of the others was different. The walls were a pale blue and the carpet a beige Berber. A couple of wicker rockers with peach-colored cushions added some color. But the walls of windows, and the sliding doors that opened to the balcony and the Gulf, were the focal points of the apartment with their unbelievably beautiful view.

"Sometimes I forget how rich Aunt Sister is," Haley sighed happily, propping her feet up on the coffee table.

"And never hit a lick at a snake."

"She got married three times."

"For her that was like falling off a log, not hitting a lick at a snake."

Haley looked at the balcony, at Mary Alice waving down to Fairchild Weatherby. "I guess you're right." She grinned. Sister gave a last wave, turned, and came in. "Y'all come on," she said. "Fairchild's going to help us unload the car."

"Why am I not surprised?" Haley said, getting up from the sofa.

"Because you take after me. Nothing surprises me." Sister headed for the door, stopping before the mirror in the hall to check her makeup. "Not even cappuccino machines being carted to the beach."

"You just wait," Haley said. "You'll be glad I brought it."

Fairchild Weatherby lives in the condo next to Sister with his wife, Millicent. Fairchild is from Toronto and arrived in the Panhandle to spend the winter eleven years ago with his first wife, Margaret, who managed to plow their Lincoln Continental into a utility pole on Highway 98 on New Year's Day, thereby knocking out all the electricity to Holiday Isle, where most of the condos are located, during a Sugar Bowl game between Alabama and Florida State. I believe the national title may have been at stake. The intenseness of everyone's sorrow over the accident touched Fairchild; total strangers wept. When Margaret died from her injuries (as did Florida State's unbeaten record), Fairchild took her home to Toronto, had her cremated, and came back to Destin where the rent was paid through March, which, he had been led to understand, was the best golf month on the Panhandle.

"Brave soul," the condo ladies said of the then sixty-year-old Fairchild. "Holding his head up through all his troubles." It also happened to be a handsome head with a lot of white hair. And they comforted him with casseroles and invitations to dinner. Millicent Abernathy, the recently widowed resident manager ten years his junior, was the most help, though. When he informed her he was thinking of moving to Florida, she advised him to do it immediately while he could still see well enough to get a driver's license. Once he had the license, she assured him, he would never be retested.

It was practical advice like this, plus the fact that Millicent was a sharp, nice-looking woman who owned a plush three-bedroom condo, that paved the path to true love. Fairchild and Millicent have been married ten years. The only flies in the ointment seem harmless: Fairchild's mad crush on Mary Alice and his tendency to call Millicent "Margaret." Millicent is still the resident manager, and Fairchild plays a lot of golf, having discovered that March is only one of the great months.

"How come Fairchild has a British accent?" Haley asked. We were sitting on the deck of The Redneck Riviera restaurant an hour later eating boiled shrimp. Quite a stack of shells lay on the newspaper between us.

"He's Canadian," Sister explained.

"Canadians don't have British accents," Haley said. "They talk just like we do."

I turned and looked at her. "Surely you jest."

"Well, you know what I mean." Haley dipped another shrimp into the bowl of red sauce in the middle of the table.

"He's a retired insurance executive," Mary Alice said.

Haley grinned. "Well, that explains it." She popped the shrimp into her mouth. "How come I get the impression," she said as soon as she finished chewing, "that he could eat you with a spoon, Aunt Sister?"

"Because it's true." Mary Alice picked up a shrimp and examined it. "He says I'm a luscious Southern peach."

I spluttered into my iced tea. "Fairchild Weatherby said that? My, my, what would Millicent say?"

"She's not worried. She knows they don't make a spoon with a handle that long." She held the shrimp toward me. "What's this?"

"The black thing? Looks like part of a bay leaf."

"Good. I knew if it was a fly it was boiled, but even so—" Sister peeled the shrimp and dipped it into the sauce. Haley opened another package of crackers.

"Fairchild says Millicent's making tons of money in that development over on the bay. Remember, Mouse, when her first husband bought a lot of that land for something like ten dollars an acre and everybody thought he was crazy? Paying ten dollars an acre, for worthless piney woods. I'm sure it's the one Berry's coming down to see. Fairchild says lots are selling like hotcakes over there." Sister motioned for the waitress to bring her another beer.

"I hate to see them develop all the land around here," Haley said. "We're running all the poor animals out, the bears and foxes. The butterflies. There weren't nearly as many monarchs here last fall. Did you notice?"

"Bears? I've never seen a bear down here, not even when we were children. Have you, Mouse?"

"There used to be some raccoons that came up and got in the garbage at Wilhite Apartments in Panama City. That's where we usually spent our vacations," I explained to Haley.

"Raccoons are not bears. Besides, that was during World War II. German submarines used to come right up in the Gulf. You could see them firing on ships at night. Or being fired on. Daddy told us it was fireworks."

I quit peeling a shrimp and looked up, startled. "It wasn't fireworks?"

"It was ships firing at each other. It was the *war*, Patricia Anne. For heaven's sake! Daddy just didn't want us to know it." Sister took a long swig from her bottle of beer. "There were more mosquitoes then, too."

Haley probably didn't understand this synaptic leap, but I did. I remembered lying on a blanket on the warm sand with Daddy and Mama and Sister, watching the "fireworks" in the Gulf and swatting at mosquitoes that dive-bombed us like kamikazes. Daddy and Mama would puff on cigarettes and blow smoke over us to make the mosquitoes go away. Secondhand smoke and ships firing at each other created one of my best memories. Damn. Sometimes we just learn too much.

Sister nodded her head toward the dark Gulf. "That's one reason the fishing is so good here. All those sunken boats."

I looked at the peaceful water rippling with white edges against the beach. Beyond that, a few lights from buoys and fishing boats dotted a black expanse that blended into the horizon and seemed to continue forever. I shivered.

"Rabbit run over your grave?" Sister asked.

I nodded.

"Some key lime pie, ladies?" The waitress, obviously a college student working a summer job, asked. A groan from all of us was our answer. "I'll bring you some coffee then." We watched her walk away in the short flowered sarong that was the uniform at the Redneck.

"She looks like Dorothy Lamour," Sister said.

"Who?" Haley asked.

Mary Alice and I looked at each other. "Like I told you, I'm going to be sixty-four next week," she said.

I nodded. "Then that makes me fifty-nine."

"What are you talking about?" Haley asked. "And who's Dorothy Lamour?" Sister and I laughed.

We drank our coffee slowly and contentedly. I had talked to Fred before I left the condo. He was going to have dinner with Alan and Lisa and the boys, and seemed excited about his meeting the next day. He missed me. And I missed him. A very nice miss.

The early dinner crowd was thinning out and the bar crowd was getting larger and noisier.

"Let's mosey on home, girls," Sister said. We were pushing our chairs back when we heard our names called.

"Hey, y'all. Fairchild told me you were in Destin."

The Millicent Weatherby who was walking toward us holding a drink was not the Millicent we had known for years, first as Tod Abernathy's wife and then Fairchild's. Though obviously Millicent, she looked spectacular. Her hair, which had been a salt-and-pepper gray, was now a soft, sun-streaked blonde pulled back casually and held by a large barrette. A 160-pound matronly body had become a tanned 110 encased in a size six jumpsuit, off-white and silky. Heavy gold earrings shaped like turtles brushed against tan, unlined cheeks.

"Lord, Millicent! You look wonderful!" Sister exclaimed.

"Thanks." Millicent smiled. At least her smile was the same, sweet and a little timid. "I'm helping on the big development on the bay. You know that scrub pine I never thought would amount to a hill of beans and tried to talk Tod out of buying? Hah!"

"We heard about it. What are you doing?" Mary Alice asked.

Millicent's smile became a grin. "You're looking at an officer of the Blue Bay Ranch Corporation, honey. A lot of it's PR, like making talks to groups about the advantages of community living. Even made a video. Anyway, I decided the plump old resident manager look wouldn't get it."

"The resident manager look was fine," I said.

"Sweet Patricia Anne." Millicent gave me a light hug. Her earrings banged against my shoulder. "How are you, Haley?" she asked.

"Fine, Mrs. Weatherby. And I can see that you're fine."

Millicent swirled around, giving us the view from all directions. "I don't look like a sixty-year-old broad from De Funiak Springs, do I?"

"No, you don't," we assured her.

"I don't even have angel wings anymore." She bent her elbow to show us there was no loose skin swaying in the breeze under her upper arms.

"I'm impressed," Sister said. "Where's Fairchild? Is he overwhelmed at having a new glamorous wife?"

"He's home watching the Braves. I'm meeting someone for a drink, and then the Blue Bay folks are having a birthday party for one of the sales staff."

I noticed Millicent hadn't answered the question Sister had asked about Fairchild's reaction to her new image. I tried to imagine how Fred would react if I showed up completely renovated. He'd have a fit probably.

"Come over and see the development while you're here," Millicent said. "Jason Marley's doing it. Do you know him, Mary Alice?" Sister shook her head no. "Well, he's just the best. It's new and yet old-fashioned at the same time. You'll love it."

We promised her that we would. She gave a little wave goodbye and disappeared into the crowd around the bar.

"Can you believe that?" Sister asked.

"Jealousy over you probably drove her to it, not sudden wealth," Haley said.

"It seems so out of character," I said. "Millicent has always struck me as being very comfortable with her life and her looks. Down-to-earth. You know what I mean?"

"The broad from De Funiak Springs and no bones about it," Mary Alice said.

"Right."

We paid our checks and went down the steps to the beach. The Redneck Riviera is only a short distance from the condo so we had walked. We pulled off our shoes and waded in the edge of the water. There was a slight breeze, and we could hear music from the radios of lovers hidden in the dunes.

"I hope they're practicing safe sex," I murmured as we heard the romantic "Unchained Melody."

"I hope they're not practicing," my sweet daughter said. "Sex in the sand can be painful."

I trusted she was talking about an experience with her late husband Tom. They had come down here frequently.

Other than that exchange, we were lost in our own thoughts. Even Mary Alice was quiet. We walked along, our feet in the warm water, and felt totally relaxed and safe. When we got to the condo we rinsed the sand from our feet at the stile that allows easy access over the seawall. At the top of the stile is an uncovered deck with benches on each side where residents gather to enjoy the sunset or just visit. As we started up the steps, we realized Fairchild Weatherby was sitting there alone.

"Evening, ladies," he said. "You been to the Redneck?"

"Had great boiled shrimp," Haley said.

"I'm full as a tick," Sister added. "What are you doing, Fairchild?"

"Just enjoying the evening."

"It's a lovely one," I agreed.

Sister sat down on the bench across from Fairchild and

leaned forward. "Fairchild, let me ask you something. Do your earlobes ever get numb when you get tired?"

He seemed slightly startled by the question. He reached up and rubbed both his earlobes. "No, I can't say that they do."

"Mine do. Do you think I should see a doctor about it?"

"I don't know. I guess it wouldn't hurt."

"What we need," Haley said, "is to call it a day. I'm exhausted."

We left Fairchild sitting on the stile and trudged to the elevator. I realized I was exhausted, too. I also realized that none of us had mentioned seeing Millicent at the Redneck.

"Are your earlobes really numb?" I asked Sister.

"Of course not. But I remember they were one time. Both of them."

When we got to the apartment, there was a message on the answering machine for Haley to call Philip. She took the phone into the bedroom and shut the door. Sister went to get a shower, and I wandered out to the balcony. Fairchild had been joined by a man who was so bald the stile lights seemed to bounce from his head.

I was glad he had someone to talk to. Later on, after everything had happened, I was glad I had the memory of him sitting peacefully that warm night, his white hair gleaming like a halo.

## Chapter
### 4

Haley and I were sharing the bedroom with twin beds. It's still known as the "children's room" or the "elevator room." It has been years since it truly was the "children's room," packed with sleeping bags and giggling kids. But it's still the "elevator room," the one closest to the noise of the opening and closing elevator doors out in the hall. Since there are only four apartments on each floor, that's usually not a problem.

"Everything okay?" I asked Haley as she came to bed. She had talked to Philip for at least a half hour.

"Nothing's changed." She held out a bottle of body lotion. "You want some? It's freesia."

I took the bottle and poured some into my hand. "Ummm. This smells great." I handed the lotion back to her and wished I could think of something to say that would comfort her. She looked both fragile and woebegone in an oversized blue T-shirt emblazoned with the Olympic torch and the words "Atlanta, 1996."

"Would it help," I asked, "if I said he's an asshole?"

"Sure it would." Haley reached over, kissed me, and then crawled into her bed. "Aunt Sister can think of a lot better names, though."

"Aunt Sister's had a lot more practice using them."

Haley laughed and opened the latest John Grisham; I settled down with an Elmore Leonard, an old one I had never read and had found, like a present, in a used paperback store.

The elevator opened down the hall.

"Think that's Fay-uh-chile?" Haley asked.

"Probably. Millicent's sure done a turnaround, hasn't she?"

"I don't see how she's managing this place and doing the real estate thing, too."

I yawned. "The condo association board is responsible for the big decisions. And most of the units are owned by permanent residents. Millicent's been manager so long, things run like clockwork." I yawned again. "And I think she'd miss knowing all that's going on here. Besides, Fairchild's here in case of an emergency."

"I'd like to see that new development on the bay that she's involved in."

I yawned again and rubbed my eyes. Elmore's words were getting fuzzy. "We'll see it. You can bet on that if your Aunt Sister's new boyfriend is interested in it." I put the book on the nightstand and turned out my light. "Don't let the bedbugs bite, sweetheart."

"You too, Mama. 'Night."

The sheets were cool and crisp; the air conditioner made

a slight humming noise. My sweet Fred over there in Atlanta. Sleep tight, darling.

Fred and I are at the World Trade Center.

"Get in the elevator," he says.

"Are you crazy?" says a woman's voice behind me. "It's not my fault!"

"Stupid! Stupid! Stupid!"

But it's not Fred. It's a man I've never seen before. His face is contorted with anger. "Where's Fred?" I ask him, grabbing his arm.

"You stupid bitch! Get in the goddamned elevator!"

The elevator closes and I wake with a start, my heart pounding. In a moment I remember where I am, and by the light filtering around our blinds, I can see that Haley is sleeping soundly. I get up, tiptoe out, and go into the kitchen for a glass of milk.

Damn! What a vivid dream!

Which is how I happened to be in the living room early the next morning when the pounding on the door started. I hadn't wanted to disturb Haley, but the dream had left me wide awake. I took a glass of milk and one of Sister's magazines listing 250 ways to satisfy a man in bed, and lay down on the sofa. The twentieth way was to massage his feet with oil. While I was thinking about what a mess this would make on the sheets, and how much Shout you would have to use before you washed them, let alone how he would break his neck if he so much as walked into the bathroom, I went back to sleep. Consequently, I was the one that the pounding woke up.

In lieu of a sheet, which I had been too lazy to get from

the linen closet during the night, I had spread my robe over me.

"Wait a minute," I grumbled inaudibly to the person beating on the door. I pulled my robe on. "Wait a minute."

I shuffled barefooted down the entrance hall and was almost hit in the head with Fairchild's upraised fist when I opened the door. "God!" I said, jumping back.

"Sorry!" He lowered his hand and his arms hung loosely by his side. "Is Millicent here, Patricia Anne?"

"What?" I asked, still half asleep. "What time is it?"

"About six." Fairchild shuffled from one foot to the other. "Have you seen Millicent?"

"This morning? Of course not."

"She didn't come home last night."

"Where could she be?"

"I don't have any idea. I was hoping she might be here."

"Why would she be here?"

"I was just hoping she was."

I realized we were getting nowhere fast and I was feeling a desperate urge to brush my teeth and comb my hair. "Come in, Fairchild," I said. "I'll make us some coffee."

"What's the matter?" Mary Alice asked behind me. A glance told me she had not only combed her hair and brushed her teeth, but was also wearing a flimsy pink peignoir.

Fairchild rubbed his hands across his eyes, overcome by worry over Millicent or the sight of Mary Alice's pink peignoir. Maybe a little of both. "Millicent didn't come home last night," he repeated.

"Oh, you poor darling." Mary Alice brushed me aside and took Fairchild by the arm, guiding him in. "You just come right in and tell us all about it. Fix us some coffee, Mouse."

"You fix it," I said cheerfully, heading for the bathroom.

"What's going on?" Haley murmured as I fumbled in my suitcase a few minutes later for some shorts and a top.

"Nothing," I said. "Go back to sleep. It's just Fairchild visiting."

"What time is it?"

"Early." I slipped on my clothes and went back into the living room where Mary Alice and Fairchild were ensconced on the couch.

"Coffee," Sister mouthed over Fairchild's shoulder which she was patting.

I stuck my tongue out at her, but I headed for the kitchen. I was in need of a caffeine fix, too.

"What time was it when we saw Millicent last night, Mouse?" Sister called.

"About eight thirty? Nine?" I got the coffee from the refrigerator where Mary Alice keeps it and filled the top of the Mr. Coffee. "I had already talked to Fred, but he called early because he figured we'd be going out to supper a little later since we'd just gotten here." I leaned across the counter that separates the kitchen from the dining and living area. The Gulf, I realized, looked blue this morning. Unusual. "Look, y'all. The water's blue this morning. Reckon that means anything like 'red sky at morning'?"

They both looked out at the Gulf, but neither said anything.

"I guess not," I said.

"We had come straight from the Redneck when we saw you, Fairchild," Mary Alice explained.

Fairchild shook his head. "She's never done anything like this before. I think I ought to call the sheriff, don't you?"

"She said she was having a drink with someone," I said.

"Maybe they got to partying and she decided it wasn't a good idea to drive home."

"Millicent isn't much of a partier. You know that."

"She looked in a party mood last night." I could have bitten my tongue the minute I said it. Sister glared at me. "I mean she looked pretty. And happy."

"Younger." Fairchild put his head in his hands.

"Now, just a minute." Sister got up in a swirl of pink, opened the end-table drawer and got out a pencil and note-pad. "I'm sure she's all right, Fairchild. Why don't we make a list, and Patricia Anne and I will help you make some calls. Millicent could even have gone up to De Funiak Springs to check on her family."

"Not without telling me."

"Well, we'll make a list anyway. Fetch us some coffee, Mouse, when it's ready."

Fetch? I was to *fetch* Mrs. Mary Alice Tate Sullivan Nachman Crane some coffee?

"And would you like cream and sugar?" I asked sweetly.

Fairchild looked up at me. "Cream, please, Patricia Anne." The worried expression on his face made me feel guilty; I got the tray out for the coffee.

"Let's start with friends," Mary Alice said. "Is there some friend she might have decided to spend the night with?"

"Her best friend is Emily Peacock. You know Emily. Lives over in Emerald Towers. I got her answering machine."

Mary Alice nodded. "Anybody else?"

"I called Eddie and Laura Stamps next door. They haven't heard from her, but Laura's calling around."

I carried the coffee into the living room and put it on the table in front of them. Sister handed Fairchild a cup and poured some cream in it. "Say when."

"When."

"Mouse," Sister said, "I think there are some sweetrolls in the freezer."

"I couldn't swallow a bite," Fairchild said.

I took my coffee and sat down in a chair across from them. "Who was she meeting at the Redneck last night?" I asked.

"Probably some of the folks from Blue Bay Ranch. She told me, but I was watching the Braves game."

"She told us about Blue Bay Ranch," Mary Alice said.

"Running out of names if you ask me." Fairchild studied his coffee. "Anyway, that's where Jason Marley and the rest of the crew like to hang out. At the Redneck. "

"Jason Marley sounds like his face should show up on a door knocker," I said. Sister and Fairchild both looked at me blankly. "You know, like in Scrooge. Jacob Marley, the partner. Scrooge thinks he's seeing him because he's eaten a greasy supper, but he's really there to tell him he'll be visited by the three spirits." They continued to look at me. "Write his name down, Sister." I bent to my coffee.

"I expect Laura's already called him," Fairchild said.

"What about relatives in De Funiak Springs?" Mary Alice asked.

"There's a brother and a sister. The sister has a bad heart condition, though, and the brother is considerably older. I'd hate to alarm them unnecessarily."

"You could just call them to chat, couldn't you?"

"I could do that." Fairchild put his cup on the tray and rubbed his hands across his eyes again. "I think what I should do, though, is call the sheriff."

"Then that's what you ought to do. Here," Mary Alice reached behind her, got the phone, and handed it to Fairchild.

"I'll call from my apartment." Fairchild stood up. "I might

drive over to the development and look around first. I just
had a thought that maybe she went back to work and
dropped off to sleep over there."

"Very possible," Mary Alice said. I agreed but didn't believe it for a minute. The way Millicent had looked the night
before had sent me a clear message: there was another man
in the woodpile.

"You sure you don't want us to call anybody? Jacob Marley?" Sister added as we followed Fairchild to the door.

"Not yet. But thank you for your help." Another rub of
the eyes. "When I woke up and realized she hadn't been
home, I panicked."

Mary Alice patted his arm. "Everything's going to be all
right. You let us know, now."

"I will. I'm sorry I bothered you so early."

"Don't worry about it. You call us." Sister gave the de-
parting Fairchild a little wave and closed the door. "Another
man in the woodpile," she announced. "Our no-longer-so-
prim resident manager had herself a rendezvous last night,
and they went to sleep. It happens to the best of us."

I decided not to pursue that remark. I took my coffee out
to the balcony and watched a single great blue heron wading
in a small tidal pool. Several joggers had already made it to
the beach, and the horizon was dotted with fishing boats.
There wasn't a cloud in the sky and later it would be hot.
But right at that moment, it was about as perfect as it gets.

Mary Alice followed me in a few minutes with sweetrolls
and more coffee. "I'll bet you it's that Jacob Marley," she
said, handing me the sweetrolls and a napkin.

"Jason," I corrected.

"Poor Fairchild." Sister sat down in her swirl of pink.
"Did you notice, Mouse, how his eyes looked like tragic

pools of brimming tears? How his hands lay in his lap, lonely as an empty bird's nest?"

I looked around at Sister. "What the hell are you talking about?"

"Practicing my similes and metaphors for the writers' conference. Pretty good, huh?"

"In all my years of teaching English, I promise you I've never heard anything quite like it."

"Thanks. That's what my creative writing instructor at the university said, too." Sister bit into a sweetroll and wiggled it around on her tongue while she blew over it. "Hot! Hot!"

"You want some ice?"

"It's okay." Sister took another bite and wiggled it around, too, exclaiming, "Hot!"

"Why don't you wait until they cool?"

"They're not as good cool."

I suppose that made sense.

"I'm thinking about sending the story I'm working on now to some literary journals," she said. "I brought it to have it critiqued at the conference."

"Have I read it?"

"I don't think so. I'll let you read it today. It's about a wheelchair repo man."

"A wheelchair repo man?"

"It's real sad. He works for this company that sells wheelchairs and when the customers don't pay for them, they send this guy out to get them back. It's chock-full of angst and existentialism."

"Sounds like a winner. Nothing quite like a good dose of angst and existentialism."

"It's good, Miss Smarty Pants, and don't you go being smartass about it until you read it. You just thought you were the only person in this family who knew about angst and existentialism, didn't you?"

Fortunately, someone banged on the door again and saved me from answering.

"Dear God. Grand Central." Mary Alice got up, brushed the crumbs from her peignoir, and headed toward the door. I followed her, curious, half-afraid that it was Fairchild with bad news.

It was Millicent. Not the Millicent of the night before at the Redneck, but an older, tired version with no makeup and uncombed hair, wearing the same outfit she had had on at the Redneck, which had obviously been slept in.

"Good morning, y'all. I'm sorry Fairchild bothered you. I had a couple of drinks and I'm not used to it, and I just plain went to sleep in the parking lot at the Redneck." Millicent smiled wanly. "I'm real embarrassed about it."

"Don't worry your head about it, Millicent," Sister said. "It happens to all of us sometimes. We're just happy to see you're okay."

"Thanks." Millicent looked relieved.

"You want some coffee?" I asked.

Millicent shook her head. "I've got to go calm Fairchild down. Did you know he was about to call the sheriff?"

"He was scared," Sister said.

"I know. I'm sorry."

"Her eyes were tragic pools of brimming tears," I said as Sister closed the door. I scooted down the hall out of her reach.

"Hmmm," Sister said. "Hmmm."

"And what was that 'it happens to all of us' bit? I've never gotten drunk and passed out in a parking lot."

Sister looked at me, looked through me. "What *have* you

done, Patricia Anne?" She walked into her bedroom and shut the door.

Oh, God. I walked back heavily to Sister's balcony where the sweetrolls I had acted a fool about cooking stared at me accusingly. What *had* I done? Had I ever been as kind, as generous, as much fun as Sister? I sat down wearily while angst and existentialism covered me like a blanket.

"You okay, Mama?" Haley was dressed in pink shorts and a white T-shirt. Her strawberry blonde hair and olive skin seemed to glow in the sunlight reflected from the beach. *Well, I had done this,* I thought. I had produced this golden woman.

"I'm okay," I said. "Just thinking."

"You look sad. You're sure you're all right?"

"I'm fine. What time is it?"

"About ten. What was all that commotion early this morning?"

I was explaining Millicent's disappearance when Mary Alice walked out onto the balcony and handed me several sheets of paper. "Here," she said, and went back into the apartment.

"You and Aunt Sister have a fight?" Haley asked.

"Not really. I think I'd better read this right away, though."

"I'll go get some cereal."

I took the story into our bedroom, shutting the door so I could concentrate. And somewhere in the middle of the wheelchair repo man's angst, mine began to disappear. By the time I finished, I was laughing so hard I was sobbing. The repo man was a Poor Soul: Charlie Chaplin eating his shoes, Buster Keaton with the wall falling around him. In one scene a ninety-year-old woman in a wheelchair was chasing the bumbling repo man, hitting him with her cane while he tried to apologize. Woody Allen could play this part, I thought.

The door opened. "Well?" Sister asked.

"It's great!" I said truthfully. "He's Everyman with a conscience and the job from hell. I wonder why that's so funny."

"Funny?" Mary Alice scowled. "It's not. It's sad, Patricia Anne." Then, after a pause, "Come on, let's go to the beach."

Frances arrived about three; we had left a note on the door that we were at the beach. Mary Alice and I were in the shade of a huge umbrella, both of us half-dozing, half-reading, with Factor 45 sunscreen coating us, and Haley was taking a dip in the water when Frances flopped down on the sand beside us. She had on unwrinkled linen beige pants (don't ask me how) and every strand of her blonde hair was caught in her usual chignon.

"Hey, y'all," she said. "Did you order this weather?"

We admitted that we had. Eighty-three degrees and a nice sea breeze in June is a day to be savored in Destin.

"You want a Coke or a beer?" I asked. "Or do you want to go unpack first."

"Beer first."

"You got it." I reached in the cooler and handed her one. "You want one, Sister?" I asked. We were still being polite to each other. She took one.

"I thought you were going to be at a writers' conference, Mary Alice," Frances said.

"It doesn't start until tomorrow. It's a three-day thing with a reading on Friday night."

"Hey, Frances!" Haley called.

"Lord, look at that child's shape!" Frances waved. "Did any of us ever have a waist like that?"

"Patricia Anne did," Sister said graciously.

"But you had boobs and I didn't." We smiled at each other.

Frances looked at us, puzzled, but she was too polite to ask us why we were being so nice to each other. Instead, she scooped her hand into the sand and said, "Goodness, this is wonderful."

Haley came up, got a towel, and found a place in the shade of the umbrella. There were two little girls building a sandcastle close to the water, and WUWF was playing Beethoven's Sixth, nice beach music. There was no hurry; there was no supper to cook, no sweet Woofer dog to walk. Bless his heart. But Mitzi would be good to him.

We finally left the beach, almost in slow motion. We helped Frances unpack her car, got her settled, took showers, decided we would have dinner at The Summer House, an old Victorian mansion on the bay. We even dressed for dinner, as much as you ever dress in Destin: a sundress for Haley, skirts for Sister and me, and a split skirt for Frances. And we set out for The Summer House.

We were headed into another beautiful sunset. "Drive down to the end of Holiday Isle, Aunt Sister," Haley said. "We can show Frances all the blue herons, and maybe we'll see the green flash." And Sister turned left and drove down Holiday Isle.

The road ends at a dune. We got out and clambered up so we could see the sunset. To our right, across a large inlet, was Destin Harbor, where fishing boats were being berthed for the night. To our left was the Gulf. We were standing on a small spit of beach that tends to disappear during storms and then rebuild. It's a favorite place for seabirds, particularly the herons. The water is shallow enough there for good fishing.

We came down the dune and walked toward the water. The sun was in our eyes, but we saw several of the huge birds had waded into the water.

"This is so beautiful," Frances said.

Mary Alice reached down and picked up a beer can. "Drives me crazy when people dump trash off the boats."

"There's a whole garbage sack," Haley said.

And that's exactly what it looked like, a white plastic sack filled with garbage at the edge of the water. And that's what we thought it was until we were right on it. Sister was slightly ahead, so she was the first one to see what was really lying on the beach, close enough to the water to be lapped by small waves. "My God!" she exclaimed, stepping back, holding out her arms to stop us. "It's a person!"

# Chapter
## 5

For a moment, there was utter confusion. I think Frances screamed. I know she stepped back into me, knocking me flat on my behind on the hard sand. I remember her arms whirling like windmills as she tripped over me and tried unsuccessfully to keep her balance.

"Is he dead?" Haley asked, looking around Mary Alice at what we had thought was garbage.

"Definitely." Mary Alice took a step closer.

"Dear God," Frances moaned into the sand.

"Are you hurt?" I whispered. I don't know why I was whispering. It just seemed the thing to do.

"Dear God," Frances moaned again. "A dead body."

Mary Alice and Haley were creeping toward the form at the edge of the water as if it might do something unexpected, like sit up and say, "Trick or treat." I sat up and a pain shot through my tailbone. "Shit!" I muttered.

The sun was close to the horizon, shining right into my eyes, but I saw Sister and Haley stop. Sister turned to Haley and said something, and they began to back up. I groaned and got to my feet. Pain! I'd busted my butt for sure. I started shuffling toward them.

"Stay back, Mama," Haley said. Her face was strange, contorted. "It's Millicent Weatherby and you don't want to see her."

I stopped. "Millicent? Millicent's dead?"

"Run to the car, Haley," Sister handed her the keys. "Call 911."

"That's Millicent over there?" I pointed to the form in the water. "That can't be Millicent!"

Frances moaned. She was on her hands and knees in the sand, her face hidden in her arms, her behind stuck up in the air.

"It's Millicent." Sister sat down beside Frances. "I think I'm going to be sick."

"Put your head down, Aunt Sister," Haley said. "Take deep breaths. I'll be right back." She sprinted across the dune toward the car.

I sat down gingerly beside Mary Alice. And then there were several strange minutes I'll remember all my life. Everything seemed beautiful, peaceful, and surreal. The sun touched the water and I imagined I could hear the sizzle; several blue herons sailed in on giant wings to join the others on the beach. A small boat crossed the inlet to the harbor, the music from its radio louder than its engine. A moment or so after the boat's passage, its wake stirred the white bundle that was Millicent Weatherby. Millicent who was dead, whose body was being pushed higher onto the beach by small waves.

None of us spoke for a few minutes. We heard the sirens

as the rescue squad left the fire station across on the main-
land. Then another siren crossing the bridge.

"I wonder how often they see drownings," I mused.

"Too often," Mary Alice's head was still down so she was
talking to the sand. "But this isn't one of them."

"What?" I asked.

"Oh, Lord, Mouse! It looked like someone tried to cut her
head off!"

"What?" I said. "What are you talking about?"

"They're coming!" Haley called from the top of the dune.
Just at that second, the last of the sun was swallowed by
the water with a great green gulp.

"Someone killed Millicent?"

"Oh, Lord!" Sister moaned.

"Oh, Lord!" Frances echoed.

"They'll be here in a minute." Haley sat down beside me
and took my hand. "Are you okay, Mama?"

"Her throat was cut?"

"Be grateful you didn't see her, Mama. And she's been in
the water, so her body's probably damaged other than that.
You know, by sharks and things."

"Shut up, Miss Open Heart Cut People's Guts Out
Nurse," Sister said into her hands. "Lord! And to think we
saw her this morning all in one piece."

Frances burrowed her head deeper into the sand. "Oh,
God! There are pieces missing? I'll never touch seafood
again."

"Sorry, Frances," Haley apologized. "I was just speculating. Of course there aren't any pieces missing."

"Well, quit speculating," Sister grumbled.

I jumped in. "The child said she was sorry, Mary Alice."
I patted Haley's hand.

"It's okay," Haley said. "We're all just rattled."

The sirens were screaming down the Holiday Isle road now. A few of the herons, disturbed by the noise, took off, running a short distance on their stick legs before they lifted into the air.

"What do they do for broken tailbones?" I asked Haley.

"Put a shot of xylocaine in it. Cortisone. Why?"

"I think Frances broke mine when she knocked me down."

"Shut up," Frances said. "Everybody shut up."

And we did. The sirens wailed to a stop at the dune and three uniformed men and one woman came scrambling over it, carrying all kinds of heavy and totally unnecessary resuscitation equipment. We all stood up to meet them, including Sister who was about as green as the sky had been a few moments before.

"You the women who called?" the youngest of the men wanted to know.

"I did." Haley took a step toward them. "There's a body over there." She pointed toward the white form that was Millicent, and that had now washed farther up on the beach.

Lugging their heavy equipment as if they expected to perform a Lazarus miracle, the four hurried toward the body. The four of us stayed where we were. We watched as they circled the white bundle, as they conferred. Finally the woman broke away and came back to us.

"She's wet," she said. We looked at each other, puzzled.

"She's part way in the water," Sister stated the obvious.

"Was she like this when you got here?"

"Wet? Yes. Dead? Yes. Why?"

"If she's wet she belongs to the Florida Marine Patrol, not us. We're the Okaloosa County Sheriff's Department. We'll call them."

"You've got to be kidding," Haley said. "How long will it take for them to get here?"

"Depends. Sometimes they're right in the harbor. Sometimes not." She turned around and yelled at one of her cohorts, "Buddy, get the marines." Then she turned back to us. "Sorry about this, but it's out of our jurisdiction." She shook hands with Mary Alice who was standing closest to her. "I'm Lisa Andrews. Are you ladies okay?"

"Been better," Sister admitted. "We know the lady."

"Really?" Lisa Andrews took out a notepad. "Who is she?"

"Her name is Millicent Weatherby. She's resident manager at Gulf Towers where I have a condo."

Officer Andrews looked up from her writing. "Fairchild's wife?"

"Yes. You know Fairchild?"

"Sure. He's one of the head honchos in the Polar Bear Club. Bunch of old fools get naked and go swimming every winter, freeze their balls off. Get arrested every time because their wives call and tell us when they're going. Scared they're going to have a heart attack. That's his wife?" She motioned toward the water.

We all nodded.

"I think I've talked to her." She turned and screeched, "Buddy! You get the marines?" We all jumped.

"They're out of the boat," he answered. "They'll be here in a few minutes in the van."

"Well," Lisa Andrews said, "I guess there's no hurry. Why don't y'all sit down and make yourselves comfortable?"

We sat and looked over the darkening harbor. Lisa Andrews went over and joined the three men who were huddled around Millicent's body.

"What," Frances wondered, "if someone got killed in the dunes and it rained."

"You'd have to wait on the Marine Patrol," Mary Alice said.

"My tail hurts," I said, but nobody was paying any attention.

In June, twilight lasts a long time, but we were about to run out of light when the Florida Marine Patrol officers finally made it over the dune.

"Where the hell you been?" Lisa Andrews called when she spotted them.

"Home eating supper," one of them said.

"You probably shouldn't have! Wait till you see this!" Lisa Andrews sounded gleeful.

"I think I hate that woman," Sister said. "Don't you hate women like that, Mouse?"

"Women like what? My tail hurts. I may need to go to the emergency room."

"You know. Trying to act tough."

"Maybe she *is* tough," Frances said. "Women in her position have to be, have to develop a tough veneer."

"The guidance counselor has spoken," Mary Alice said.

Frances began to cry. "I think I better just go home tonight. I wasn't expecting the vacation from hell."

Haley put her arms around her. "It'll be all right as soon as we get away from here, won't it, Aunt Sister?"

"I'm sorry, Frances," Sister said. "I'm just upset."

"I'm in pain," I said.

"Ladies?" A large man with thinning hair and a round, babyish face had walked up. He was dressed in the uniform of the Florida Marine Patrol. "I'm Lieutenant Major Bissell. I'd like to ask you a few questions."

"Please hurry," Mary Alice said. "I need to go to the bathroom."

He smiled. "I'll make it quick as I can." He took out the usual notepad and pen. "Your names?"

We supplied that, our addresses, where we were staying in Destin, and why we were there.

"I'm going to the writers' conference, too," he said, beaming at Sister. By now it was so dark, he had had to turn a penlight on to see his notepad.

"Good," Sister said. "I'll see you there. Now, tell me, would I be breaking one of your laws if I made a quick trip back in the dunes?"

"I think it would be all right."

"Just don't get wet," Frances called as Mary Alice climbed up through the sea oats. I could tell I was going to have to keep these two apart.

"Lisa says you knew Mrs. Weatherby, the victim."

"We've known her for years," I said. I explained that she and her husband had the condo next to Sister's.

"I knew her, too," Lieutenant Major (what kind of a title was that?) Bissell said. "Destin's still a small town in the wintertime." He flicked his pen off and on with his fingernail. "She showed me some property in the new development. It's beautiful, but too rich for my blood." He cleared his throat. "She was a nice lady."

"Lieutenant Major Bissell—" Haley began.

"Just Lieutenant. Major's my first name. Confuses everybody, including me."

"Lieutenant Bissell, I saw Mrs. Weatherby's body. I know you have a murder case on your hands."

"I think we're safe in saying she didn't die of natural causes."

I remembered what Sister had said about Millicent's throat and shuddered.

"Well, who'll tell Mr. Weatherby about it?" Haley continued. "Is there some policy that you have to be the ones to do it?"

"We usually do. Why?"

"We all know Fairchild very well, especially my aunt. I know it'll be hard, but I think it should come from us."

What a wonderful child I had raised. When Sister got back from her trip to the sea oats, it was all settled. The lieutenant would go with us, but Mary Alice would be the one to break the news of Millicent's death to Fairchild.

"You volunteered me to tell Fairchild?" It was too dark to see the expression on her face, fortunately. She was quiet for a moment and then sighed. "Well, so much for having to pee."


He knew when he answered the door, when he saw all of us, including Lieutenant Bissell, when Mary Alice held out her arms. He had had a similar visit when his first wife Margaret centered the utility pole on Highway 98.

"Millicent?" he asked, the blood draining from his face. "What happened?"

"She was killed, Fairchild," Sister said.

He looked confused. "But the lights are still on."

"She didn't hit a utility pole, Fairchild. We found her body on the beach."

"Millicent drowned? She never went near the water."

Sister looked imploringly at Lieutenant Bissell, who stepped forward and suggested that we all go in and sit down. Just at that moment, the elevator opened and Eddie and Laura Stamps, the couple who live in the apartment on the other side of Sister's, got out. Like Sister, they had owned their apartment for years, but they had retired and moved from Atlanta three years ago to become permanent residents. In their mid-sixties, the Stampses both had the tanned, extra crispy skin of people who spend most of their time on golf courses and boats. They stopped when they saw us standing at Fairchild's door with Lieutenant Bissell.

"Patricia Anne? Mary Alice? Is something wrong?" Laura asked.

"It's Millicent," I said. I remembered that Millicent had been her close friend and I couldn't say the next words.

Laura walked toward us with Eddie trailing her. "What about Millicent?"

Haley answered the question. "She's dead, Mrs. Stamps."

Laura's hands flew to her chest. "Dead? Millicent's dead? Where's Fairchild?"

"Here I am, Laura." Fairchild's voice was shaky and frail. Lieutenant Bissell backed up so the Stampses could get through the door to Fairchild. They both embraced him.

"What on God's earth?" Eddie Stamps asked. "What's happened?"

Fairchild shook his head. "She drowned."

"Get out of the hall, everybody," Sister demanded. "This is like playing sardines."

We all followed her except Frances, who told me she was going to go find the aspirin, maybe a Valium, maybe several of each, and headed next door.

Fairchild and the Stampses sat on the sofa and the rest of us gathered around. There was a half-played game of solitaire on the coffee table, and a Gilligan's Island rerun was playing loudly on TV. Lieutenant Bissell reached for the remote and turned it off.

Sister leaned forward. "Fairchild, Millicent didn't just drown. She was killed. We found her body on the beach at the end of Holiday Isle. That sandbar down there where all the herons are."

"Millicent was killed?" Fairchild still looked puzzled.

"You mean murdered?" Eddie Stamps asked.

"Yes, sir." Lieutenant Bissell's voice seemed to boom in relief that the word had finally been spoken. "I'm sorry."

"Oh, God!" Laura put her head in her hands, and Eddie put his arms around her shoulder. A large man whose white hair drew a perfect circle around a tanned scalp, his arm seemed heavy on her thin shoulders.

"Excuse me," Fairchild said. He got up and made a dash for the bathroom.

Laura began to sob. "We were going to see if Fairchild and Millicent wanted to go to dinner." Eddie's fingers tightened on her arm.

"Let's get out of here, Mama," Haley whispered to me.

I looked around Millicent's living room. This morning she had walked into this room and allayed Fairchild's fear; it would never happen again. Suddenly, the fact that she had not come home last night loomed as an important piece of information that Fairchild would have to tell the lieutenant.

"Lieutenant," I said, "you don't need us for anything, do you?"

"I'll need to talk to you later."

"We're going next door, then." I looked at Mary Alice who had reached over and was moving a red four to a black five on the solitaire game. "Mary Alice?"

"I think I'll stay a while, see if Fairchild's going to be all right."

"Okay. If you need us just holler."

"All of a sudden, I couldn't breathe in there," Haley said as I closed the door behind us. She shuddered. "I knew exactly how Fairchild felt when he opened the door and saw us standing there with the policeman. We didn't have to say a word. He knew, just like I did with Tom."

I nodded.

"And then when he found out she was murdered!" Haley began to cry.

"Come on, honey," I said. "Let's go see if Frances has taken all the aspirin and Valium."

"I'm so glad you didn't see her, Mama. Who would have killed Millicent like that?"

"God knows, honey." I led my weeping daughter into Sister's condo where my best friend sat on the sofa with an afghan over her head. "Frances?" I said. "What are you doing?"

"Saying my mantra and freezing."

"Why don't you turn the air conditioner up?"

"You mean down?"

"Whatever. So it's not so cold." I've never figured out if that's up or down.

"I did turn it down." Frances's voice was muffled. "I think I'm in shock."

"No you're not," Haley said, wiping her cheeks with the back of her hands.

"Yes, I am."

"No, you're not. I know what shock's like."

Lord! "I'm going to make some hot tea," I said. I went into the kitchen and put the water on to boil. Then I reached up in the cabinet, took down a bottle of bourbon, and put it on the tray with the tea cups.

"Did you take any Valium?" I asked Frances as I brought the tea to the living room.

She lowered the afghan. "No."

"Then pour a slug of this into your tea. And you, too," I said to Haley.

"It'll taste awful," she said.

But Frances was already lacing her tea with the bourbon. "I had an aunt used to do this."

"So did I," I said. "A toddy for the body."

"And another aunt drank paregoric." Frances sipped the tea and made a face.

"One of my great-aunts did," I said.

"Which one?" Haley asked.

"Aunt Ida. You know, Haley, the one who got hurt when the fish hit her on the head. Came right through the window. Nobody would have believed her if her brother and his wife hadn't been standing there. A three pound big mouthed bass. Whack, right on the side of her head. Knocked her cold."

"Where did it come from?" Frances draped the afghan around herself like a cape.

"Best they can figure, a little twister sucked some of the fish from the pasture pond. There were several out in the yard just flapping around."

Haley poured some bourbon into her cup and held it up. "To Aunt Ida," she said.

"To all the Aunt Idas," Frances said. "Bless their hearts."

By the time Fred called, we had each eaten a sandwich, and we were in the middle of a three-hand bridge game that none of us could concentrate on. He sounded very excited about the Metal Fab merger. Everything was going to be great, better than great. Check and see if any of the condos in the building were for sale.

"Ha," I said, and didn't tell him about Millicent Weatherby. What I told him was to be careful, that I loved him.

I had just hung up when Mary Alice came in. We all wanted to know how Fairchild was.

"Dr. Harris down on the second floor came up and gave

him a sedative," she said. "Laura's called some people and they're beginning to come in. Bless her heart. She's so upset, I thought we were going to have to get the doctor to give her something, too."

Mary Alice looked tired. "How about a toddy for the body, Sister?" I asked. "And I'll fix you a sandwich."

"Thanks, Mouse."

"Did Lieutenant Bissell ask Fairchild any questions?" Haley wanted to know.

"A few. He was very nice. He'll get around to being tougher, though. Poor Fairchild."

"I wonder where Millicent spent last night," I said from the kitchen. "Who she spent the night with."

"You know what puzzles me?" Sister said. "She had on the same clothes, the same clothes she had on at the Redneck and this morning. Now wouldn't you think if she had slept in that outfit like she said, that she couldn't wait to take a shower and change? Millicent was meticulous. She certainly wouldn't have gone to work in those clothes."

"Seems to me that after a night like that she would have just gone to bed and caught up on sleep." Haley said.

Mary Alice sighed and propped her feet on the coffee table. "I told Major about the clothes. He made a note."

"Major Bissell?" I stuck some bread in the toaster.

"Uh huh. He's having a story critiqued at the writers' conference, too. I hope he doesn't get so tied up on this case that he doesn't get to come to it."

"If Millicent was having an affair, maybe Fairchild did her in," Frances said.

"Not Fairchild," Sister said emphatically.

But I knew what Frances was thinking. Anybody is capable of doing anything if they are pushed too far. I had taken the same psych courses she had.

The phone's ringing startled me. Haley looked up expectantly, but it was a neighbor from downstairs. That was the first call. In the next hour there were at least ten more, residents of the condo and friends of Millicent who had heard about the circumstances of her death and our discovering the body.

"I'm unplugging the phone," Sister said finally. And she did. We watched the late news and heard that a woman's body had been found on the beach at Holiday Isle, that identification was being withheld pending notification of the next of kin.

A woman's body. Such cold, uncaring words. Tears stung my eyes. Millicent Weatherby, you were a good old broad from De Funiak Springs. How could you have met such a violent death?

# Chapter
## 6

After Haley and I were in bed, we heard the elevator open and close several times. The sound brought the dream I had had the night before popping up from my unconscious. The memory was so vivid that I asked Haley if she had heard anything out in the hall the night before.

"Like what?" she asked, looking up from her book.

"Like two people arguing. One was calling the other one a stupid bitch and saying to get on the elevator."

"You heard two people arguing out by the elevator?" She put her book down, interested. "Was it a man and a woman?"

"I don't know,' I admitted. "I think one was a man, but it was like a dream, a real clear one."

"I didn't hear anything," Haley said. "What were they arguing about?"

"I have no idea. It probably was a nightmare." I picked

up my book and began to read again. In a moment, Haley did the same. After about five minutes, though, she pushed her cover back and announced that she had to go make a phone call. I don't know how long the call lasted, but I certainly knew who it was to. By the time she came to bed, I was sound asleep.

"Psst!" Sister said into my ear. "Psst, Mouse!"

I came straight up. "What's the matter?"

"Are you asleep? I thought you might like to take a walk on the beach."

"Are you crazy?"

"Shhh. Don't wake Haley up."

"What time is it?" I whispered.

"Don't know. I didn't look."

"Yes, you did. It's the middle of the damn night. What time is it? Two? Three?"

"It's late," Mary Alice admitted, "but I can't go to sleep. Come on, let's go down to the beach."

"Absolutely not. I'm going back to sleep." I pulled the sheet over my head.

"What's the matter?" Haley mumbled.

"Do you want to go for a walk on the beach?" Sister asked her.

"Now?" Haley's voice sounded confused. "What time is it?"

"God knows. " I said, uncovering my head. "Go back to sleep, honey."

"Y'all are missing the Perseid meteor shower," Sister said.

"That's not until August. Go away."

She did. I heard the bedroom door close, heard Haley's breathing resume the pattern of sleep, heard the elevator door open and close. Shit! Sister didn't have a bit of business going to the beach by herself in the middle of the night. I scrambled out of bed, fumbled around in the dark for some clothes, and tiptoed from the room. Sister was sitting on the living room sofa reading a magazine.

"Oh, good," she said. "You changed your mind."

Ten minutes later, we were walking barefooted along the great shallow sea that is the Gulf of Mexico. There were no waves tonight, simply a curling of warm water around our ankles as our feet sank into the sand. Haze haloed the lights over the stile behind us.

"Everybody on the sixth floor is awake," I said, looking back toward the building where the four apartments were a streak of light across an otherwise dark building.

"A sad night," Sister said. "The people in the end apartment, the one next to Eddie and Laura, may be getting ready to go to work, though. They both work for Delta Airlines. He's a pilot and she's a flight attendant. Maybe vice versa. Anyway, they're real nice. Remember I told you about them, Mouse? When they moved in back in the spring?"

"They're the ones with the teenage daughter?"

"Uh huh. Jack and Tammy Berliner. Their daughter's name is Sophie."

"And they fly out of Atlanta? That's not exactly commuting distance."

"They've got a Cessna, I understand. And they don't work every day. They'll make a flight and then be off for a couple of days. It seems to be working out okay. Millicent says the move was mainly for Sophie and she thinks it's done her good. She's not quite as weird." Sister stopped walking. "Oh, my. Poor Millicent."

We stood at the edge of the water. Beyond us, some flounder fishermen were shining their lanterns into the water. Above us, the stars wheeled hazily.

"I hope he was good," Sister said.

"Who?"

"The man Millicent was with last night."

"Oh, for heaven's sake. Maybe she just went to sleep like she said she did."

"I hope not. I hope she was with some strong, virile man who made love to her all night."

I was getting caught up in this. "A sweet and gentle man."

"I got a big one!" one of the flounderers shouted.

"To each his own," Sister said.

The next morning, it was about nine o'clock when I woke up. Haley's bed was empty. I put on my robe and went to see what was going on. Haley and Frances were sitting on the balcony drinking coffee and passing a pair of binoculars back and forth.

"Good morning," I said. "What are y'all looking at?"

"Porpoises," Haley looked up. "There's a whole bunch of them out there. How's your tailbone?"

"Not as bad as I thought it was going to be. Did your Aunt Sister get off to her writers' conference?"

"Bright eyed and bushy tailed. She's been gone a long time," Frances said. "She left you a Post-it on the refrigerator."

I headed into the kitchen, bleary eyed, amazed as always at my sister's energy. She couldn't have had more than three or four hours' sleep and she was bright eyed and bushy tailed? I took the Post-it from the refrigerator. It said, "Patricia Anne, please take care of Fairchild."

Take care of Fairchild? What was I supposed to do to take care of Fairchild? I poured a cup of coffee and went back to the balcony.

"She wants me to take care of Fairchild," I said.

"I know. I saw the note." Haley handed Frances the binoculars. "Look, Frances, right to the left of that bait boat. See the fin? Reckon that could be a shark?"

"Could be. I swear I haven't been more than ankle deep in the ocean since I saw *Jaws*. Frances trained the binoculars in the direction Haley was pointing.

"I guess I'd better get dressed and go see about him," I said. "See how he fared last night."

"Mary Alice checked before she left. She said he's doing pretty good. Still wrought up, of course, but who wouldn't be?" Frances handed the binoculars back to Haley. "It's a porpoise."

"You're probably right." Haley put the binoculars on the table. "If he's real wrought up, Mama, maybe that doctor that lives downstairs needs to check him out again."

"I'm still pretty wrought up, myself, from finding the body yesterday," Frances said. "I sure didn't sleep much last night."

"You could have gone for a walk on the beach with Mary Alice," I grumbled. I went to get a shower and get dressed. Fairchild was one of my favorite people. I didn't need a reminder from Sister or a description of him as "real wrought up," whatever that meant, to go see about him.

Fifteen minutes later, as I stepped into the corridor, I almost bumped into a beautiful blonde woman who was carrying a covered dish toward Fairchild's door. A quick dodge and some juggling saved the contents.

"I'm so sorry!" I said.

"It's okay." She smiled at me. "We almost had breakfast pizza all over us, didn't we?"

"I should have been more careful."

"No harm done." She smiled again. "I'm Tammy Berliner. I live down the hall."

"It's nice meeting you, Tammy. I'm Patricia Anne Hollowell, Mary Alice Crane's sister."

"It's nice meeting you, Mrs. Hollowell. I've heard her talk of you."

"Don't believe a word. And call me Patricia Anne, please." I motioned to the pizza. "You on your way next door?"

She nodded. "I can't believe this has happened. Can you?"

"No," I said. "I can't. We've known Millicent for twenty years, the nicest person you'd ever meet. Fairchild, too."

"I know. Can you knock on the door for me?"

I did, and Laura Stamps answered. My first thought, as usual when I see Laura, and which I had the decency to feel guilty about, was that it was a shame they hadn't invented sunscreen years ago. Laura's tanned, leathery skin looked like a mask this morning. With cracks in it.

"Come in," she said, taking the dish from Tammy and nodding toward the living room. "Fairchild's in there."

"How is he?" I asked.

"More hungover from what that fool doctor gave him last night than anything else." Laura disappeared into the kitchen.

"That's breakfast pizza, Laura," Tammy called. "It's for eating right now if anybody wants some."

It sounded good to me. I hadn't had anything but a cup of coffee but didn't feel comfortable diving into his food without speaking to Fairchild first. So I stepped into his living room where women were perched everywhere, on the arms of the sofa, on the footstool; those young and thin enough were sitting on the floor. Fairchild sat in his recliner, looking dazed. Or panicked.

"Hey, Fairchild," I said, stepping over several women to

kiss him on the cheek. Mary Alice's cryptic message had suddenly become clear. "I came to get you. There's a policeman next door who wants to talk to you."

He looked up in surprise. "Now?"

"He can wait if you can't come now." I looked straight at him and saw him catch on.

"I'll come." He came up out of the recliner with an agility that was amazing in a man his age. "Right now."

"Good," I said. Nobody seemed to think it strange that a policeman would be next door to question Fairchild, and no one saw me grab the breakfast pizza on our way out.

"Thanks, Patricia Anne," he said as I opened Sister's door.

"You're welcome. You want anything to eat?"

"I just want to go to the bathroom and rest a while."

"Well, we can arrange that. There's the bathroom and you can take a nap on Mary Alice's bed." He seemed to brighten a little at that idea.

Haley and Frances had disappeared, probably had gone to the beach. While Fairchild was in the bathroom, I made up Sister's bed, got a pillow from the linen closet, put a fresh pillowcase on it, and located a light cotton blanket.

"Oh, my," Fairchild said, stretching out. I think he was asleep by the time I left the room.

I headed for the breakfast pizza which was nothing but mega fat grams and cholesterol: ham, cheese, bacon, eggs. Delicious. Haley and Frances showed up in time to help me finish it, Haley saying at least ten times between bites that our arteries would never be the same.

"Y'all be quiet," I cautioned them when they came in. I told them what had happened in Fairchild's apartment and that he was napping on Sister's bed.

"All those women in there consoling him? You sure you didn't pull him out of the briar patch?" Frances asked.

"I'm sure. The ladies of Gulf Towers are formidable consolers."

Haley took another piece of pizza. "Good cooks, though."

"This came from the lady at the end of the hall, the one who moved in this spring, Tammy Berliner. She's a beautiful blonde, probably just a little older than you, Haley. She's a flight attendant for Delta."

"She commutes to Atlanta?" Frances asked.

"She and her husband both. He's a pilot. Or else she's the pilot and he's the flight attendant. One or the other. Sister says they have a teenager named Sophie. I love that name, don't you? Sophie Berliner. And I'll bet she hates it. Probably wishes she had her mama's name."

"Everybody hates their name," Frances said. "It's a given."

"I hate mine," Haley said cheerfully, her mouth full of cholesterol.

I took the last piece of pizza. "Sorry. We should have gone with Letitia Maude, your papa's first choice."

"Letitia Maude Hollowell," Haley mused. "I'd have been a completely different person."

"You would have been a perfectionist," Frances said. "A Letitia Maude would do everything just so."

"Like dresser drawers. All my dresser drawers would be straight. And my closets. A place for everything." Haley dribbled water down her shirt from a glass that had condensation on it.

"Letitia Maude wouldn't have done that," Frances said.

"You're right," Haley giggled, wiping her shirt with the back of her arm. "And you know what? In Letitia Maude's kitchen, even the roach motels would be lined up perfectly."

Frances giggled, too.

I didn't feel like playing along with them. My eyes were

still puffy from lack of sleep, I had a slight tail-ache, and I was worried about the nice man asleep on Sister's bed who had just lost his wife so violently. I got up, went into the kitchen, and was putting on another pot of coffee when someone knocked on the door. Expecting Laura Stamps, who would be wondering where Fairchild was, I was startled to see the small, black-clad figure that looked up as I opened the door.

"Is my mother here?" she asked. "Tammy Berliner? She's not next door."

"No," I said. "You're Sophie?" The question wasn't a rhetorical one; I truly wasn't sure. That the blond, golden-skinned Tammy could have given birth to this child was indeed questionable. Standing before me was one of those big-eyed, waifish children you see on velvet paintings. Long black hair hung limply against the palest skin I'd ever seen. And the outfit she had on was a loose robe that reached the floor and seemed to be made of black gauze.

"I'm Sophie," she said. "I'm sorry to have bothered you."

"No problem." Who was it who had told me Sophie was less weird since they had moved to Destin? "I'm Mrs. Hollowell, Mrs. Crane's sister. Would you like to come in and have something to drink?"

Sophie scowled, and I realized that part of the wide-eyed look was caused by a liberal application of eye liner, deep purple shadow, and what couldn't possibly be real black eyelashes.

"I'm looking for my mother," she said. She turned and wafted toward their apartment at the end of the corridor.

"Nice meeting you, too," I mumbled to myself.

"Who was that?" Haley asked as I walked back into the kitchen.

"One of the Addams family children."

"Which apartment do they live in?"

I leaned across the kitchen counter. "It was Sophie Berliner." I described her to Haley and Frances.

"Rebelling," Frances said, forever the guidance counselor.

"How old did you say she is?" Haley asked.

"Thirteen or fourteen, I'd guess. Y'all want some more coffee?"

Frances got up and handed me her cup. "Neither fish nor fowl at that age. I wonder how close she was to Millicent. The black could be her way of showing mourning."

*Shit*, I thought. *The kid's just screwed up*. But I didn't say it. Instead, I took my coffee into the bedroom, lay down on my bed, and opened my book. Lack of sleep and the breakfast pizza immediately took their toll. I was so sound asleep, the pounding on the door an hour later was incorporated into my dream as Fred hanging a picture on the wall. The sound of voices brought me awake, though. I peeked into the living room and saw Fairchild and a couple of Florida Marine Patrol officers. I ran a comb through my hair, brushed my teeth (on the mirror was a Post-it that Haley and Frances had gone to the outlet mall), and went to see what was going on.

The two Marine Patrol officers jumped up as I came in. One was a pretty young woman with curly brown hair, the kind of hair that I was sure drove her crazy frizzing in the high humidity of the beach. I knew, because mine did the same thing. The other officer was a man close to retirement age who had the opposite problem. You could have counted the hairs on his head.

"Patricia Anne," Fairchild said, "this is Elaine Gregory and Tim Blankenship. They're here to ask me some questions about Millicent."

I shook both the officers' hands and asked if they wanted to talk to Fairchild alone.

"Stay, by all means, Mrs. Hollowell," Elaine Gregory said. "I understand you found Mrs. Weatherby's body."

"I didn't look at her," I admitted. "My sister did, sort of accidentally. And my daughter." I sat on the sofa beside Fairchild. "You feeling better?" I asked him.

"Yes. Thanks." But he was still very pale and the hands he kept running along the crease in his pants were shaking. Pants that Millicent had ironed. I looked away toward the water.

"We just need to ask you a few questions, Mr. Weatherby," Tim Blankenship said.

"All right."

Too placid. "He's on medication," I told the officers. And, patting Fairchild's arm, "You don't have to answer anything now, Fairchild."

"It's okay, Patricia Anne."

Officer Blankenship cleared his throat and looked at his partner. She nodded. "Mrs. Weatherby didn't come home night before last?" he asked.

"I've already told the Major Lieutenant about that. She had drinks at the Redneck Riviera with some friends and had a little too much. She went to sleep in the car in the parking lot."

"Do you know who the friends were?"

"Some people from Blue Bay Ranch, I think." Fairchild's fingers quit creasing his pants. "I'm not sure."

"We'll check," Elaine Gregory said.

"She's never done anything like that before," Fairchild looked at me. "Tell them, Patricia Anne."

"She's never done anything like that before," I said, hoping I wasn't lying through my teeth.

Elaine Gregory ran her fingers through her hair, making it spring out even more. "What time did she come in?"

"Look," Fairchild said. "I'm trying to cooperate, but where's that other fellow, that colonel what's his name. I've already told him all this."

"Lieutenant Bissell is taking a personal leave day," Officer Gregory said.

"He's at the writers' conference," I explained.

"Well, damn!" Fairchild's face was no longer pale. He leaned forward. "Look here," he told the two officers, "you find out what happened to my wife and you tell me when you are going to release her body. She's got a sick sister in De Funiak Springs and this whole thing is going to kill her. I've got to at least tell her and her brother when we can plan a funeral. You hear me? And I'm damned if you're going to keep asking me the same questions you've got the answers to there in those damn notebooks."

This was the man who had just said he would answer anything they asked? I reached over and patted his arm again.

The two officers didn't seem at all surprised by Fairchild's outburst. "Okay, Mr. Weatherby," Elaine Gregory said. "I'll read you what we have in our notes and you can tell us if we're right. Okay?"

"I guess so." Fairchild folded his arms and waited.

Elaine Gregory consulted her notebook. "Mrs. Weatherby got home between six and six-thirty yesterday morning." She looked at Fairchild and he nodded. "She said she had been sleeping in her car at the Redneck Riviera because she had had too much to drink."

"She only had a couple of drinks," Fairchild said. "But she wasn't much of a drinker."

"She was with some people from Blue Bay, you think, either the staff or prospective clients."

"That's what she said."

"Which? Staff?"

"I'm not sure," Fairchild admitted. "I was angry and relieved at the same time, so I don't remember what she said about who she was with."

Elaine nodded and continued. "You had a few cross words, and then Mrs. Weatherby came over here to tell Mrs. Hollowell she was all right."

"She did," I agreed.

"And then she went back to your apartment, Mr. Weatherby, discovered you were out of tomato juice and said she was going to run over to Delchamps Super Market to get some."

"Their Food Club tomato juice is delicious," I said. "The store brand? It's not as tart as some of the others. About twenty cents cheaper, too."

Officer Gregory cut her eyes at me. "Well, it's the truth," I said.

"And she never came home." Tim Blankenship spoke up.

"No," Fairchild said. "And if you'll consult your notes, you'll see I thought she had decided to go on to work."

"Not in the clothes she had slept in, Fairchild," I interrupted. "Millicent wouldn't be caught dead not looking neat as a pin."

*But she had been. Shut up, Patricia Anne.* I bit my lip and looked out at the Gulf again.

"Thank you, Mr. Weatherby." Elaine Gregory put her notebook back in her pocket. "We're just doing our job, trying to find out what happened to your wife."

"I know," Fairchild said. "And I'm sorry I flared up. It

just seems so unnecessary to go over the same things again and again."

"We understand. We'll try not to do that." Elaine Gregory nodded toward Tim Blankenship. "You ready?"

They started out and I followed, being polite, seeing them out of the door. I was so close that when Elaine Gregory turned suddenly, I jumped backwards.

"Oh, Mr. Weatherby, there is one new thing we need to ask you about, the insurance policy."

Fairchild was standing in the middle of the living room. "What policy?" he asked, though I could tell he knew exactly what she was talking about.

"Mrs. Weatherby's million-dollar life insurance policy naming you the sole beneficiary."

My mouth fell open. "Millicent took out a million-dollar life insurance policy? God, Fairchild, that must have cost a fortune."

He sighed and looked down at the floor. "It's not what it sounds like."

"But you are the beneficiary, aren't you, Mr. Weatherby?" Tim Blankenship asked.

"Of course I'm the beneficiary. This is some kind of deal the Blue Bay Ranch Corporation cooked up, this insurance thing. One of Jason Marley's ideas. He's the one you need to talk to."

"We will, sir." Tim Blankenship opened the door. "Y'all have a good day now."

# Chapter 7

When the door closed, I turned and looked at Fairchild.
"The insurance was a Blue Bay perk, Patricia Anne," he said. "The corporation bought it and paid the premiums. The land was Millicent's part of the corporation, you see, and she wanted to make sure I wouldn't be left out if something happened to her." Fairchild shook his head. "To tell you the truth, I didn't pay much attention to it. Millicent was ten years younger than me, so it never occurred to me that I would collect it."

I came back into the living room. "I believe you, Fairchild."

"It looks bad, though, doesn't it?"

"It won't when they find out all the details."

Fairchild sank down on one of the wicker rockers and put his face in his hands. "I wish she had just sold the land to Jason Marley; he offered her a good price for it. But she wanted to be in on the development, said she wanted to be sure they did as little damage as possible to the environment." He looked up. "Who would have killed her, Patricia Anne?"

I shook my head that I couldn't imagine. I sat down in the chair across from him and for a few minutes we were quiet, lost in our own thoughts. Finally Fairchild sighed and said he had better go next door and see what was going on.

"I'm surprised Laura Stamps hasn't been over here looking for you," I said.

He managed a grin. "She's scared of Mary Alice."

I grinned back. "Smart woman."

"Thanks for the R and R." He got up. "I needed it."

"Mary Alice left me a note reminding me to rescue you."

"She did?" He looked pleased.

I handed him the Post-it that was in my pocket. "I would have done it anyway."

"Thanks." He left the apartment looking much better than he had when he came in.

I fixed myself a sandwich and went to the balcony to eat it. I missed Fred and wanted to talk to him. I missed Woofer and wanted to talk to him, too.

"You look woebegone," Mary Alice said behind me.

I jumped. "What are you doing home? The conference isn't over for the day, is it?"

"It is for me. All they're doing this afternoon is poetry." She said *poetry* as if it were something ridiculous.

"I love poetry," I said.

"I like some of it, too," she admitted, plunking down in the chair beside me. "I like that woman's poetry, you know, that book you gave me Christmas. She makes sense."

"Mary Oliver?"

"Yeah. She's not at the conference."

"Too bad. Who is?"

"I don't remember." Sister held out a manila envelope. "We swapped short story manuscripts this morning and we're to critique them and take them back tomorrow."

"That sounds interesting. Did you see Major Bissell?'

"God yes, Mouse." Sister rattled the manila envelope. "I hope this isn't his story. Lord only knows what he'd write about. You know what he told me? Just came right out and told me while I was eating a doughnut and a kiwi?"

"What?"

"That Millicent's throat wasn't cut. He said it was torn, like some animal had ripped it right through the jugular and the carotid."

"Dear God!"

"You should have heard him describe what the blood must have been like."

"Don't tell me."

"Well, *spurting* and *fountain* were included."

"Thank you for sharing that," I said, putting my sandwich down.

"See?" Sister said. "I couldn't finish my snack either, and they'd put out all kinds of good stuff during the break." She looked down at the beach. "Where are Haley and Frances, and what's been going on?"

I told her they were at the outlet mall, described my rescue of Fairchild, and related the visit of the two Florida Marine Patrol officers. I even managed to remember the details, as many as Fairchild had related, of the insurance policy.

Sister was amazed. "Millicent had a million dollar life insurance policy?"

"A perk of the Blue Bay Ranch Corporation, so Fairchild says. But he's the beneficiary."

"You know, Mouse, I remember when Tod Abernathy bought that land over on the bay. You probably do, too. We thought he'd lost his mind spending a thousand dollars or some such amount on that worthless property. I thought Millicent was going to divorce him. And now it's Blue Bay Ranch."

"Beats all. Fairchild said Millicent wouldn't sell the property outright because she wanted to have a say-so in its development. She didn't want the environment disturbed."

"You know, that could be why someone killed her." Sister saw the look on my face. "I'm serious. She could have found out they were breaking some environmental law, maybe the wetland thing, and was going to squeal on them."

"Tell that to the lieutenant colonel tomorrow."

"Lieutenant Major. In the meantime, let's ride over there and see what those ranches look like. It's just what I've always wanted, a ranch on the beach."

"You want to wait on Haley and Frances?"

Mary Alice shook her head. "They wouldn't be interested."

"Haley said she wanted to see it."

"We can go back any time. We're just scouting."

I had grown accustomed to the seatbelt on Mary Alice's Jaguar, so when it grasped me I wasn't surprised. In fact, it gave me a sense of being pampered. "You're safe now, ma'am," the clasp proclaimed. And then Mary Alice peeled out of the parking lot.

"Slow down," I screeched.

"My Lord, Patricia Anne, I'm barely moving." Which was true when she said it, because by this time we were headed down Highway 98. Mary Alice has maxed out on the number of speeding tickets she can receive on 98 in a three-year period without having to go to driving school. It is, she claims, the fault of the Okaloosa County Sheriff's Department, who actually enforce the ridiculous thirty-mile-per-hour speed limit with unsportsmanlike shenanigans such as popping out from behind billboards and the Greek Orthodox church to nab innocent speeders.

So we drove sedately down 98, past the Mid-Bay Bridge to a huge billboard that proclaimed the entrance to Blue Bay Ranch was one-quarter mile on the left. The billboard, which did not have a policeman behind it today, featured a bikini-clad girl (much girl, small bikini) in cowboy boots, lassoing a sea horse.

"That's just downright tacky," I said, studying the sign.

"I know," Sister agreed. "I saw it on the way to the conference. They've got a pretty entrance, though."

Soon I noticed a split-rail fence wending through the stunted palmettos and saw-briars. "To keep the sea horses in, I suppose." I pointed toward the fence.

I thought it was funny, but Sister didn't even smile, just clicked on her left turn signal and pulled into the double driveway that made a "U" in front of an honest-to-God log cabin with a sign announcing it was the visitors' center. A small parking lot was on the side of the building, and I expected Mary Alice to stop there. Instead, she headed out one of the roads that angled from the "U" like antennae toward the bay. A man stepped from a guard house at the entrance to the road and she slowed.

"Ma'am," he said politely, "do you have a visitor's pass?"

"No," Sister said. "We're not visiting, just looking." And she drove on.

"I don't think that's what he meant," I said, nervously looking back at the guard standing in the middle of the road scratching his head.

"Then he should say what he means."

"I suppose so." What was the worst thing they could do to us? Run us out? I relaxed and looked around.

Other than the road, not much clearing had been done. Red flags and stakes with numbers on them marked the boundaries of lots. Tall pines leaned away from the Gulf, pushed constantly by the prevailing winds. Between them were the typical vegetation of the coastal piney woods and a lot of Sold signs.

"I'll bet there are rattlesnakes in here big as a tractor tire," I said.

"Looks about like it did when Tod Abernathy bought it," Sister said. "Any money Millicent got offered for it, she should have taken."

And then the road branched. We were almost to the bay when Sister said, "Look, Mouse. Can you believe that?"

It was a fairy-tale house, the only problem being that the imaginative architect had incorporated every fairy tale from Rapunzel and her tower to what looked suspiciously like a big shoe, but which must have been some kind of garden room. Painted a shrimp pink and trimmed in white ginger-bread, the house perched on the edge of Choctawhatchee Bay.

"It looks like about five houses squashed together," Mary Alice said, slowing so we could get a good look.

"It looks embarrassed."

"And there's a blue one."

Five houses had been completed or were close to comple-tion, five enormous houses, all rainbow colored, all mirrored in the bay. These, I realized, were situated on what was the prime location in Blue Bay Ranch. A couple of them already had piers and boat houses, but only the pink house seemed totally finished and occupied. A concrete block seawall prevented erosion by pushing the bay's tides down the beach for others to worry about.

"Lord have mercy," Sister said. "Who would ever have thought."

"Boggles the mind," I said. "Millicent was really in on something big, wasn't she?"

"Yes, she was. Bless her heart."

"This doesn't look like one of those community developments, though. You know, with the sidewalks and all."

"Let's stop by the visitors' center and get some brochures on our way out." Sister was forced to turn around in a pale lavender house's driveway since the road was blocked by a bulldozer, and we headed back the way we had come. As we passed the guard shack, she let the window down and called "Thank you." The man inside actually waved.

"Act like we're interested in buying some property," she said. "They'll jump on us like chickens on a June bug. You can find out all kinds of stuff that way."

"What kind of stuff is it we want to find out?"

"Well, personally, I want to know how much that pink house cost. Those folks got taken to the cleaners, I'll bet you." Sister pulled into the parking lot and we got out of the car. "I think this log cabin is cute, don't you? Those rocking chairs across the front?"

"I don't understand it."

"What's to understand? You sit on the porch and rock."

"I mean I don't understand this whole ranch bit. Did you ever hear of a ranch where the Intra-coastal Waterway runs right by the bunkhouse?" But I was speaking to Mary Alice's back as she disappeared into the log cabin.

We didn't have to act as if we were interested in property in order to have the sales staff jump on us like chickens on a June bug. They had spotted the Jaguar as it pulled into the parking lot. The first woman to get to Sister was skinny, in her forties, and had greenish-blond hair, something that happens sometimes in Florida given the amount of sun and chlorine people are exposed to. Her name tag read Lolita.

"Hello, hello," she smiled. "I'm Lolita Brown. Welcome to Blue Bay Ranch where your own personal rainbow ends."

Mary Alice looked at her. "My personal rainbow ends here?"

"She means the places cost a pot of gold," I said.

"Hush, Patricia Anne. That's not what she means at all, is it, Lolita?"

"Of course not." And then Lolita did something that made me decide that if I ever won the lottery and bought a place at Blue Bay, it would be from her. She grinned and said, "Well, maybe a little pot."

We introduced ourselves and declined the guided tour she offered. At her insistence, we admired the huge map on the wall that showed the configuration of all the building sites, denoting the ones that were sold with a pale pink, magic markered $x$. The prices were also marked on each lot, increasing in price as they neared the water.

I pushed my bifocals up and looked at the numbers. "Two hundred and twenty thousand dollars for a lot?" I gasped.

"Close to the bay with a view of the bridge," Lolita explained. "As you can see, there aren't many of them left."

"And the ones on the bay?" Sister asked.

"Are all sold. Many of them are already built on."

"We rode around there," Sister admitted. "I especially liked the pink house."

Lolita beamed. "That belongs to Mr. Jason Marley, the chairman of Blue Bay. It's a beauty, isn't it?"

"I've never seen anything quite like it," Sister said truthfully. "I don't suppose there's any chance he'll be selling anytime soon?"

"I wouldn't think so. He loves that place even though he's a widower and needs all that room like he needs a hole in his head." Lolita sighed a little wistfully. "Here," she said, going over to a desk and handing us several brochures, "take these home and look them over. I don't think you could go wrong here at Blue Bay."

We thanked her and left, promising that we would be back for the guided tour. I looked down at the first brochure. On the cover, the girl in the bikini lassoed the seahorse. Tacky.

"Well, what do you think?" Mary Alice asked as we got into the car.

"I think it's tacky," I said.

"I mean about Blue Bay Ranch."

I thought for a moment. "It's like they can't decide what they want to be. The split-rail fence and log cabin and even those houses on the bay. How would you describe them?"

"*Colorful* comes to mind." She turned onto Highway 98. "And I thought it was interesting that the pink one belonged to Jason Marley. Think about it, Mouse. You saw those numbers on that map that showed how much the lots cost. Whose property is it?"

"Millicent's. But I'm sure the property was her contribution to the Blue Bay Ranch Corporation."

"And where was Millicent living?"

"Gulf Towers."

"In the same condo that she and Tod Abernathy bought twenty years ago, still working as resident manager to pay the assessment fees."

"Maybe she didn't want one of those pink houses."

"She probably didn't, knowing Millicent. But I'd be willing to bet you her death had something to do with what's going on over there. We're talking *millions*, Mouse."

"Reckon Fairchild knew the extent of Millicent's estate?"

Mary Alice shrugged. "I doubt it. I doubt Millicent really believed it, that land going from a joke when Tod bought it for a thousand dollars to being worth a bundle. I just hope she realized it was valuable enough to get some good legal advice."

We passed the miniature golf course, the Wal-Mart, the new bungee jump where people were actually lined up to pay twenty-five dollars to jump from a tower attached to rubber bands.

"What are we doing to our beaches?" I asked.

"Nothing hurricanes won't take care of eventually." With that, Sister turned into Gulf Towers.

"I'm going to go check on Fairchild," she said, turning left as we got off the elevator at the sixth floor.

"I'll see where Haley and Frances are." I went into our apartment and saw that it was empty. A glance from the balcony showed me they were at the beach. I put on my bathing suit, slathered Factor 45 sunscreen all over me, and went to join them.

"Hey, Mama," Haley said, looking up from her book as I approached. "Where've you been?"

"Your Aunt Sister and I went over to Blue Bay Ranch to look around. It has to be seen to be believed."

"I wanted to go," Haley said.

"Me, too." Frances looked slightly pink.

"You better get under the umbrella," I said, handing her the sunscreen. "We'll take y'all back tomorrow."

"What's it like?" Haley asked.

I tried to explain the split-rail fence, the log cabin, the brightly colored houses that seemed to have been designed by architects who were familiar with every school of design and were determined to show it.

"Sounds cute," Frances said.

I looked to see if she meant it. She seemed to. "How long have y'all been out here in the sun?" I asked.

"A while." Haley closed the book she was reading. "We saw Sophie Berliner."

I sat down in the shade of the umbrella. "Here at the beach?"

Haley nodded. "Had to be her. Fit your description exactly, complete with the black gauze outfit. I know she was burning up."

"Making a statement." Frances settled into the shade beside me.

"Anyway," Haley continued, "she came over the stile like some kind of crow, sort of creeping along."

"And the lifeguard came to attention," Frances added. "Like someone had poked him with a stick."

"We found out why when she got to the water. She shucked off that black gauze and had on a bathing suit that was almost nonexistent. And the kid's got a shape like you wouldn't believe, Mama."

"She's only a child, Haley!" I protested.

Haley and Frances both laughed. "Some child!" Haley said. "I'll bet pacemakers were popping on all over the beach."

"How about that," I said. "You should have seen the skinny Lolita who showed us the layout of Blue Bay. Sounds like they should swap names."

"Sophie's doing just fine with the one she's got," Haley said.

"Have y'all seen Fairchild?" I asked.

Haley reached for the sunscreen. "I looked in on him for a minute. I thought you might be over there."

"Was he overwhelmed with women?"

"Nobody was there but Laura Stamps from next door. She was fixing him some lunch."

"Had he heard anything? Did he say?"

"I didn't ask. I just told him we were next door if he needed anything."

I remembered what Mary Alice had said about Millicent's throat looking as if it had been torn by an animal and told them.

"Lord!" Frances said. "A shark?"

"A shark wouldn't have just torn her throat," Haley said.

"He didn't say it was an animal. He just said that it wasn't cut with a knife or something like that."

"Vampires?"

Haley and I both looked at Frances.

"You're right," she said. "Vampires just leave teeth marks, don't they?"

We continued to look at her.

"What?" she asked. "What?"

"Vampires, Frances?"

"You're right. This is the Florida panhandle, not New Orleans." She reached for a beer from the cooler.

I turned over the book she was reading and looked at the cover. Anne Rice.

Frances turned a little pinker. "I guess there's a logical explanation. Right?"

Haley and I both nodded.

Mary Alice came over the stile and joined us. "Did Patricia Anne tell you about Blue Bay Ranch?" she asked Haley and Frances as she stretched out on a beach towel.

"I'm surprised Millicent and Fairchild weren't building a house over there," Haley said.

"Didn't Laura say she and Eddie were?" I handed Sister the sunscreen bottle. "Here, put some on your face."

But nobody could remember.

Sister handed the bottle back to me. "I'm just going to be here a minute. I've got to go read the short story I got at the conference this morning. Critique it."

"I'll go with you," I said. "We need a few things from Delchamps. We're almost out of bread, for one thing."

Haley looked up. "Get some of that no-fat caramel popcorn. I love that stuff."

"And those no-fat cookies, too," Frances chimed in. "The chocolate fudge kind."

"Some of that fruit dip and some apples." Sister sat up. "That stuff's great with those real crisp apples. Not the Delicious ones, the rounder, fatter ones. We need some of those, too."

"And tonight's two movies for the price of one night. See what you can find, Mama. And you better check before you leave. We may need some more Diet Coke."

"Does Chinese suit everybody tonight?" Sister asked. "We can just call it in."

I pushed up from my chair. "We really lead a gastronomically deprived life, don't we?"

They had the decency to smile.

# Chapter 8

That night we watched the movies while we pigged out on Mu Shu pork, almond chicken, and shrimp fried rice. Then Sister disappeared into her bedroom to critique the story she had been given at the conference. When Fred called, I told him about Millicent's death, leaving out the part about us finding the body. When he jumped to the conclusion that she had drowned while swimming, I let well enough alone.

"That's terrible!" he exclaimed. "She was such a nice lady. How's Fairchild holding up?"

"Pretty good, I guess. He's surrounded by a harem of women wanting to console him." I thought for a moment. "Just like you would be." I could imagine Fred's grin 250 miles away. "It's the truth and you know it. I'm not going to be stiff in the grave before you're married again."

"I'll never marry again," Fred said emphatically. "No way."

"Why not? What's wrong with marriage?"

"Nothing, honey. I just could never be married to anyone but you."

Bull. I wouldn't be stiff in my grave.

"When's Millicent's funeral going to be?" he asked, changing the subject.

"Fairchild hasn't made all the arrangements. Sister and I'll go, though."

Our talk ended with Fred's usual admonishment. "Do not," he said, "and I repeat, *do not* let Mary Alice get you mixed up in any of her harebrained schemes."

"Like what? Bungee jumping?" The mental picture of Sister jumping from a tower and bouncing on rubber bands like a yo-yo was an awesome one. Probably it was to Fred, too. "She's at the writers' conference every day," I assured him.

"I wouldn't put bungee jumping past her."

"I love you, too," I said. And I did. Forty years, and the thought of any woman other than me consoling him was infuriating.

Frances and Haley were sharing a box of Kleenex and watching Elizabeth Taylor die beautifully in *The Last Time I Saw Paris*. Haley looked up from the floor where she was sitting in some kind of semi-yoga position. "What did Papa have to say?"

I sat on the sofa beside Frances. "He said not to go bungee jumping."

Elizabeth Taylor gasped for breath.

"That pneumonia sure got to her in a hurry," Frances said.

"Getting locked out in that snow and rain, and she'd already had it once." Haley wiped her eyes.

Elizabeth Taylor cashed it in. The music, "The Last Time

I Saw Paris," soared. I reached for a Kleenex. "At least Van Johnson didn't get married again before she was stiff in her grave."

"You know," Frances said when the credits were rolling and Haley was crawling over to hit the rewind button, "one of the security blankets of my life is that Elizabeth Taylor and Debbie Reynolds are older than I am."

"I know what you mean," I agreed.

Mary Alice came in carrying the manuscript she had been critiquing. "Damn," she said, looking at the TV. "She's already dead."

"I can run it back," Haley offered.

"Just to where she's locked out. I love it when she's collapsing against the door and it's snowing and raining." Sister put the manuscript on the coffee table. I picked it up and looked at it. On the cover page, she had written in red magic marker "Medical help is available."

"What kind of critique is this?" I asked. "Medical help is available?"

"The poor fellow is impotent and suffering. I think he needs a penal implant."

"Penile," Haley said from the floor.

"Whatever. He needs one of those things you pump up."

"But, Sister, it's just a character in a story."

"No way. He knows too much."

"I knew a man had one of those," Frances said. "You really couldn't tell the difference." We all looked at her. "Well, that's what his wife said."

"Y'all ready?" Haley asked. "I think I've got Elizabeth Taylor at the door."

Sister reached for a Kleenex. "Let her rip."

\*      \*      \*

It was early the next morning that Sister got the phone call. She was talking as I went into the kitchen, and she pointed toward the carton of orange juice on the counter and handed me her empty glass.

"No," she said. "I'm sorry, I'm on my way out. I've got to be at Sunnyside at the conference by nine. Can't you just tell me on the phone?"

I handed her the refill on her orange juice. "Who is it?" I mouthed.

"Laura," she mouthed back. And then into the phone, "We'll be through about four." A pause. "Sure, I'll call you tonight. Can't you at least tell me what it's about though?"

I poured myself some juice.

"Okay. I'll see you then." Sister hung up the phone, looked at me, and shrugged her shoulders.

"What was that about?" I asked.

"Damned if I know. Laura says there's something she's got to tell me about Fairchild and Blue Bay Ranch. She wouldn't tell me on the phone, though. Said it was," Sister held up her fingers like quote marks, " 'too complicated.' "

"Complicated? What's she talking about?"

"Doesn't make sense, does it?"

"Maybe you better go talk to her now. Be late to the conference."

"Don't be silly. You know how melodramatic Laura can be."

I'd never known Laura to be melodramatic about anything. "Go talk to her," I insisted.

"I don't have time. You go." And with that, Sister sailed out of the door.

Fifteen minutes later, showered and dressed, I was knocking on Laura's next-door apartment. There was no answer. I turned, walked past our apartment, and knocked on Fairchild's door. Laura opened it, and when she saw it was me, she looked disappointed.

"Hey, Patricia Anne," she said. "I thought you were Mary Alice."

"She's gone to the writers' conference. She said you sounded upset. Anything I can do to help?"

"I'm sorry, Patricia Anne. I don't mean to be rude, but this is something I need to talk to Mary Alice about."

"Sure."

"But come in for some coffee, won't you?" Laura opened the door wider. "I was just straightening up a little. Fairchild's not here. He and Eddie have gone to De Funiak Springs to make funeral arrangements. They're releasing Millicent's body tomorrow."

"Have the police said anything about what they think may have happened?"

"They know she didn't drown; they know that much. She bled to death."

"So she had to be dead when she was thrown into the water?"

Laura held up her hands in a "who knows?" gesture and shrugged. "You want anything in your coffee?"

I nodded that I did. "About a half teaspoon of sugar."

"Let's sit on the balcony. Go on out. I'll bring the coffee."

It was another cloudless day, and would probably be hotter than the day before. A perfect beach day. The procession of young parents juggling floats, coolers, and kids over the stile and onto the sand brought back memories of Fred and me herding our three to the beach. I could have told them that as soon as they were settled under an umbrella, the kids would have to go to the bathroom. It was a given.

"Here we go." Laura put a tray with two cups on it on a small glass table and we sat down.

"It feels strange being here without Millicent," I said.

"Yes, it does." Laura picked up her coffee and blew across the steam. "Lonesome." Tears filled her eyes. As she brushed them away, she parted her bangs and I noticed a large bruise on her forehead.

"Are you okay? I asked.

She saw I was looking at the bruise and smiled. "Eddie hasn't been abusing me, Patricia Anne, if that's what you're thinking. We're building over at Blue Bay, you know, and I bent down too quickly over the corner of a kitchen cabinet. Saw stars." She pulled her bangs back into place.

"You're lucky it didn't break the skin."

"Bumps and bruises seem to be par for the course when you're building a house."

"Mary Alice and I went over to Blue Bay Ranch yesterday. I had no idea it was going to be such a fancy development."

"Millicent was sitting on a gold mine. I don't think she ever understood it, which makes you realize what a mindset money is. If you're born poor, I wonder if you can ever feel wealthy."

I thought about that a minute. "Mary Alice seems to have the hang of it. Of course, we weren't poor when we were children, just very middle class."

Laura nodded. "So was my family." She put her coffee on the table. "We'll be moving in about a month. The boathouse is already finished."

"What color is your house? We probably saw it."

"It's lavender. My favorite color."

"I remember it. It's beautiful."

"Thank you," Laura said, so obviously pleased at my compliment that I felt guilty for lying. The color didn't bother me. After all, this was Florida. It was all the turrets, gables, and gingerbread.

"Are you selling your place here?" I sipped my coffee.

"Yes. We've already had several inquiries. You interested?"

"Don't I wish." I looked out at the water and the sailboats. Maybe it wasn't such a farfetched idea. Fred had sounded pretty excited about the Metal Fab merger. But then I remembered that only a few months ago he had been scared the business was going to go belly up. I sighed. "I don't think so."

A black-clad figure approached the stile. "That's the child who lives next to us," Laura said, pointing. "Look at that outfit. Looks like she's on her way to a coven meeting."

I looked down at Sophie Berliner. "Haley says she has an unbelievable figure. Maybe she doesn't know how to cope with it yet."

"She knows. She's just weird. Pops up everywhere and scares hell out of you. Like one day, I went in the laundry room and she came up from behind the washing machine. My heart nearly stopped."

I grinned. After all those years of popping into the girls' bathroom at school, I was pretty sure what had been going on. "Did you smell cigarette smoke?"

"Hell, I didn't wait to find out. I dropped the clothes and went and told her father."

"What did he do?"

"Nothing. Laughed." Laura put her cup on the glass table. Her hands were shaking. "You see, that's the problem. They let her get away with everything." She reached in her pocket, pulled out a pack of cigarettes as if my remark about smoking had reminded her, and lit one. She picked a piece of tobacco from the tip of her tongue, "Millicent thought Sophie was handed down, too. Thought everything she did was amusing."

I watched the black-robed figure head down the beach. "She'll turn out fine."

"The father's about twenty years older than the mother," Laura said, managing to talk and exhale smoke at the same time. "Second family."

Which was what Haley was asking of Philip Nachman, I thought, to father a second family. Jack Berliner might have jumped into the role eagerly, but it was something Philip didn't want and shouldn't be forced into. Suddenly I felt very sad and angry. I stood up to leave.

"I don't need to know the details about why you called, Laura," I said. "I just want to know if Fairchild is in serious trouble."

Laura stubbed her cigarette into her coffee cup; it sizzled fiercely. "Oh, God, we all are." And with that, she got up and walked out of the apartment.

I was so surprised, I sat there for a moment thinking she would come back. When she didn't, I rinsed out the coffee cups and put them in the dishwasher. As I left, I turned and looked into the condo behind me; it suddenly seemed as empty as a shell.

And what in hell had Laura meant by saying we were all in trouble?

I didn't mention Laura's remark to Haley and Frances, but when they wanted to go to Sunnyside for lunch I was very agreeable. It's a small community so I was hoping we might run into Sister. I wanted to tell her what Laura had said, to encourage her to get in touch with her as soon as possible. As for Haley and Frances, they were hoping to find out the impotent man's reaction to "Medical help is available." But the writers' conference participants were meeting in a building known as "The Nest," so we were informed by the waitress at Billy and Jo's. And their meals, she said indignantly, were being catered by The Catfish Market in Panama City, though Billy and Jo's food was ten times better, a hundred times better, and they had even offered to throw in a brownie.

"Did Aunt Sister," I asked Haley as soon as the waitress had left with our cheeseburger orders, "happen to mention that she was meeting in The Nest and eating food from The Catfish Market?"

"Didn't say a word." Haley grinned.

"Sounds kind of nice to me," Frances said. "I like catfish."

"But she didn't get a brownie thrown in, Frances."

"Maybe she got something else, like one of those smushy lemon things with the graham-cracker crumbs on the bottom. Or even a slice of poundcake."

I looked over at Haley who was studying the beach. "After lunch," I said, "let's go see Blue Bay Ranch. It's on the way home."

They both nodded yes, but Frances was not to be sidetracked.

"You know what else she might have gotten?" she asked. "A cupcake with something on it. Maybe a marzipan shell, since we're at the beach."

"Or a catfish," Haley said.

I kicked her lightly.

"Will they let us in at Blue Bay?" Haley asked quickly.

"We'll tell them we're visiting Eddie and Laura Stamps," I said, "if they stop us."

They didn't. In fact, no one was at the guard house. A sign in the window said, "On patrol. Back in 1 hour."

"Good. We'll be able to steal a lot of stuff in that amount of time," Haley said.

"When you get to the fork, hang right," I directed Frances.

"Looks like a bunch of nothing in here," Haley said. And just then we broke through the spindly trees and scrub bushes onto the bay where the five rainbow houses perched.

"My Lord!" Frances stopped the car. "Look at that pink house. Have you ever seen anything like it?"

"I love the blue one!" Haley, who was sitting in the backseat, leaned forward excitedly. "Look, Mama. Isn't that the cutest thing you've ever seen in your life?"

"No! The pink one! It's gorgeous!" Frances insisted.

The houses still looked to me as if some visually challenged architect had designed them. But I was in the minority here, so I kept my mouth shut while they ooohed and ahhhed.

"The lavender one is Eddie and Laura's," I said finally.

It was wonderful, too. Did I think it would be all right if they got out and looked?

"Sure," I said. What did I know? I even got out and looked around some myself, peeked in the windows of Laura's lavender house, which glistened with new paint and wallpaper, walked down the pier and admired their boat. I had to admit that being on the bay would have its advantages.

"Most gorgeous place I've ever seen in my life," Frances announced. "When I say my mantra, I'm supposed to imagine myself in a beautiful location. I'm going to be in that pink house from now on." She had turned around in the Stampses' driveway and we were headed back toward the highway. We waved at the guard, who was back on duty, and at Lolita, who was standing on the porch of the log cabin. "That's going to be my place from now on." Frances's voice was determined. "Yep. You can bet on it."

*    *    *

"Hey," Mary Alice said that afternoon. "Where have you been?" I had just gotten off the elevator, and she was unlocking the condo door.

"Guess." My arms were full of grocery sacks. I went into the kitchen to put them down.

"How did the workshop go?" Haley called. "Is the guy going to get medical help?"

"I hope so. The instructor read my story to the class. Everybody laughed."

"It's a funny story." I put the yogurt into the refrigerator. "You want some grapes?" I held out the bowl.

Sister shook her head no. "I went by, but Laura's not at home. Then I stopped in to see Fairchild. I'm fixing to go over to Emerald Waters for him. I just stopped by to get a beer and go to the bathroom."

"What are you going to Emerald Waters for?" I folded empty grocery sacks and put them in the pantry.

"Fairchild doesn't think Emily Peacock knows about Millicent's death. She's in Savannah visiting her sister, but the number up there doesn't answer. I told him I'd go check with the neighbors and see if they know if she and her sister were going somewhere else."

"I'll go to Emerald Waters with you," I said. It would give me a chance to tell Sister about my talk with Laura. That, plus the fact that Elizabeth Taylor was gasping her last breath again on TV. Time to return that video to Delchamps.

"She said what?" Sister asked. We were about halfway to Emerald Waters and I had just gotten to the "we're all in serious trouble" bit.

I repeated Laura's words.

"See, Mouse? I told you how melodramatic she is."

"Hmm." Sister hadn't seen her face; I had.

We pulled through the gates of Emerald Waters and into

the crowded parking lot. Built a couple of years after Gulf Towers, this apartment complex was caught by the dune laws that required all construction to be behind the natural dunes. So Emerald Waters was farther from the water and there was no seawall. Its architecture was similar to that of Gulf Towers, though, the only difference being that there were six apartments on each floor opening onto an outside corridor.

"E. Peacock. Eleven-o-six." Mary Alice turned from the directory and examined the lobby, which was all rattan furniture, huge potted plants in oriental urns, and some nice seascapes on the wall. "This place is nicer than Gulf Towers," she announced.

"Hmmm." Yes, it was, but I was planning on a future.

"I think those Japanese pots came from K Mart. We need to get some for our lobby."

"It would be nice," I agreed. "Are you going to ask the resident manager, or just go up to the eleventh floor, or what?"

The decision was made by an empty resident manager's office.

The view from the eleventh-floor corridor was spectacular. We were looking down on a series of rainbow-colored shops that are called The Mediterranean Village. Across 98, children were zipping down the water slide at Big Kahuna's.

"She has a better view, too," Mary Alice said.

Apartment 1106 was the one on the western end of the building, the corner one, which meant that Emily probably did have a better view. "Hmm," I said.

Sister marched up to 1105. "Mrs. L. Snodgrass," she said, and knocked. No answer. I watched the children at Big Kahuna's.

"Let's try the next one," Sister said. "You know what

Fairchild said his blood pressure was this afternoon? Two-hundred-twenty over one-ten. I hope some of these folks know where Emily is. Take one worry off him."

I turned to trail along behind her, and that's when I noticed that Emily's door was slightly ajar.

"Sister," I said. "Emily's door's open. Maybe she's back."

"Oh, good. Knock."

I did, and there was no answer.

Sister opened the door and called, "Emily! It's Mary Alice Crane!"

No answer. This, of course, is when we should have turned around and left, located the security guard. This, of course, is not what we did.

"Emily? You here? You okay?" Sister walked through the open door with me right behind her.

The foyer in these apartments is formed by the kitchen wall. One has to turn right into an L-shaped eating area and living room with a wall of windows opening onto a balcony.

"Emily?" Sister called again. And then we were in the living room and Emily Peacock was slouched against the end of the sofa, her head turned as if she were looking at the water and the sun. But she was looking at nothing; the hole in her right temple guaranteed that.

"Oh, God!" Sister said. She rushed past me, and I could hear her being sick in the kitchen. But I walked the length of the room, opened the balcony doors and walked out into the fading sunlight. I sat in a plastic, stackable chair and watched parents herding tired children in from the beach, sailboats headed toward the pass, and gulls walking along the sand. The body behind me on the sofa was as unreal as the body on the beach had been.

Sister came onto the balcony. "I need a mint or a piece of gum." I reached in my purse and handed her a package of

Certs. "We need to call 911." she said. "Go call them, Mouse."

"You know what I've been thinking?" I asked. "I've been thinking that Fred and I need to take a long vacation. Maybe a cruise to Alaska. If he really closes this deal on Metal Fab, we can do a little traveling and I think we should. Don't you?"

Sister's normally olive skin was pale green. "Go call 911, Patricia Anne."

"No."

"What do you mean, 'no'? There's a dead woman, a very dead woman, sitting in there."

"I'm not going back in there," I said. "I'm just going to sit here and think about Alaska. I've given myself permission not to be drawn into any more of your traumas."

"*My* traumas?" Sister's hand went for my upper arm. When we were children, she perfected a pinch that is very painful but doesn't leave a bruise. The secret is in the twist. She hasn't used it in a long time, but with Mary Alice, one always has to be prepared.

I jerked my arm back just in time. "That's childish."

She sank down onto a chair and put her head in her hands. "I'm sick," she said, rocking back and forth.

She looked sick. Her hands were shaking, which frightened me. I got up and looked through the sliding doors at Emily Peacock; sightless eyes stared back at me. A few strands of gray-blonde hair had stuck to her cheek as blood had welled from her temple. Not as much blood as one would have imagined, but God only knew what was on the other side of her head, the side that we couldn't see. One thing was certain, the essence that had been Emily Peacock was gone. All that was on that sofa was a hull.

I did the decent thing; I went inside, holding my breath

as long as I could, and called 911. Then I scooted back to the balcony and Mary Alice.

"The rescue squad is coming." And, sure enough, just as we had two days before, we heard the sirens again in the distance as the crew left the fire station and headed down Highway 98. "At least this time the body's not wet. We won't have to wait on the Marine Patrol."

Mary Alice shivered but didn't say anything.

"I think she committed suicide," I said. "There's a pistol by her on the sofa."

Mary Alice looked up. "You saw a pistol?"

"Right by her side."

"Why would she do that?"

"How should I know? I hardly knew her." I thought for a moment. "Upset about her best friend Millicent's death?"

Mary Alice shrugged.

"You feeling any better?" I asked in a moment.

"I guess so. Are you?"

"I wasn't sick."

"Just doing your wandering off into never-never land like you always do when there's an emergency. I swear, Patricia Anne, I don't know how you raised three children."

"Hey," I said. "There's a big difference in stumped toes and dead bodies. Besides, I don't drift off into never-never land."

"Of course you do. It's like you change channels. Click, here's the Travel Channel. Doesn't Alaska look like a fun place! Click, and look how beautiful Greece is."

"Shut up!"

Mary Alice started rummaging through her purse, which is huge. She confided to me once that a big purse can make you look like you've lost twenty pounds. Which is fine. The only problem is that she can never find anything, such as a package of mints.

"What are you looking for?" I asked.

"A Kleenex. Oh, look what I found." She held up her tiny cellular phone. "I forgot about this. We could have called 911 from out here. I'm sorry."

I sighed. The sirens were getting closer. "Maybe you should call Haley and Frances and tell them we're going to be tied up here a while. Don't tell them why. Just tell them to go on out to dinner and not wait on us."

"Don't be silly. There's nothing we can do here. As soon as the policemen come, we'll leave."

I snatched the phone away from her and called Haley.

"Hi, Mama," she said, "what's up?"

"Not much," I said truthfully, hoping my voice wasn't shaking so much she would notice it. "I'm with your Aunt Sister and we're running a little later than we planned. Y'all don't wait on us for dinner."

"Fine. Tell Aunt Sister that Berry West is here from Birmingham. He and Frances are out on the balcony having drinks. He's real nice. Jason Marley's here, too."

"Your Aunt Sister says that Berry's an Adonis."

"Like I said, he's real nice."

I said goodbye, handed Sister the phone and smiled pleasantly. "Berry West and Jason Marley are there. They're on the balcony having drinks with Frances."

"Snake shit!" Sister grumbled.

The same rescue squad, firemen, and policeman answered this call that had answered the one from the beach.

"What is this?" Lisa Andrews said, stepping onto the balcony. "Y'all made this call, too?"

We admitted that we had.

She called back into the living room, "Buddy! It's the same women found the body on the beach."

Buddy stuck his head out. "Y'all ain't invited to any of my parties."

"They wouldn't want to come, anyway." Lisa Andrews got out her notepad and flipped back a couple of pages. "Okay, let's see. You're Mrs. Crane and Mrs. Hollowell. Right?"

We nodded yes.

"And you," she pointed toward Mary Alice, "Mrs. Crane?" Another nod. "You have a place at Gulf Towers, and you, Mrs. Hollowell, are visiting."

"We're sisters," I said.

"You sure don't look like it."

"Well, we are," Mary Alice narrowed her eyes. "And we came over to find out if anybody knew where Emily Peacock, who happens to be lying in there dead, shot in the head on her own hide-a-bed, might be. We came because Fairchild Weatherby asked us to and his blood pressure is sky high. He was worried she didn't know about Millicent's death, and we found her lying in there dead as a door nail. Dead as a door nail." She caught her breath.

"Wait a minute. I can't write that fast." Lisa Andrews flipped over a page in the notepad. "How do you spell Peacock?"

"P-E-E-C-O-C-K."

"P-E-A," I said, giving Sister a hard look.

"Thanks. And you didn't get to talk to her?"

"I tried, but she had trouble answering," Sister said.

This time it was Officer Andrews who narrowed her eyes. "Have you touched anything? Moved the body at all?"

"Lord, no, we haven't moved the body." I said. "The door was ajar and we called and came on in. I guess we touched the doorknob and my sister was sick in the kitchen sink." Officer Andrews smiled a little at this piece of news. "Oh, and I called you from the phone. Other than that, we've been out here."

Lisa Andrews looked up, looked at the salmon-colored sky, the darkening bay water. "It's a nice view, isn't it?"

We hadn't exactly been siting there admiring the view. But Lisa Andrews was right. Lights were being turned on along the beach and we could hear voices. I didn't turn to see what was going on behind us, though I sensed busyness.

"Know anything about her family?"

"She was supposed to be visiting a sister in Savannah," Mary Alice said. "She was a widow when she moved down here. I really don't know."

"Lisa!" A man called from inside.

"Coming!" She closed her notebook. "Listen, y'all go on home. I've got your address and phone numbers. You ladies might even do us a favor and stay home for a few days." She turned and started into the condo. "We'll be in touch."

"Who's going to tell Fairchild and the rest of her friends?" I asked.

"Y'all can do it if you want to."

"Smartass," Mary Alice muttered. I'm sure Lisa Andrews heard her.

We wasted no time getting out of there. Several people were crowded around the door, drawn by the commotion of the rescue vehicles and the sheriff's department.

"Is something wrong with Emily?" an elderly woman asked.

"Dead," Mary Alice announced. The spectators gasped, parting before her six feet, 250 pounds like the Red Sea before Charlton Heston.

"Lord, Sister," I said, running to catch up. "You could

have been a little more tactful. That lady could have had a heart attack.''

Mary Alice hit the elevator button and looked back at the crowd. ''You mean break it to them gradually? Like that old cat on the roof joke? Emily's up on the roof?''

''Something like that.''

''Emily's dead, Mouse. Dead as she'll ever be. And I think I'm going to be sick again.''

Fortunately, that didn't happen. Nor were we the ones who had to break the news to Fairchild about Emily's death.

# Chapter 9

Traffic was heavy between Emerald Waters and Gulf Towers; it seemed to take forever to get home.

"You okay?" I asked Mary Alice, who kept rubbing her hand across her throat.

"You mean am I going to pull a Pukey Lukey? No." Pukey Lukey is a cousin of ours who was the bane of our vacations during our childhood. Show him a car and he got carsick.

"I'll drive if you need me to."

"My Jaguar? Good God, no!"

"It's just a car," I said huffily. "And I'm a damn good driver."

"You're a terrible driver."

"I'm an excellent driver."

"You're not."

"Yes, I am." I felt the sting of tears. I wiped them away angrily.

We rode in silence for a few minutes. I closed my eyes and saw Emily Peacock's sightless eyes staring through me, staring straight into the setting sun.

"I could never shoot myself," I said.

"Me neither. And right on her new living-room sofa." Mary Alice pulled into the turn lane. "Did you notice that floor in the foyer? I'll bet that parquet's going to be hard to keep up at the beach." Mary Alice pulled into the turn lane.

"It looked like it had an acrylic finish on it." I thought for a moment. "You know what? She was looking out at the bay. She wanted her last look at the world to be a beautiful one."

"If she still thought the world was beautiful, how come she killed herself?"

I couldn't answer that. My whole body felt heavy, achy, as if I were coming down with something. We parked, went into the lobby, and waited for the elevator.

"What are we going to tell Fairchild?" Sister asked. "No telling what this will do to his blood pressure."

What was this "we" business? Then it just popped out: "You could tell him Emily's on the roof." In a moment the elevator opened and the young couple who got off were greeted by the sight of two old sisters hanging on to each other, laughing and crying.

The note on the refrigerator said that everybody was at The Flamingo and we should join them when we got in.

"The Flamingo? I don't think so. Not tonight." Mary Alice took the note down and threw it in the garbage. "I wish I had some ginger ale. Remember, Mouse, how Mama always gave us ginger ale when we were sick to our stomachs?"

"I could drive over to the grocery in your car and get you some."

"A Coke will do."

"I'll fix it. I need one, too."

When I brought the drinks out to the balcony, Sister said, "I'm serious. I don't know how I'm going to tell Fairchild about Emily's's death. Do you think I ought to call the doctor downstairs to go with me?"

I handed her her Coke. "Wouldn't hurt."

"What's his name?"

"I have no idea, but Eddie and Laura called him, didn't they? Maybe he's a personal friend."

"Maybe."

We sat quietly for a few minutes. There was still a tiny streak of orange on the western horizon.

"You know," Sister said, "chances are that the two deaths are connected. I just don't see how."

"Emily was distraught about Millicent's death and just couldn't take it?"

"She didn't even know about Millicent's death."

"Maybe she did. Maybe she was the one who killed her."

Sister rolled her damp glass across her forehead. "Cut her throat like an animal? I don't think so. Emily was one of the sweetest people in the world."

"You can't go by that."

"I know." Sister shivered.

"Did you get to talk to Major Bissell today?"

"No. He came late and left early." Sister got up. "I'm going to get some aspirin."

"Take it with some Maalox."

"I'm taking it with some bourbon." She went inside and pulled the sliding door shut. That's why, a few minutes later, she didn't hear the scream, a scream of such desolation and terror that I jumped straight up, the back of my neck tingling, my heart racing. The next scream sent me banging into the glass door, trying to find the handle, finding it and almost falling inside. Mary Alice looked up, startled. "What's the matter?"

I pointed to the balcony with one hand. The other held my heart in my chest.

"What?"

"Scream," I managed to say.

"Oh, that's just kids, Mouse. For heaven's sake. They do that all the time."

I shook my head no. Mary Alice looked at me questioningly and walked out onto the balcony. I stayed behind her.

"I don't hear anything," she said.

"It was a scream, damn it, right here."

She came back in and shut the door. "A kid on one of the balconies. Probably on the floor below us."

"I think it was next door in Laura's apartment."

"No one's there. I just called."

"Nobody would answer the phone if somebody was trying to kill them."

"Get real, Mouse."

Just at that moment there was a loud knock on the door. We both jumped a mile.

"Don't open it," I whispered.

"I'll look before I do." Mary Alice marched toward the door. "Damn," she muttered, her eye to the peephole. "It's that dickless Tracy."

"And a good evening to you ladies again, too," Officer Lisa Andrews said, stepping inside the foyer as Mary Alice opened the door. The evening dampness was doing a number on her curly hair, I noticed.

I almost threw myself on her. "Scream! Right next door. Something awful's happening!"

Lisa Andrews backed up a couple of steps. "What?"

"For heaven's sake, Mouse," Mary Alice said. And then

to the officer, "It's kids yelling. You know how it is in the summer. Patricia Anne's just nervous."

"I think the scream came from next door," I said.

But I was ignored. Mary Alice turned to Lisa Andrews. "What do you want? We told you everything we know. We even came home, as you suggested so politely."

"Have you already told Mr. Weatherby about Mrs. Peacock's death?"

"No," Sister admitted. "I'm worried about him. He doesn't look well at all. We were going to see if we could get the doctor from downstairs to go with us."

"What's the doctor's name?"

"I don't remember. The Stampses next door would know but they're not home."

"Probably murdered," I muttered.

Lisa Andrews smiled patronizingly at me. "I'll check it out, Mrs. Hollowell." And almost as an afterthought, "Mrs. Peacock left Mr. Weatherby a note."

"A suicide note?" I asked. "Why would she leave it to Fairchild?"

Lisa Andrews shrugged, informing us that she would find the Stampses and Fairchild and tell them about Emily's death. We didn't argue with her.

"Might not hurt to have that doctor with you," Mary Alice said.

Lisa Andrews nodded and informed us that she would get back to us later, that we should stay available. Sister closed the door behind her. "Pissant."

"I'm just glad she's the one telling them."

"Yeah. I'll go over after while and find out what's in the note." Sister sat on the sofa and propped her feet on the coffee table.

"Let her be the one who finds a third body." I shivered.

"Kids, Mouse. They do it all the time."

Another knock on the door. This time I looked through the peephole and saw Sophie Berliner. "It's the child from down the hall," I told Mary Alice.

"Some child!" Sister said.

But when I opened the door, I saw that Sophie did, indeed, look like a very young teenager. The black robe was gone, and in its place were jeans, sneakers, and a tee shirt with a picture of Homer Simpson on it. "Is Haley here?" she asked.

"She's gone to The Flamingo for dinner. She should be back soon. Can I help you with something, Sophie?"

"Some turtles are coming in at Navarre! They've been spotted in the water, and Millicent and I were supposed to be on patrol tonight." She paused. "Anyway, Daddy's taking me, and Haley said she wanted to see them."

Mary Alice had come up beside me. "They're coming in to lay their eggs?"

"Yes, and I've got to go. But tell Haley maybe some will come in tomorrow night."

"I will," I assured her. "She'll be sorry she missed it."

"They're so big!"

I looked at the child's face, flushed with excitement, and realized for the first time that she was going to be a beautiful woman.

She turned toward the elevator. "I've got to go."

"Sophie," I said, "wait a minute. Did you hear somebody screaming a few minutes ago? A real, loud scream?"

She giggled. "That was me doing my Tarzan yell. Daddy was down on the stile and he knows when I do the yell, I need him." She punched the elevator button. "Why? Did I scare you?"

"I was considering going to someone's rescue."

Sophie giggled again. The elevator opened and she stepped in, giving Sister and me a backward wave.

"See?" Sister said. "I told you it was a kid."

She gloats when she's right. "Think you can keep down some soup now?" I asked. "Some Chicken and Stars?"

She could, and so could I. In fact, I thought I had myself pretty much under control until Fred called to say he was home, at which time I took the phone into the bedroom, closed the door and bawled. I told him about finding Millicent's body and how her throat was torn; I told him about finding Emily's body and how her eyes had stared toward the water. "Oh, Fred," I ended, sobbing.

"What?" he was saying, "What? Tell me again, honey."

So I told him again, this time a little slower and a fraction more sensibly. When I finished, there was a long silence. Then Fred said, "I'm coming down there."

It took me several minutes to convince him to wait until the next day, that I would worry too much about him driving down two-lane Highway 31 in the dead of night.

"Where is Haley?" he asked.

"At The Flamingo."

"And Mary Alice?"

"She's in the living room."

"Y'all stay put. I'll be down there tomorrow. You and I'll stay at the Holiday Inn."

Sister looked up from something she was writing when I came back in. "When's the knight in shining armor arriving?"

"Tomorrow," I admitted.

"I figured." She closed her notebook. "What did he say?"

"He said to stay put until he gets here. He said we'd stay at the Holiday Inn."

"Don't be silly, there's plenty of room here. But, Mouse, that man treats you like a child."

"I know it," I agreed. I wasn't about to say how much better I felt just knowing he was coming. I nodded at the notebook. "What are you writing?"

"I've started a new short story. Gets my mind off things. They keep telling us we should write about what we know, so this is going to be about a manic-depressive man who marries two lesbian sisters. At different times, of course."

"Of course. This is something you know?"

Sister grinned. "You bet. They live in Birmingham."

I hoped she wasn't serious.

She got up and announced that she was going to check on Fairchild and did I want to go? I didn't. To my chagrin, she took the notebook with her. In a few minutes she was back with the news that the doctor had sedated Fairchild, that his blood pressure was soaring, and that Eddie was there and was comparatively calm. He had told her that the note from Emily said simply "Fairchild, forgive me."

"For what?" I asked. "Killing Millicent?"

"That's what it sounds like, doesn't it?"

"Or does she want forgiveness for killing herself?"

The door opened and Haley called out, "Hey, y'all." She came into the living room followed by Frances, Berry West, and the man I had seen Fairchild talking to on the stile the night we had walked back from the Redneck, the night before Millicent was killed. He was younger than I had thought that night, probably in his late fifties, but my view had been from above, and the light had been shining on what I had thought was a totally bald head. But there was no mistaking; this was the same man. I had seen his face several times as he looked up toward the apartments.

Berry hugged Sister and then me as I was introduced to

him. A handshake would have sufficed, but the hug was nice; he smelled like The Flamingo's grilled grouper with an underlay of expensive soap.

The other man was Jason Marley, who had apparently accompanied them to dinner.

"I told Jason how much we loved his pink house," Frances gushed.

"It's unbelievable," I said, truthfully, shaking his hand.

Sister pointed vaguely toward the chairs. "Y'all have a seat. Can I get anybody a nightcap?"

"You have any bourbon?" Berry asked.

"Sure."

"Bourbon and water then."

"Same for me," Jason said.

"I'll get it." Haley headed for the kitchen while we sat down. "Why didn't you and Mama come to The Flamingo, Aunt Sister?"

Mary Alice and I looked at each other. "Your mama and I went over to Emerald Towers to see if we could locate Emily Peacock."

"That was early, though."

Mary Alice, Berry, and I were sitting on the sofa. Jason was in one of the rockers, and Frances had chosen a pillow on the floor on which she was perched as if she were riding sidesaddle. "Wait until she tries to get up," Sister had mumbled. Now she said, "Emily was dead when we got there. She had apparently committed suicide."

There was the silence of shock. Then we heard a glass crash into the sink, and Frances came up from the floor with such agility that I was right proud of her.

"You found another body?" She looked accusingly from Mary Alice to me.

I could sense Sister bristling. "Yes, we did, Frances. Too bad you weren't there."

"I wish I hadn't been," I said.

"You found a dead body?" Berry said. And then, "Jason, are you all right?"

Jason Marley was leaning forward, the palms of both hands pressed against his eyes. He didn't look up when he said, "God, not Emily. Emily's dead? What happened?"

"She shot herself, Jason." Sister's voice was gentle, but the words were harsh with finality.

"Oh, God," he said. "Not Emily."

Haley came in from the kitchen with a paper towel wrapped around her bleeding hand and a glass in the other. "Jason?" she said. "Here, drink this. It'll make you feel better." She handed him his bourbon; he stared at it as if he weren't sure what it was.

"I'm going to get me one," Frances said, disappearing into the kitchen.

"What's going on?" Berry asked.

We explained that Emily Peacock lived at Emerald Towers and that we had found her body, apparently a suicide, when we went to tell her about Millicent.

"You've found two bodies?" He was beginning to sound like Frances.

"This place is chock-full of bodies," she called from the kitchen.

"Shut up, Frances," Sister said. Then to Berry, "Yes. Emily Peacock and Millicent Weatherby."

"Millicent Weatherby is the woman who owned all the property on the bay?" Berry looked over at Jason Marley.

"*Was!*" Frances again. I might have to belt her one.

"She was." Jason took a long drink from his glass. "She was the majority stockholder of Bay Ranch. Emily was a stockholder, too." He shook his head sadly. "Both of them dead. I can't believe it!" He turned up the glass, finished the drink, and stood up. "I'm sorry, but I think I'd better call it a night. Berry, I gave you a key, didn't I? Just come on over any time. You know which room is yours. Thanks, ladies, for the good company. I enjoyed dinner. I hope to see you again soon." He called "Good night" as he closed the door.

"Well, my goodness," Mary Alice said. "Reckon he's all right?"

"I'd say he was just very upset and needed to be by himself," Haley said.

"Is your hand cut much?" I asked.

She peeled the paper towel back and examined it. "It's okay. I'll put a Band-Aid on it."

Frances had come back into the living room and now she sat in the chair Jason had vacated. "Could Jason be worried about Blue Bay Ranch, Berry? Will the two deaths mess things up?"

"I doubt it. I'm sure everybody in the organization will be emotionally upset but, knowing Jason like I do, everything will be okay legally."

"But the land was Millicent's," Haley said. "Won't that hold things up until her estate is settled?"

Berry leaned over and put his glass on the coffee table. "No, the land belongs to Blue Bay Ranch Corporation. At least that's usually the way these things are set up." He held his fingers in a triangle. "See, this finger is Jason. He wants to develop the land and has the financing to do it. Now," he wiggled the other finger, "this is Millicent who owns the land. So they form a development corporation with her land and his money." His thumbs formed the base of the triangle, the corporation. "The land and the money are now the Blue

Bay Ranch Coporation, not Jason's and Millicent's, except
they are stockholders, of course."

"So wouldn't Fairchild inherit Millicent's shares?" Haley
asked.

"I doubt it," Berry said. "Usually, in a case like this, the
original shares revert to the company. It's for the protection
of the development. I expect Millicent had a hefty insurance
policy for her husband, though, that the company paid for
so he wouldn't be left out in the cold if she died before the
development was completed."

"A million dollars," I said.

Berry nodded. "I figured it would be a good one."

"So any shares Emily Peacock had in Bay Ranch would
revert to the company, too," Sister said.

"I imagine so, if we're talking about the original charter
here."

Haley spoke up. "So what you're saying is that now the
two women are dead, Jason Marley is the principal share-
holder of Blue Bay Ranch."

"Hell, he may be the only one." Berry looked at Haley
and shrugged.

"What were y'all doing over at Emerald Towers anyway?" Haley asked. Berry had said good-night and left not
long after Jason had and the four of us had somehow ended
up at the dining-room table. Sister, I noticed, was sipping
plain Coke again.

"I volunteered," Mary Alice said. "Fairchild was trying to
locate Emily to tell her about Millicent's death. He didn't
think she was at home but figured some of her neighbors
would know how to get in touch with her at her daughter's."

I pressed my fingers against my temples. "It was awful.
She'd been there for two days."

Sister got up. "The Chicken and Stars may make a return visit." She disappeared into her room and shut the door.

"Do, Jesus!" Frances said. "The surgeon general ought to label this place as hazardous to your health."

Haley turned to me. "Do you think it was a suicide, Mama?"

"She left Fairchild a note saying she was sorry. Who knows?"

"Maybe we ought to talk Aunt Sister into going home."

"Fat chance. We couldn't get your Aunt Sister out of here with a crowbar. Besides, Officer Andrews has informed us we have to stay at her beck and call."

"You know what?" Frances was shredding a paper napkin into strips and making a neat stack. "I read a book one time about all these women who decided to do away with their husbands, collect the insurance, and travel. They went all over the world. Had a great time."

Haley and I looked at her. She tore another strip and placed it on the stack.

"So?" I asked.

"So maybe that's what we've got here. We've got two widowers, already. Fairchild and Jason Marley. Three counting Berry West. Now what are the odds against that?"

"They're killing their wives so they can travel?" I asked.

"Of course not." Frances gave me a withering look for being a smart aleck. "It's got something to do with Blue Bay Ranch." Another strip hit the pile. "Mark my words."

"But Emily committed suicide. And she didn't make anyone a widower."

"But her death made them richer. Except for Berry."

True. After we were in bed, I kept thinking of all the wealthy widowers involved with Blue Bay Ranch. Before I put out my light, I did remember, though, to tell Haley that

Sophie had come by to get her to go see the turtles coming in to lay their eggs.

"I'm sorry I missed that," Haley said.

"Well, she said they would probably come in tomorrow night, too. She said she's on patrol protecting the nests, that Millicent had been taking her."

Haley put her book down. "That was why Millicent didn't want to sell the land over on the bay, wasn't it? I wonder if Jason Marley will remember there's such a thing as the environment."

"I hope so. You know, he's younger than I thought he was. I saw him talking to Fairchild the other night and I could have sworn he was bald."

Haley giggled. "Mama! You thought that rug was his hair? It wasn't even on straight when he left."

"Well, I guess you just inherited your father's power of observation, not your mother's." I turned off my light and closed my eyes. Smartass child!

"Mama?"

"What?"

"I'm really sorry you and Aunt Sister were the ones who found Emily. I know it must have been awful."

"It was." I heard the elevator open and close. Probably the Berliners coming back from the turtle watch. The elevator. *"Stupid! Stupid! Get in the elevator, you stupid bitch!"* I sighed and turned on my side. Damn it! Why did I keep remembering that dream?

Sometime during the night, I came awake to hear Haley snoring slightly. Heavy breathing, she would call it. And though the elevator didn't open, I lay awake for a long while and realized that I hadn't told Haley that Fred was coming to Destin. I also realized that she hadn't talked to Philip the night before. Whatever that meant.

# Chapter 10

I awoke the next morning to the sounds of Haley trying to get dressed without making any noise. The dresser drawer creaked as she opened it; she dropped what may have been a shoe.

"What are you doing?" I mumbled.

"There's a heavy fog. I'm going to go for a run."

Fogs are a rarity in June along the Florida Panhandle. The humidity is there, but the temperature usually doesn't drop below the dew point. When it does, and fog forms, it's like a cool blanket that muffles sound. By eight or nine o'clock, it's gone.

"If you'll keep it to a brisk walk, I'll go with you," I said.

"I'm about ready. Why don't I go run a little while and meet you back at the stile?"

That suited me. As much as I like walking in the fog, I also need a coffee jump start.

"What time is it?" I asked.

"About seven. Want a cup of coffee? I've already made it."

"Bless you, my child."

After Haley left, I pulled on a pair of baggy white shorts and a T-shirt I had bought at a garage sale, which proclaimed in large blue letters that I was a Happy Camper. Then I took my coffee into the living room and admired the fog, which was so thick it feathered onto the balcony. The beach was barely visible, and the water and fog were one.

Mary Alice wafted into the room in the pink peignoir that had almost blinded poor Fairchild. "What are you doing up so early?" she asked.

"Going walking in the fog. Haley's already gone. You want some coffee?"

"I'll get it. I didn't sleep worth a damn last night. Did you?"

"Better than I thought I would."

"I even got up and worked on my story some, the one about the manic-depressive man who marries all the lesbians. But I really couldn't get into it. You know?"

"Hmmm."

She went into the kitchen, poured herself a cup of coffee, and came back. "So I told myself, I said, Mary Alice Tate Sullivan Nachman Crane, you don't know these people well enough, don't know what makes them tick."

"You don't know a wheelchair repo man, either."

"But I've had some pretty sad jobs. Some that would suck the very soul from you."

"I don't remember you having any sad, soul sucking jobs."

"Well, I did. Like the summer I kept the Bishop kids."

"All you did was baby-sit."

"But I was seventeen. And the three-year-old would hold her breath until she passed out. Scared me to death the first few times she did it." Mary Alice sat on the sofa and reached for the remote. "My whole seventeenth summer."

"The three husbands being buried together would make an interesting story," I said.

"That is nice, isn't it? Ecumenical. A Catholic, a Jew, and an agnostic. I swear, though, it's not a perfect situation. If one of them has a birthday and I take him flowers, I don't want the others to feel left out so I have to buy them some, too."

"Only fair."

Sister looked at me suspiciously. I bent to tie my shoe.

"Are you going to be at the conference all day?" I asked.

"It finishes at lunchtime. Then there's the reading tonight."

"And Major Bissell's hanging in there?"

"Actually, he's pretty good. The story he brought to be critiqued was a mystery where they caught the killer because of a matchbook. They figured out he was left-handed because of the way the matches were pulled out. Think about it, Mouse, how you pull matches from a folder. Which side."

"He was writing about what he knows." I slipped on a nylon windbreaker. "Be careful going down 98 if the fog hasn't lifted. You want us to wait for you to go to lunch?"

Sister shook her head no. "Some of us will probably eat down there." She turned the volume up on "Today," where Martha Stewart was busy demonstrating herbs that would grow happily on your kitchen windowsill. "This woman," Sister grumbled, "obviously does not have a Bubba Cat." Which made me think of my Woofer and miss him. He loved to walk in the fog, skittering from lampposts to trees as if the moisture had brought out all kinds of messages.

Eddie Stamps from next door was sitting on the stile drinking a cup of coffee. The fog was so dense, I wasn't sure it was him until I approached the steps.

" 'Morning, Patricia Anne," he said. "I saw your daughter a while ago. She said she was going running."

" 'Morning, Eddie. Which way did she go?"

"Toward the jetties."

"If she's not back in a little while, I'll head that way." I sat down beside him on the bench. "Rough news last night. How are you this morning?"

"Okay, I guess. I stayed with Fairchild again. He was still asleep when I walked down here. I need to get out some, thought I'd take the boat out this morning." He gestured toward the water. "Looks like it's going to be a while, though. Suits me; I like the fog. Laura hates it."

"Laura said you went with Fairchild yesterday to make the arrangements for Millicent's funeral."

"It's in the morning in De Funiak Springs, that little chapel on the lake. You know where it is?" He leaned over to pick a sandspur from his pants leg and then threw it behind the stile, into the sea oats. "Those things hurt like hell when you step on them."

"Have you heard anything more about Emily?"

"No." He ran his hand through his white hair. Beads of moisture flew backward. He looked at his wet hand in surprise and then wiped it against his khaki pants. "I'll tell you what, though. I never would have figured Emily Peacock as a suicide."

"She wasn't depressed?"

"Depressed? Hell no. Happy as a lark. Said she and Jason

Marley were planning on getting married this fall. Least that's what she told Laura."

"Really?" If it were true, it explained why Jason had been so upset the night before. What a horrible way to learn about the death of someone you loved! And then I remembered that Emily had been dead for two days with the door to her condo open. If they were engaged, how come Jason hadn't been checking after not hearing from her for that long?

"Could they have broken up?" I asked Eddie. "Could that have been the reason she did it?" It sounded like a fairly logical explanation to me.

"Could have been, I suppose." Eddie didn't sound convinced. He squinted over my shoulder toward the building. "Is that Fairchild?"

I turned and saw a figure approaching through the fog. It was Fairchild, all right, dressed in a navy terry bathrobe that he lifted like a lady does an evening dress as he came up the stile steps. On his feet were flip-flops that seemed to be giving him more trouble than the long robe. Is there some law of nature that makes men incapable of walking in flip-flops?

"Good morning," he said. "I am going swimming. Patricia Anne, if you are easily shocked, I suggest that you avert your eyes." And with that warning, he stepped out of the flip-flops and shucked the robe, folding it neatly and laying it on the bench beside Eddie. Then, naked as a jaybird, he crossed the beach, walked into the water, which had to be chilly, and started swimming.

"Lord!" I said, remembering that Deputy Andrews had said Fairchild was a member of the Polar Bear Club.

Eddie laughed. "It's the fog. Drove Millicent crazy."

"He makes a habit of swimming nude in the fog?"

"Thinks no one will see him. He's not an exhibitionist, just likes swimming in the buff."

"But what about his blood pressure?" I looked toward the water where I could hardly see the swimmer. "Will he be all right?"

"Sure. I'm glad to see him out there. Must mean he's feeling better."

I wasn't convinced. "Maybe. But the doctor's got to have him on all kinds of medication, I'm sure. And, to tell you the truth, if I were a man it would make me nervous as hell to be swimming out there naked with all those hungry fish."

Eddie laughed again. "Fairchild hasn't got a thing to be nervous about."

How on God's earth had I gotten into this anatomical discussion with this man I hardly knew? I got up and said I'd walk toward the jetties and meet Haley. Eddie said he'd wait for Fairchild, keep an eye on him.

What is it about fog that is so beautiful? Like snow, it brings its own mood, its own quietness. The blurring of the familiar demands that you notice things you usually take for granted. And at the beach, it is especially beautiful. The horizon disappears, and you can't tell which is water and which is sky. Vapor swirls around you as you walk, and gulls huddle together on the sand as if the weight of the air were too much for their wings.

I had just started down the beach when I saw Haley coming toward me. She was running along the edge of the tide where the sand was packed tightly and (granted, I'm her mother; I'm partial) looked like a nymph just emerging from the water. The illusion was shattered, though, when she stopped in front of me, breathing hard, and asked if that wasn't a man out there swimming bare-assed.

"It's Fairchild. He thinks no one can see him in the fog," I explained.

" 'Morning, Fairchild!" Haley shouted. "Take your Vasotec?" The figure in the water raised his arm in a wave.

I grinned. "Don't do him that way."

"Are you kidding? I think it's great. It'll relax him. If more men would do that, we wouldn't be unclogging so many arteries in our operating room."

Which reminded me. "Your papa's coming down tonight." We had started walking toward the Redneck Riviera.

"Why am I not surprised? Coming to the rescue."

"Which is pretty nice after forty years of marriage, Haley."

"But, Mama, you're a capable, intelligent woman. It's patronizing."

"Of course it is." I chose not to admit that I had called him blubbering. Someday I would get it straight in my own mind how much I wanted Fred to look after me. In the meantime I said, "It's his way of showing love. Mine is letting him do it."

Haley laughed, which didn't surprise me. Lord, I had sounded pompous. But the way I look at it, a marriage is a separate entity from the couple who forms it. And whatever it becomes is always a surprise.

We huffed on down the beach, reached the Redneck, and turned around automatically. The fog was beginning to burn off and a few people jogged toward us now, making me wonder if Fairchild had made his exit from the water yet.

I stopped, leaned over, and rubbed my right calf. "Wait a minute. I'm getting a cramp."

Haley jogged a circle around me while I sat on the damp sand and kneaded the muscle. "You need to take some calcium."

"I do take calcium. Go on. I'll be there in a minute."

"I'll wait." Haley bent and stretched and then sat down beside me. A round patch of sunlight, a perfect spotlight, brushed down the beach toward us. Several appeared on the water. "There goes the fog," she said. "Look at the sky."

I did; blue holes were scattered across it.

When we got back to the seawall, rinsed the sand from our feet, and climbed the stile steps, there was no sign of Eddie or Fairchild. The sun was out and the lifeguard was putting up the beach umbrellas. For some reason, I remembered what Eddie had said about Emily and Jason Marley, that they were going to be married, and told Haley.

"Do you think it's true?" she asked. "He certainly was upset last night."

"I don't know. She'd been dead for two days right in her apartment. I wonder why he wasn't trying to find her, especially to tell her about Millicent's death."

"Maybe he was trying. She was supposed to be out of town."

"Ask me, he wasn't trying very hard."

"True." Haley looked under the bench for a missing sandal. "You know what I wonder?" She came up with the miscreant hooked around her finger. "I wonder how that Blue Bay Ranch thing is set up. If it's like Berry said, then Jason Marley came out with a bundle when those women died."

"What are you saying?"

"That he would have had a motive, God knows, to kill them."

"You sound like your Aunt Sister, Haley. You're forgetting it was a murder and a suicide."

"Who says?"

I thought about this for a moment. Mary Alice and I had

both just jumped to the conclusion that Emily had killed Millicent because of the "Forgive me" note. But what reason would she have possibly had? They were good friends.

"Nobody says," I admitted. "It just seems to fit. The note and all."

"Why?"

I tried to think of an answer. "God knows. That's probably one of the things the police are trying to figure out."

"Hey, y'all!" We looked up and saw Frances waving from the balcony. Next door to her, Fairchild leaned against the bannister in his navy robe and looked down at us, too. Smoke from the fat cigar he was puffing on floated in the air like the fog had earlier.

Laura Stamps was posting the information about Millicent's funeral on the bulletin board beside the elevator when we came into the lobby. "Did you hear about this?" she asked us.

"From Eddie," I said.

She looked at the notice. "I added that instead of flowers, memorials be made to the Wildlife Rescue Service. Fairchild says that's what she would have wanted, and I agree."

"That's very nice."

Laura stuck the card of thumbtacks back in her pocket and got on the elevator with us. "I still can't believe it. Millicent and Emily both."

"Do you think there's any chance it was a murder-suicide?" Haley reached over and punched the button for the sixth floor; the door closed with a slight clang.

"I don't know," Laura said. "It's got me so upset, though, that I think tomorrow after the funeral we're going to Houston to visit my sister. There's nothing going on over at the new house that can't wait."

"Do you think Emily's funeral will be here in Destin?" I asked.

The door opened at the sixth floor, and we stepped out.

"I have no idea." Laura turned to go to her apartment and then turned back to say, "But I can tell you good and damn well mine won't be!" She went in and shut her door.

"Lord! She really is upset!" I said.

"Beat up, too," Haley said.

"What?" I fished the key from my pocket.

"You didn't see anything, Mama? You didn't see the bruises on the back of both her arms?"

I shook my head no.

"You could see them when she was tacking up the notice; her sleeves were pulled up. And then there's one on her forehead, too."

I unlocked the door. "She bruised herself over at the house. Hit her head on a kitchen cabinet."

"The bruise on her head could have come from walking into a door or falling; the bruises on the back of her arms, though, are consistent with someone having grabbed her. Hard."

"Damn," I said, remembering my dream of someone being forced onto the elevator. Could it have been real, not a dream? Could it have been Laura? I was about to remind Haley of the dream when Frances called, "Why are y'all standing in the door?"

"Because I can't walk and put two and two together at the same time," I said.

"Well, long as you haven't found another body. I'm fixing to scramble me an egg. You want one?"

"Sure," Haley said. I declined and went out on the balcony. Haley followed me in a moment.

"I'm sorry, Mama," she said. "I shouldn't have said what I did about Laura. You were already upset."

"No, darling. It's fine. I'm just wondering if this has been going on all the time, and your Aunt Sister and I have missed it. I'm assuming it's Eddie."

"Laura has bruises, Mama. We can't assume anything from that. Even the ones on her arm could have an innocent explanation. Maybe someone grabbed her to keep her from falling."

"I hope so." I thought about little, skinny Laura with her sun-damaged skin and hair. What did we really know about her and her life? "Remember I told you I dreamed about someone being forced on the elevator? Maybe it wasn't a dream."

"But nobody else heard anything, Mama."

"Your egg's ready, Haley," Frances called.

"Go get your breakfast, honey," I said. "I'm okay."

And I was. Just very sad.

In a few minutes she was back. "Here's the protector of the turtles, the defender of the nests."

Sophie Berliner giggled as she followed Haley onto the balcony. She was wearing her usual black robe which, the more we got to know the child, didn't seem so strange.

"How did last night go?" I asked. "See any turtles?"

"Two. We marked two nests." She and Haley sat down at the table, Haley with her eggs, Sophie with orange juice. "My dad thinks one of them is too close to the water so we may move it back farther in the dunes. We have to get someone from the Wildlife Service to help us, though. It has to be done just right."

"But won't the mama turtle get upset if it's moved?"

Sophie gave me a look that I can only describe as disgusted. "She lays her eggs and leaves, Mrs. Hollowell. Turtles don't sit around on their eggs like chickens do."

"Sounds like the perfect setup," Haley said. "Just lay the eggs and leave."

"Well, they're okay unless rattlesnakes or ghost crabs get them," Sophie said.

Haley took a large bite of scrambled eggs. Had she no shame? "Ummm, good. You want some, Mama?"

I shook my head no. "Rattlesnakes? There are rattlesnakes on the beach?"

"Millicent said those woods over on the bay are full of them."

"Do the turtles lay their eggs on the bay beaches, too?" Haley asked Sophie.

"A lot of them do. That's one thing Millicent hated about them building those houses over there. She said the turtles have a hard enough time as it is." Sophie propped her feet on her chair, the black robe tight around her knees. "Did you know they cry when they lay their eggs? Real tears."

At this, Haley put her fork down and pushed her plate away. "Because they're hurting?"

"Millicent says they're not. She says she thinks they're marking the nests with their tears." The child stopped for a moment. "Said. Millicent said." She loosened her robe and stood up abruptly. "Anyway, my mom's coming in today, and she'll take me tonight. But if you'd like to go, I'll call you."

"That would be wonderful, Sophie," Haley said.

"You have to be absolutely quiet and you can't have a light."

"Okay."

"Once they dig their nests and start laying their eggs, you

can shine a flashlight on them. It's like they don't even see the light then."

"Can I go, too?" I asked.

"You'll have to be quiet."

"I can do that."

Frances came out onto the balcony with her eggs and toast. "You want some more juice, Sophie?" she asked. "Or a Coke?"

"No, thanks. I have to go." The child gave a wave and disappeared into the living room. In a second, though, she stuck her head back through the door. "I have my nipples and my navel pierced," she announced. And with that, she left.

"Good Lord!" Haley exclaimed. "Do you think she really does? Surely we'd have noticed in that bikini."

Frances and I, old veterans of this war, just grinned at each other.

# Chapter
# 11

"**P**apa's coming to protect us," Haley said when I told Frances about Fred's plans.

"Don't knock it," Frances pushed her empty plate back and sighed. "You know, I haven't smoked in—how long has it been, Patricia Anne?—God knows, and I'd give an eyetooth for a cigarette right this minute."

"Take a deep breath and you can get a whiff of Fairchild's cigar," I said. "He's over there on the balcony smoking up a storm."

"At least he's not inside." Haley took the last sip of coffee and sighed contentedly. "That was delicious, Frances. Thanks."

Frances nodded. "He'll be smoking in the living room by afternoon."

"You think so?" Haley asked. "Millicent hated those cigars."

Frances nodded again. "I'm telling you. In the living room. When my Aunt Isabel died, they laid her out at home—you know how they used to do—and damned if my Uncle Douglas didn't go in there right over the casket and light up a cigar and blow smoke on her. And Aunt Isabel just lying there and smiling, decked out in her wedding dress that wouldn't button anymore but you couldn't tell it since the buttons were in the back. Made my mama so mad she said, 'Douglas, this is a sin and a disgrace doing my sainted sister this way. God'll punish you, sure as anything.'"

"Did he?" I asked.

"What? God punish him? Not that I know of. He's still living up in Lanett, working on his third wife." Frances licked her finger and stabbed toast crumbs from her plate. "Which reminds me. Have y'all ever been to The Little White House at Warm Springs? It's not far from Lanett."

We admitted that we hadn't.

"A dump," Frances declared. "We'd go over there every time we went to see Aunt Isabel. She and Mama both thought Roosevelt was handed down, and they'd look at that pitiful little kitchen and say things like, 'Here's where the cook was fixing meatloaf the day he died.' One time we were walking through the dinky, tiny bathroom, not even a shower, and Aunt Isabel looked at the toilet and grabbed her chest and said, 'My God! He peed here. Right here in this toilet.'"

Haley and I both laughed, and Frances smiled. "Lord! How did I get off on that subject?"

"I always thought the place would be elegant," I said. "Not big and pretentious, but elegant."

"Don't kid yourself. It's worth a trip, though. He drove his own car around Warm Springs with all these hand controls, and they had the gate to the driveway fixed so that if he bumped it, it would open. Stuff like that's interesting."

We thought about that for a moment.

"And it was a pretty steep grade down to the house," Frances added.

"We need to make the trip, Mama," Haley said, grinning. She got up, collected the dishes, and started through the door. "Frances, can I borrow the car for a while this morning? I need to go into Fort Walton."

"Sure," Frances said, her mind obviously still on The Little White House. "Looks like Mrs. Roosevelt or even his girlfriend Lucy whatshername would have hung some curtains, doesn't it? Or bought a refrigerator? They had an icebox. And this was in the forties. They had electricity, so there wasn't any excuse."

When Frances ran out of things to say about The Little White House, I told her about Fairchild's morning swim and Laura's bruises.

"You don't think it happened like she said?" she asked.

"I suppose it's possible; I hope so."

"How long have Eddie and Laura been married?"

"Forty-something years. Would a spouse start beating on the other after all that time?"

"Well, not usually. But anything could have happened, clinical depression, a slight stroke."

Haley stuck her head out the door and asked for the car keys.

"In my purse," Frances told her. "What's she going into Fort Walton for?" she asked me as we heard the door shut. But I had no idea.

"Maybe she's getting something to wear to Millicent's funeral," Frances said. "I'm sure she just brought beach stuff."

"Which reminds me." I pushed my chair back. "I need

to call Fred and tell him to bring a suit, and me a dress and heels."

Frances got up, too, stretching. "I'm going to put on my bathing suit and mosey on down to the beach. Do you think it'll be all right with Haley for me to move in with her, let you and Fred have the middle room?"

"Sure, thanks. Fred mentioned the Holiday Inn, but I'd rather stay here. Long as he and Sister aren't at each other's throats." Which probably meant we would spend that night at the Holiday Inn.

Haley and Mary Alice came in together about noon. Both were excited, Mary Alice because her wheelchair repo man story had been selected to be read at the writers' conference that night, and Haley because she had gotten the information on the setup of Blue Bay Ranch.

"You go first, Aunt Sister," Haley said graciously. "I've got some photocopied stuff to show you, some stuff I found at the courthouse."

Mary Alice was beaming. "Well, they chose a couple of stories and mine was one of them. I came on home because if I'm to read it in front of the whole crowd, I've got to go buy something to wear. I think something black so I can wear it to the funeral tomorrow, too. Eight o'clock and everybody is invited."

We all assured her that we would be there.

"And I'm going to call Berry. He'll want to know."

"Major Bissell's reading, too." Haley said.

"Oh, I forgot to tell you. He's the other reader. I just knew it was going to be that impotent man, but he didn't make it."

"That's great. We'll come cheer you both on." Haley spread the papers on the coffee table. "Now, look at what I found."

"What are these? Legal papers?" I asked.

"I've been to the courthouse looking up these records." She rearranged some of the documents. "Okay, here's the history of Blue Bay Ranch."

We looked at the legal documents and waited while Haley paused dramatically.

"Tod Abernathy bought the land from a man named Sellers Magee in 1971. Paid him ten dollars an acre for 942 acres of land on Choctawhatchee Bay that nobody figured was worth a dime. When Tod died in 1982, the land still wasn't worth much. But Millicent hung onto it. I don't know if she knew how much it would be worth one day or not. She probably just didn't think much about it.

"Anyway, developers gradually began to build around the bay. They built Sandestin and Indian Bayou. And here Millicent was, sitting on almost a thousand acres of prime land. But she had also seen what some of the developers were doing to it and didn't want that to happen to her land." Haley held up a couple of xeroxed papers. "You ought to see the stipulations she put in here."

"When did Jason Marley enter the picture?" Sister asked.

"Three years ago. He's a real estate developer from Montgomery. Made millions building shopping centers. He went along with all of Millicent's plans for the property, apparently, and they formed the Blue Bay Ranch Corporation. And here's where it gets interesting." She held up another sheet of paper. "Voila! The shareholders of Blue Bay Ranch."

Mary Alice, Frances, and I looked at the paper blankly; none of us had on our reading glasses.

"Well?" Haley asked.

"Well what? We can't see the damned thing," Sister admitted.

Haley poked her finger at the piece of paper. "Laura and

Eddie Stamps are stockholders! And Emily Peacock. With Millicent and Emily gone, Eddie and Laura and Jacob Marley own the whole kit and kaboodle of Blue Bay Ranch."

"Jason," I corrected.

"But I don't understand," Frances said. "What about Fairchild? Berry mentioned it last night, but how come he doesn't get Millicent's part?"

"I looked that up, too," Haley said. She sat on the sofa with the photocopied papers before her on the coffee table, and motioned us to gather around like a teacher does a reading group. We gathered.

"It's a common business practice," she explained. "Millicent had the land and Jason Marley had the money to develop it. He wasn't about to risk his money in a deal she could back out on, and she wasn't about to risk her land. So they formed Blue Bay Ranch Corporation, a joint tenancy from which both of them were planning on making a bundle of money. In this type of corporation, in case of the death of either partner, what they put into the corporation originally stays there, doesn't go to their heirs." She paused. "Are you with me?"

I nodded. "That's why Millicent had Blue Bay buy her a million-dollar insurance policy for Fairchild."

"Right. And I'm sure Jason Marley has one, too, made out to his heirs."

"But Eddie and Laura?" Mary Alice asked. "How do they fit in?"

"Well, Millicent and Jason could have done it fifty-fifty, but if they hadn't agreed about something, the whole company would have come to a standstill."

"I don't understand," Frances said.

"You know, like the vice president not voting unless there's a deadlock. With two people owning equal shares in a business, deadlock could happen easily, something as simple as Jason wanting to cut down some trees that Millicent didn't want cut, and neither giving in. Just all sorts of things. So it's a common business practice to have someone else own a small share of the stock, enough to make a voting difference."

Haley's knowledge of "common" business practices was on par with mine, but what she was saying sounded reasonable. "So Eddie and Laura Stamps are the tie breakers," I said.

"Two of them. Emily was the other." Haley looked at the paper. "It broke down this way: Millicent owned forty-seven percent, Jason owned forty-five, the Stampses had four, two each, and Emily had four. The Stampses and Emily paid $2,500 for each of their shares. Like a present, considering what they were investing in."

"Eight shares doesn't sound like enough to shake a stick at, let alone make a difference," Mary Alice said.

"Sure it would, Aunt Sister. Neither Millicent nor Jason could do anything without the consent of at least one of the others. Jason had to have both of the others. Millicent was real smart in that deal."

"Plus, the other three were her close friends," I said.

Frances looked puzzled. "I thought they were all friends. I'm getting all these people confused," she added.

"They were Millicent's friends first," Sister explained.

Frances nodded as if that had cleared things up.

"Anyway," Haley said, "with Millicent and Emily dead, fifty-one percent of the shares revert to the corporation, which now consists of only Jason, Eddie, and Laura."

We were all quiet for a moment, absorbing this information. Then Frances spoke up. "Does this mean that Eddie and Laura get four percent of the fifty-one? How much would that be?"

"Go figure," Sister said.

"That sounds reasonable, but that's not how it worked. The way it was set up, if Millicent died, Jason would receive six of her shares, which would make him the majority stockholder. The rest would go to the Stampses and Emily Peacock, half and half."

"Isn't that a strange way to do it?" Sister asked.

"Common business practice." My daughter was proving the adage about a little knowledge.

"Now I *am* confused," Frances said. "Who owns what?"

"Eddie and Laura Stamps own a piss pot of real estate, Frances, that they paid ten thousand dollars for," Sister said.

"That about sums it up," Haley agreed. There was a knock on the door, and she put the papers on the coffee table and got up. "I expect that's Major Bissell. He was at the courthouse looking up the same thing. That's when he told me he was reading tonight. We're going to lunch."

"Well, do," I murmured to Sister.

Major Bissell came in with a grin on his round, babyish face. "Hey, ladies. Mrs. Crane, I heard you and I are going to be the readers tonight."

"How about that? I wondered where you were this morning."

"Had to do some work." He nodded toward the papers on the coffee table. "Some interesting stuff there, isn't it?"

"About like a spider web," Sister agreed.

"Best story plots in the world are at the courthouse. No way you could spend much time there and have writer's block." He turned to Haley. "The Crab Trap suit you?"

"Fine."

"Would the rest of you like to join us?" He actually

looked as if he meant it, that he would be pleased to have the three of us traipse along with them to lunch.

We didn't, of course, but we spent at least fifteen minutes after they left talking about what a nice young man he was.

"Dr. Philip Nachman just might have something to worry about here," I said.

"Hmmm." Which might have been an agreement from Sister. She was studying the photocopies Haley had left on the table. Now she put them down and looked at Frances and me. "You know what? Eddie and Laura killed Millicent. It's as clear as the nose on your face."

"They had a motive," I admitted.

"I thought y'all had decided Emily killed Millicent and then committed suicide," Frances said.

"I'm ruling that out," Sister said. "That doesn't make sense. It was the Stampses."

"Jason Marley had the same motive," I said. "He's Mr. Blue Bay Ranch now and can do anything he wants with the property."

"Oh, Patricia Anne, don't be ridiculous!" Frances got up from the floor and stretched stiffly. "That man lives in a pink house!"

So much for all the psych courses Frances had taken.

After lunch, Frances settled down to watch her favorite soaps, and Mary Alice and I went next door to talk to Fairchild.

"Go away!" he yelled through the door when we knocked. "Leave me alone, damm it!"

"It's me, Fairchild," Sister called. "Me and Patricia Anne. Are you okay?"

An eye appeared at the peephole. "Are you by yourselves?"

"Of course we are."

We heard the scrape of the chain in the security latch, and the door opened. "Come in quick," a disheveled Fairchild said.

We practically jumped inside, and Fairchild shut the door and locked it.

"What's the matter?" Sister asked. "What's going on?"

"That damn woman sheriff is driving me nuts." He led us into the living room. "She's been here twice today, asking the same questions."

I tried to soothe him. "She's just doing her job, Fairchild."

"Bull! Is wanting to know how often Millicent and I had sex doing her job? Wanting to know when the last time was?" He plunked down in his recliner. Sister sat on the sofa across from him and leaned forward with interest.

"What did you tell her?"

"I told her it was none of her damn business."

"What else did she ask you?" My sister knows no shame.

"Stuff about money. They're hung up on the insurance policy Millicent left me. I told that woman, I said, 'Lady, you're going to have to look a hell of a lot farther than here to find a killer.' And I said, 'Don't think for a minute that Emily Peacock did it, either. She loved Millicent like a sister.'"

"What did she say to that?" I asked.

"That she would be back later." Fairchild sighed, crossed his arms, and scowled out at the Gulf. "There wasn't nearly this much fuss when Margaret died."

"That's the way it goes, Fairchild," Mary Alice said. "My third husband, Roger Crane? He died on an airplane halfway across the Atlantic. Fortunately, we were coming this way. But they put us off in Nova Scotia or somewhere and took Roger to the hospital and him already dead and blue.

And then I had to figure out how to get him to Birmingham. And I thought to myself, now why didn't they just let us stay on the plane to Atlanta? It would have been so much simpler. And all the insurance companies wanting to know how come the death certificate had latitude and longitude on it for place of death."

I reached over and picked up a photograph album from the coffee table. It opened to a picture of Millicent, Laura, and Emily Peacock sitting at one of the concrete picnic tables the state of Florida has placed in its state parks. All three women were smiling at the photographer, and beyond them the Gulf was a blue line. Emily was caught by the camera as she lifted what looked like a forkful of potato salad.

Fairchild nodded toward the album. "That sheriff woman was looking at that."

"Tell me about Emily," I said, studying the picture. "I've never known her as well as I have Millicent."

"Kind. Into environmental stuff like Millicent was. In fact, I think that's how they got to be such good friends, out saving turtles and stuff. Giving folks hell for picking sea oats. They even went to Tallahassee and lobbied to get a law passed about the sea oats."

Mary Alice reached over, took the album from me, and looked at the picture. "How much was Emily involved in the development of Blue Bay?"

Fairchild smiled. "She and Millicent kept Jason Marley from doing a lot of stuff over there. Stuff they thought might harm the environment. That man found out he better not cut down a butterfly bush or dump anything in the bayou." Fairchild smiled again. "Funny thing is he got to thinking their way. He, was telling me a few nights ago that he saw a porpoise coming up into Sellers Magee Bayou. He sounded real pleased."

Mary Alice handed the album back to me. "That's a nice picture, isn't it, Mouse?" She pointed to it. "Especially of Emily."

"I need to get some copies of these made for her daughter Barbara," Fairchild said. "She got in from Atlanta a little while ago."

"Is that where Emily will be buried?" I asked.

"Barbara said her mother had requested no funeral. She wanted to be cremated and have her ashes sprinkled in the bay. So that's what they're going to do." Fairchild paused. "The Stampses are pretty shook up, especially Eddie. The same folks from the sheriff's department keep bothering them, too. Asking them if Millicent and Laura had had an argument, trying to get Laura involved. I swear it's a mess, isn't it?"

"They'll figure it out, Fairchild," Mary Alice assured him.

He put the backs of his hands to his eyes to wipe away tears. "It won't bring Margaret and Emily back."

"Millicent," Sister mouthed to me.

I looked at the picture again, at the three smiling friends enjoying a picnic on the beach. And then I studied the picture, studied the rest of the pictures while Sister comforted Fairchild with stories of her husbands' deaths.

I broke into the middle of Philip Nachman's demise in the shower, which flooded the bathroom, to say we had to go. Right now. Mary Alice looked at me, surprised, but, give the woman credit, she didn't argue with me. "We'll check with you later, Fairchild," she said, and after we were in the hall, "What's the matter?"

"Emily Peacock didn't commit suicide."

"I don't think so either."

"But I *know* she didn't." I waited for Sister to ask how I knew.

"How do you know?"

"Emily shot herself in the right temple, didn't she? Remember how she was slumped over on her left side?"

"I don't want to think about it."

"And the gun had slid from her right hand. Now," I made Sister wait a moment, "think about that picture. She's eating potato salad, right?"

"I think it was slaw."

"I think it was potato salad, but whichever, she's eating it with her left hand. The fork's in her left hand."

"Maybe she already had something in her right hand, like a cracker."

"Nope. That's why I looked at some more pictures. Emily was left-handed."

Sister thought about this a moment and a slow grin began to light up her face. "Mouse," she said, "that's pretty good."

A compliment from Sister!

When we went into the apartment, Frances was sitting on the sofa with the afghan over her head again.

"Woe," she moaned through green-and-blue crocheted squares. "Oh woe."

"What the hell is she talking about?" Sister asked me. "Whoa like a mule or woe is me?"

"Woe is me," Frances wailed.

"Is David all right?" She hadn't heard from him since he left for London with his new wife. I snatched the afghan from her.

That put the spark back in her. "Of course he is. Doesn't have time to call his mother because he's getting his brains screwed out by that hussy, but other than that, I'm sure he's fine."

"Then what's the matter?"

Frances snatched the afghan back. "The murderer just

called. He said, 'Millicent Weatherby, Emily Peacock, Laura Stamps, Mary Alice Crane.' And then he laughed."

Mary Alice and I both sat down. Frances disappeared under the afghan, forcing me to snatch it away again.

"What are you talking about?" Mary Alice asked. "That's all he said? Just the names?"

"And then he laughed. Like this." Frances gave a very credible creepy laugh. "It was a warning. No doubt about it. You're after Laura Stamps, Mary Alice."

"Did you say anything?" I asked.

"I just said 'what?' and he said the names again and then laughed. God! You should have heard him!" Frances shivered and reached for the afghan.

A banging on the door made us all jump.

"Don't open it!" Frances said, covering her head.

"It's Laura," I said, looking through the peephole and opening the door.

"Phone call!" she gasped, almost ricocheting off the walls in her hurry to get into the apartment. "God! I'm next."

"Told you," came from under the afghan.

Laura plunked down into a wicker rocker and leaned over, her head between her knees. "Woozy," she said.

I brought her a glass of water and glanced over at Sister who seemed to be taking this remarkably well.

"He laughed like this. Heh, heh, heh," Frances said.

Laura looked up. "He called here, too?"

"I'm fourth on the list," Mary Alice said.

"Tell them about his laugh, Laura," Frances mumbled.

Laura took a sip of her water; the glass was shaking. "It was awful. And, believe you me, I'm taking it seriously. I'm getting the hell out of Dodge as soon as I can, and I suggest you do the same, Mary Alice."

"I'm reading tonight," Sister said, remarkably unconcerned, "and Millicent's funeral is tomorrow. Maybe then."

"What did the voice sound like?" I asked.

"Like a robot," Frances said. "You remember the tall robot in *Star Wars*? Him."

I thought about this for a moment. "Exactly what did he say, Laura?"

"He said, 'Millicent Weatherby, Emily Peacock, Laura Stamps, Mary Alice Crane.' And then he laughed that god-awful laugh."

"Could it have been a tape?"

Frances stuck her head out from the afghan. "I asked him 'what' and he said it again."

"So did I," Laura said.

Sister got up. "He could have planned on that. Anybody want anything from the kitchen?" None of us did.

"Come walk to my apartment with me, Patricia Anne," Laura said. "And then I'm going to lock myself in. I'm going to call the police, too."

"Sure," I agreed. And I did. When I came back, Sister was coming out of the kitchen with a ham sandwich.

"Want one?" she asked.

I shook my head no. "How come you're not more worried about the phone call?"

"Well, Lord, Mouse. I'm fourth on the list and Laura's still fine."

# Chapter
## 12

"Y̲ou see, we were looking at some pictures of Emily Peacock and realized immediately that she was left-handed and that whoever killed her hadn't known that. They put the gun in her right hand, shot her in the right temple." Mary Alice stuck her finger to her temple. "Bang." It was a couple of hours later and she was explaining what "we" had discovered to Major Bissell. He and Haley had come in from a leisurely lunch at The Crab Trap and had been confronted with our news.

"I think Lisa Andrews from the sheriff's department already knows this, Mrs. Crane. In fact, I understand suicide was ruled out pretty early." Major Bissell ran his hand through his thinning blonde hair. "It was sharp of you to notice it, though."

Mary Alice's eyes narrowed and I stepped between her and Major Bissell quickly and inquired about lunch, which he declared had been great—good food, good company. He and Haley smiled at each other, a cat-that-swallowed-the-canary smile. I glanced at my watch. How long had they been gone?

"Lisa Andrews told Major about the phone call, too, Aunt Sister. Called him at The Crab Trap."

"And we'll look into it, ma'am. Keep our eyes open. Since the only thing you have in common with the two victims is ownership of your apartment here, though, I wouldn't worry if I were you."

"Thank God!" Sister smiled sweetly. Laura had called an hour ago to inform us that the sheriff's department considered the call a prank. Some prank! The old folks at Gulf Towers were really on one today!

"We're looking forward to your reading tonight," I said quickly.

"I've never read in front of an audience before," he admitted. "I'll probably be pretty nervous."

"Do you want me to read it for you?" Mary Alice asked.

Bless his heart, he thought she was being nice. In fact, that's what he said. "That's very nice of you, Mrs. Crane. If you see I'm not going to get through it, just shove me aside and take over."

"I'd be happy to."

Major Bissell took Haley's hands, held them for a moment and said he would see her later.

"Tonight," she promised.

"Have mercy," Mary Alice muttered. She turned and headed for the balcony. "Patronizing punk," she said to me as I joined her.

"I think he meant well," I said in Major's defense.

"He was patronizing, Patricia Anne. Policemen tend to be that way, or haven't you noticed? Policemen and the teenagers who carry out groceries at the Southern Super Market. They may be the worst. One of them called me 'Sweetheart' the other day. Can you believe that? 'Do you want me to put these eggs in front, sweetheart?' That's what he said, exactly. I considered hitting him over the head with my purse. It might have killed him, and he'd have dropped the eggs, but I don't think any jury would have convicted me. Do you?"

"Justifiable homicide," I agreed. I waved to Frances on the beach. "I hope she has on enough sunscreen."

"Sharp. He thought it was sharp of us to figure out Emily hadn't shot herself."

"Well, it was."

"I'm not about to tell him Eddie and probably Jason Marley are the murderers. See how long it takes him to figure that out."

"Hmmm." Laura had been dropped from her list of suspects, I noticed.

Haley came out to the balcony. "He's a nice man, isn't he?"

"Hmmm." It was Sister's turn.

"I got the stats for y'all. Thirty-three years old, Mama. Never been married. Graduate of Florida State. Born in Fort Walton. His father's a charter boat captain, owns The Lucky Marie berthed at Kelly's Wharf. His mother's a church secretary."

"You got everything but his sperm count, didn't you?" Sister said. "I hope he's doing better there than he is in the hair department."

Give Haley credit: she laughed. "What's the matter with you, Aunt Sister?"

"She thinks he was patronizing," I explained. "And one of the baggers at Southern Super Market called her 'Sweetheart' the other day."

"I can talk for myself," Mary Alice said. "He was patronizing."

"He's nice, though." Haley waved at Frances. "I hope she's got on a lot of sunscreen. That sun's hot today."

"I thought you looked a little flushed when you came in," I said.

"I think it's time for me to go to the beach." And with that, Haley left.

"Look what you did," Mary Alice said.

The reading was to be held in a small amphitheater at Sunnyside. It's a beautiful place, a very miniature Hollywood Bowl with a stage large enough for a small orchestra, backed and partially covered by a shell that really is in the shape of a shell and that, for some reason, has always reminded me of a giant night-light. There are no seats except a few benches in front of the stage, but most of the audience bring blankets or beach towels and sit on the grassy embankment. The beach towels are more comfortable.

So late that afternoon, I left a key for Fred at the security gate and we headed for Sunnyside equipped with a cooler full of drinks, sandwiches, and snacks. Cultural events at the Sunnyside amphitheater are always accompanied by the frequent squish of a pop top being opened. Which makes them more fun.

Mary Alice, the star of the event, had left earlier. She needed, she said, to test the acoustics. I had volunteered to go with her. I was taking the phone threat more seriously than she was. She had turned me down, though, saying she needed the time alone to "center" herself for her reading. We had to tell her a dozen times that she looked fine in her green-and-white silk dress.

She twirled for our inspection. "I didn't find a black one I liked. You don't think these white flowers look like supernovas, do you?"

Did she seriously think we were going to say yes?

It was by far the warmest, most seasonable evening that we had encountered on this trip. The temperature was in the mid-eighties long after the sun had set, and the humidity covered everything like a blanket. The breeze that blew in from the Gulf was heavy, and it was no surprise to see lightning far out on the horizon. Almost any night during the summer, enough heat and wind currents collide over the Gulf to create thunderstorms. These storms usually don't affect the beaches, but they can be spectacular to watch.

So the night of Sister's reading, we weren't worried about rain despite the distant lightning. We climbed partway up the embankment and spread beach towels on the grass.

"Lord, it's hot!" Haley took a can of Coke and held it against her wrist. "I'll bet Major's sweating."

"What about Mary Alice?" Frances examined the contents of the drink cooler. "She was nervous as a cat."

"She doesn't sweat," Haley said. "She exercises self-control."

"What?" Frances came up with a Grapico. "I love these things. Yoo Hoos, too. We should have gotten some Yoo Hoos, Patricia Anne." She followed Haley's example of holding the drink can against her wrist. "So self-control can keep you from sweating?"

"That's what Aunt Sister says."

I opened the package of sandwiches and passed it to Haley. "Don't believe a word of it. Those flowers on your Aunt Sister's dress are going to get a good soaking tonight."

"I heard that." We looked up at green silk emblazoned with exploding stars or peonies. Take your pick. Sister leaned over and looked into the picnic basket. "What did you bring?"

"Pimento cheese sandwiches, tuna fish, cream cheese, chips."

Sister shook her head no.

"Some grapes? An apple?"

"You got any Tums?"

I handed her a roll from my purse. "You're not centered yet?"

She took several and popped them into her mouth. "There are a lot of people here," she said, looking around. "I didn't think there'd be this many."

"You'll do fine," I assured her.

"I'm just worried about Major Bissell," she said. "He's been in the bathroom ever since he got here."

Haley stopped unwrapping a pimento cheese sandwich. "Are you serious? Do you think I ought to go check on him?"

"Several people already have. That woman deputy, what's her name? You know, the one who looks like a blue tube?"

"Lisa Andrews?" I asked.

"The one without a waist who's investigating Emily's death. She's in there with him now."

"Maybe they're discussing police business," Frances said. She ignored Sister's look and calmly bit into a cream cheese sandwich.

There was a squawk over the speaker, which made everybody jump. "Sorry!" a voice said. In a moment, the sounds of James Galway's flute wafted through the small amphitheater. Everyone seemed to hold their breath, to look up at the darkening sky where Jupiter was now visible. When we resumed our picnicking and conversations, we were subdued, caught in the spell of the music.

"I've got to go," Mary Alice said. "There's going to be

about fifteen minutes of music to settle everybody down. Then I'm reading first. Good thing."

Haley said, "Maybe Lisa brought him some Immodium."

I said, "Don't sweat. Remember, you have to wear that dress to the funeral tomorrow."

Frances said, "Break a leg."

We ate our picnic while James Galway serenaded us and a slight breeze from the Gulf began to stir the halos that humidity had formed around the lights.

"I could get used to this," Haley said as she stretched out on a beach towel with a bunch of grapes in her hand.

"Except for all the dead bodies, it's just about perfect," Frances agreed.

And then the music ended and a tall, thin young woman came out onstage and introduced herself as Peggy Wright, the director of the Sunnyside Writers' Conference. This conference, so she told us, had been absolutely the best, with absolutely the best writers, absolutely the best weather, absolutely the best instructors, the best facilities, the best—

"No wonder Major Bissell's hiding in the bathroom," Frances murmured.

"Don't you call that something?" Haley asked. "What she's doing?"

"You call it a poor introduction," Frances said.

"No, I mean isn't there a literary term for listing things like that?"

"Are you talking about 'cataloging'?" I asked, as the woman got to the "very best stories."

"Sounds right."

" 'Take It Away, Horace.' And it will be read by its author, Mary Alice Crane of Birmingham, Alabama." Peggy Wright held up her hand dramatically and Sister swept onto the stage and to the podium. Peggy hung around for a moment or so as if there were some "absolutely best" she had forgotten to add, but a look from Sister sent her scurrying from the stage.

"I didn't know Mary Alice was calling her story 'Take It Away, Horace,' " Frances said while everyone was clapping. Whether the applause was for Peggy's retreat or for Sister's story being selected wasn't clear. Probably both.

"She looks good, doesn't she?" I whispered. And she did. The spotlight revealed a presence, a six-foot-tall, pink-haired woman in her sixties with 250 pounds packed into a green silk dress with supernovas exploding on it. If she was nervous, it didn't show. She opened her manuscript, looked at the audience that immediately quit its rustling, put on her reading glasses and gave the best damn reading I've ever heard. The audience laughed so hard at poor Horace with his job from hell that she had to pause several times. But she handled that easily, sensing the right time to continue. When she finished, she and the wheelchair repo man got a standing ovation.

"She's great!" Haley said, applauding enthusiastically.

"Great!" Frances concurred.

And she was, so good there were tears in my eyes that I realized were for the underlying sadness of the story. What a terribly thin line between comedy and tragedy. And Sister had walked that line with a perfect touch of black comedy. Damn, I was proud of her.

When everyone had settled down, Peggy Wright came back onstage and introduced Major Bissell. "Our own Lieutenant Major Bissell of the Florida Marine Patrol." The crowd, warmed by Mary Alice's performance, gave Major Bissell a good round of applause.

He looked pale, but if we hadn't known he'd spent an hour or so in the bathroom, we probably wouldn't have noticed. He had chosen to wear his uniform, and with his round face and thinning hair, the spotlight made him look eerily like a child in a man's body, a looming child-man. He read slowly and in a sibilant monotone, probably because of nervousness, but it suited the material perfectly. For Major Bissell's story was told from the point of view of a serial killer who drives the beach road at night, looking into the houses and condos, choosing potential victims, watching them for days, circling ever closer until he can stand it no more and strikes. There were many of us in the audience who realized his story was based on fact and that the killer had never been caught.

The story ended with the killer approaching a young woman who is struggling in the rain to put her groceries in her car. He has been stalking her for days, and says, simply, "Can I help you, m'am?"

The story was a good one. It didn't receive the standing ovation that Sister's had, probably because it made the listeners uncomfortable. Major Bissell's serial killer was too sane, too normal; he had a wife and children that he loved and who loved him. I think Frances spoke for us all when she said, "Wow, that gave me the creeps."

We gathered up our picnic stuff and worked our way down to the stage where Mary Alice and Major Bissell were accepting congratulations. Berry West was standing by Mary Alice, beaming.

"Wasn't she something?" he asked. We agreed that she was. Sister grabbed Haley by the arm, pulled her aside, and whispered to her. Haley nodded. Sister whispered some more. Haley nodded again.

"What was that about?" I asked her as we walked over to Major Bissell.

Haley grinned. "She's going out to dinner with Berry. She wants me to drive her Jaguar home."

"That's what all that whispering was about?"

"She was giving me instructions."

"Not to let me drive her car?"

"That, plus something about staying clear of mailboxes. She wanted to know if I'd ever hit one. She thinks it may be genetic."

"I wish she were going back with us. For all we know, Berry West could have been the one to make that phone call."

"Oh, for heaven's sake, Patricia Anne," Frances said. "I happen to know that his wife was president of the Atlanta Junior League."

"Well, excuse me!" I hated to admit that this piece of news made me feel better.

"Hey, ladies," Major Bissell greeted us.

"Your story scared me," Haley said.

"Good. It was supposed to." He grinned. "You know it's based on an actual case, don't you?"

"I do," I said. "They figure he's killed at least five women in the Florida Panhandle, don't they?"

Major Bissell nodded. "The last one last August. In one of those condos right on 98, not ten feet from the highway."

"How do you know it was him?" Frances asked.

"We know." He turned to Haley. "You want to go get something to eat? I'm starving."

Haley shook her head. "Thanks, but I have to drive Aunt Sister's car back to Destin, and I'm hoping some turtles come in tonight. I don't want to miss it if they do."

Major Bissell looked disappointed, but as we turned to leave, Lisa Andrews came up, took his arm, and asked if he were feeling better.

"Get lost, Haley," Frances murmured.

The lightning in the Gulf was not the usual jagged streaks, but a sudden glow of a cloud here and there. Like giant lightning bugs, I thought. The storms were still so far away, we heard no thunder as we walked toward the cars.

Frances and I helped Haley find Sister's Jaguar and immediately ran into a problem; we couldn't open the damn thing. Haley tried every key on the ring.

"Maybe Aunt Sister hasn't left yet," Haley said.

And then from the darkness behind us, a man's voice said, "Can I help you, ma'am?"

The three of us froze. None of us had heard him approaching.

A large hand reached over and took the keys from Haley's grasp. "You push this button on the keychain," the man said. We heard the click as the door unlocked, and then the keys were in Haley's hands again and the man was gone.

"Holy shit!" Frances said when we could breathe again.

"Some damn practical joker," Haley said.

Nevertheless, we all piled into Sister's car and Haley drove us to Frances's car. Then I insisted that we follow Haley home. To her credit, she didn't argue.

"I'll bet that man thought he was funny as hell," Frances said.

"Probably," I agreed. We were driving along Old Highway 98 where the condos sit right on the road. Just like the serial killer in Major Bissell's story, we could see right into many of the apartments where televisions flickered or families were eating supper. In one of the apartments, a woman was casually stepping out of a bathing suit. I wanted to yell at them all to close their blinds. And then I got angry at the man who had spooked us so, and because there really was a reason that these people, vacationing, happy, should be more careful.

We rode in silence for a few minutes. The traffic was light for a June night, but this part of the beach is usually quiet, family-oriented. Teenagers flock to The Miracle Strip in Panama City, and the older, nightclub group head the other way to Fort Walton. Folks along the Destin beaches rent a movie and order in a pizza. On Friday nights the Elks Club has a steak dinner for eight bucks that draws a crowd. But the men have been playing golf all day or fishing, and the women and children have been at the beach too long. It makes for early evenings. Even the restaurants, and there are some very nice ones, are usually empty by nine. *There was no room here for violence,* I thought. And yet, it happened.

"Millicent Weatherby left to go to the grocery store the morning she was killed. Right?" Frances asked.

"Fairchild said she went to get some tomato juice. Why?"

"What if the serial killer had been stalking her?"

For a second I could see Millicent standing by her car and a man coming up and saying, "Can I help you, ma'am?" The man had Major Bissell's face. I shivered.

"Unh-uh," I said. "Her death and Emily's are connected some way."

"The killer saw them together all the time. He was after them both."

"I don't think so. I don't think a serial killer would have tried to make Emily's death look like suicide."

"Well, it's possible." We were entering the city limits and Frances slowed to thirty.

"Anything's possible," I agreed. "What do I know?"

# Chapter
## 13

**M**y sweet Fred's car was in the parking lot at the condo. I felt a pleasant little blip of anticipation when I saw it, a very nice thing after forty years of marriage. The few days away from each other had been good for us.

"Papa's here," Haley said, getting out of the Jaguar. "The world is a safer place now."

"Yes, it is, Miss Smart Aleck." She and I grinned at each other. As much as she complains about Fred being over protective, I know it's part of her security, too.

"How did the Jaguar drive?" Frances asked.

"Fine." Haley reached over and got the picnic basket. "I might have enjoyed it if Aunt Sister hadn't made me so nervous. I swear if there had been a mailbox between here and Sunnyside I probably would have hit it." I knew the feeling.

We collected all the picnic paraphernalia and went upstairs. I opened the door of the apartment and called Fred's name. I had expected to be greeted with a hug, but there wasn't an answer. I walked onto the balcony and saw that he and Fairchild were sitting on the stile.

"Hey, honey!" I yelled.

Fred looked up, waved, and motioned for me to come down.

"He's on the stile," I told Frances and Haley as I sailed by the kitchen. "He'll probably want some supper, so don't put the picnic stuff up yet."

Fred was waiting for me, and his hug smelled like a chili hot dog with lots of onions. "You stopped at Porky Pete's," I said into his shoulder.

"I was starving."

"How many did you have?"

"Just two."

"Are we going to be up all night?"

"If you want to."

Lord, this man felt good. I stood there for a moment just savoring it.

"Fred's been telling me about his business deal," Fairchild said, and the two of us moved apart guiltily, remembering Fairchild's loss. "Sounds good."

"Yes, it does," I agreed. Fred and I sat on the bench across from Fairchild.

"I was telling him we'd probably be spending more time down here," Fred said, reaching for my hand.

"Well, if you're thinking about moving, get your driver's license now. Best advice Millicent ever gave me."

The three of us were silent for a moment. Fairchild took a puff of his cigar and coughed. Smoke drifted up slowly toward the light and joined the humidity in forming a halo.

"She was a wonderful lady, Fairchild," Fred said. "She'll be missed."

Fairchild nodded and puffed on his cigar. "The police think I killed her," he said matter-of-factly. "Her and Emily Peacock, too. Tried to make it look like Emily did it and committed suicide." He puffed. "But that would have been stupid. What reason would Emily have had to kill Millicent?"

Fred squeezed my hand. "They can't believe that, Fairchild."

"Sure they do. They always suspect the husband first, you know that. And I'm a rich man now. The insurance and property. Even the condo here." He gestured back over his head.

"But Fairchild, you're not the only one who gained financially by Millicent's death. Everybody in the Blue Bay Ranch Corporation came out way ahead. What about the Stampses and Jason Marley? Not only did they come out ahead on Millicent's death, but on Emily's, too."

He rubbed his eyes under his glasses and then straightened the glasses back on his nose. "The police have questioned them, but not like they have me. I spent the whole damn afternoon at the sheriff's department trying to explain about a stupid argument Millicent and I had at Albert's Fish Market the other day. And I do mean stupid. I wanted to order a fried seafood platter, you know one of those for two people? And Millicent said absolutely not, that my cholesterol was off the charts already. Anyway, I got ticked off and said something like, 'By God, I'll eat what I want to.' You know how that goes. And she said something like, 'Okay, Fairchild, kill yourself if you want to, but you're not going to kill me.' She wasn't angry, didn't even raise her voice. Just ordered a salad. Anyway, the sheriff claims I was heard threatening to kill Millicent." Fairchild rubbed his eyes again. "Can you believe that? It's almost funny."

"They're grabbing at straws, Fairchild," I said.

"What about these other people?" Fred asked. "Eddie and Laura Stamps and—"

"Jason Marley," I supplied.

"Jason's a wreck. Not only is he torn up about both women's deaths, but he's blaming himself for not following up on where Emily was when he didn't hear from her. He just assumed everything was okay."

"What about Eddie?" I questioned. I wondered if Laura had told Fairchild about the threatening phone call. Probably, I decided. And I didn't think now was the time for Fred to hear about it.

Fairchild hesitated for a moment, long enough to blow another puff of smoke toward the light. Then he leaned forward and pushed the cigar into a receptacle filled with sand. "I don't know if you've noticed anything, Patricia Anne, but Eddie has been diagnosed as being in the early stages of Alzheimer's."

I was shocked. "I haven't noticed a thing."

"I'll bet when you first saw them, Laura thought of some way to remind Eddie of your name."

I thought for a moment. "She said, 'Patricia Anne, Mary Alice, what's the matter' or something like that. It didn't seem strange the way she did it."

"She's gotten good at helping him like that, protecting him. She's told the police, of course, about his condition and has absolutely refused to let them question him without her being there. He understands that Millicent and Emily are dead and he's extremely upset about it. He's not that far gone."

"Damn," Fred said. My thoughts exactly.

Fairchild stood up and stretched slightly. "Well, I'll let you two lovebirds have the stile to yourselves. I've got to go in and make some phone calls."

"Is there anything we can do for you tomorrow?" Fred asked.

"Just be there." He started down the stile steps. "And bring Mary Alice."

Old coot.

I pinched Fred on the inside of his thigh. "You'd better not have another woman already lined up."

"Watch where you're pinching or it wouldn't do me any good if I did."

"You mean like this?"

He grabbed my hand and giggled. "Quit that!"

I didn't feel like playing, anyway. The news about Eddie's illness had shaken me. I stopped my hand's forward motion, moved away slightly and inquired about Woofer.

"He's fine," Fred said, confused at the sudden cessation of the game.

"Mitzi's walking him every day?"

"When the two of them aren't sitting in her air-conditioned den watching soaps. Mitzi says he's especially fond of 'The Bold and the Beautiful'."

"I swear, just like a male. And me not gone even a week."

A young couple came over the stile, spoke to us, and walked down the beach toward the water. When I turned from watching them, Fred was looking straight at me. "Tell me everything that's happened this week."

"It's been strange. Part of it has actually been fun, like tonight's reading. But finding the bodies!"

"I know, honey." He put his arm around me and I snuggled against him. God was in his heaven; all was right with the world.

I was trying to decide where to start my version of the week's events when he added, "This is the kind of thing that always happens when you're around Mary Alice. I swear, honey, you know I'm fond of her, but think how often I have to get you out of scrapes she's gotten you into."

For a moment I felt that I couldn't breathe, as if I had suddenly been immersed in an icy lake. Fred sensed my stiffening. "That's not exactly what I meant to say. What I meant to say is that Mary Alice leaps before she looks. You know that, and she pulls you with her a lot of times."

"And you have to come rescue me."

Fred shifted his weight uncomfortably. "Sometimes."

"What does that have to do with what's happened this week?"

"Well, finding the bodies and all."

I stood and looked down at him. There were all sorts of things I wanted to say to him but, give me credit, I kept my mouth shut, just turned and walked away.

"What's the matter, honey?" the jackass called. But I didn't turn around to answer.

"Where's Papa?" Haley asked as I walked into the apartment.

"Digging a hole and pulling the dirt in on top of himself."

"What did he do?"

"Pushed the overprotecting button too hard."

"Mama, just ignore it like you tell me to do."

"Better yet," Frances put in her two cents' worth, "just enjoy it."

"Enjoy someone treating you like you're a child? Blaming everything that happens on your sister?"

"Of course." Frances was sitting on the sofa flipping through the latest issue of *Cosmopolitan*. "Long as he doesn't blame everything on you. That's what usually happens to me." An article caught her attention. "Lord have mercy. Did y'all know sex is going to be different in the next millennium?"

"How?" Haley asked.

"Don't know. Haven't read it yet."

I walked to the balcony and looked down at Fred sitting on the stile by himself. Haley came up behind me.

"He looks sad, Mama."

"Hush. He said he has to get me out of scrapes."

"He looks very sad."

"Then you go let him rescue you."

"There's someone at the door," Frances called. "I'll get it."

Haley and I stepped back into the living room as Tammy Berliner came in. "Good," she said. "I was hoping you were here. I just got in and found a note from Jack and Sophie. They've gone to Navarre and said for me to bring you to see the turtles if you were home and wanted to come."

Of course we wanted to come. Should we bring flashlights? Blankets?

"No lights," Tammy said. "Jack and Sophie will have flashlights, for later."

Blankets? Sure, we might have to wait a while. And insect repellent. The dunes were full of no-see-ums on a hot, muggy night like this. And mosquitoes.

"I'm going to ask my father if he wants to come. Okay?" Haley said. "He's sitting on the stile."

"Sure. It's really something to see. How about I meet you in the parking lot in about ten minutes. I just got in from work and need to put on some jeans."

We agreed that would be fine.

"Go get your father," I told Haley.

\*       \*       \*

It was the beginning of one of the most haunting and memorable evenings of my life. The five of us piled into our car (Fred insisted on driving) and headed toward Navarre Beach.

"Don't they come in at Destin?" Fred asked Tammy.

"Too built up. They come in along the National Seashore where it's dark. Any light, even a match being struck in the dunes, will send them right back into the water."

"Are they endangered?" Frances asked.

"The loggerheads, the kind that usually come in and lay their eggs along these beaches, are considered threatened. There are five types of sea turtles that nest along the United States' coastline. The other four are on the endangered list. Leatherback turtles are almost extinct."

"That's terrible!" Haley exclaimed.

Tammy, who was sitting on the front seat with Fred, turned to look at us. "Y'all don't want to get me started on this. I'll preach to you all night, and lose my temper, to boot."

"I'd like to hear about it," I said.

"Well, I can't spout out the numbers like Millicent could. But I know that something like 55,000 loggerheads drown in shrimp nets every year in spite of the turtle excluder devices that are supposed to let them escape, and thousands choke on plastic trash or get caught in boat propellers. And if they survive to return to their nesting site, condominiums have been built there. It's a pretty bleak outlook for animals so hardy they've been around since the age of the dinosaurs."

"And man is doing them in," Fred said.

Tammy nodded. "The only good thing is that man is beginning to realize what he's done. There are more and more people becoming aware of the sea turtle's plight and trying to help. There's a real active volunteer group here along the Panhandle."

We were all silent for a moment and then Tammy spoke again. "Jack grew up here, in Mary Esther. He says when he was a boy, he and some of his buddies would come out to the beach at night and turn turtles on their backs. They can weigh up to four hundred pounds, you know, so it was a big deal to upend one. Or they would ride them. Now one of the things he does as a volunteer is talk to school kids, tell them how the turtles just can't deal with what we're doing to them and how they should never bother them. And Sophie's on call for nesting watch. Millicent brought her out here one night and she was hooked."

"That's wonderful," Frances said.

"It's a drop in the bucket, but it's a start."

"The people on nesting watch," Fred asked, "how do they know when to go to the beach? Or is someone there every night?"

"People call. There's a Turtle Watch Hotline. The turtles tend to come in close to the beach during the late afternoon and rest until night, and people in boats spot them, or even helicopter pilots from Eglin Field. They're good about calling. Volunteers walk the beaches every morning looking for nests and staking them, but it's good if we can actually tag the female turtles. There are all kinds of studies being done on their migration patterns."

The mention of Millicent had made me think of Blue Bay Ranch. "Do any turtles still nest on the bay beaches?" I asked.

"Sure," Tammy said. "If it's dark enough. That's one of the things that bothered Millicent about Blue Bay. They've already lost their nesting spots over on the Niceville side of Choctawhatchee Bay to developments. That's why she in-

sisted on keeping part of the property as wilderness."
Tammy pointed. "Turn left up here, Fred. We have to go
over the bridge."

We went through the small resort town of Navarre Beach
and soon were driving between high dunes that marked the
National Seashore.

"How will we find them?" Fred asked.

"We'll see the car. It'll be no problem."

And it wasn't. On this deserted strip of beach, the Berliners' Bronco was the only parked car. Fred pulled off the
road and parked behind it.

"Okay," Tammy said. "No lights. No talking. If the turtle
is already laying her eggs, nothing we can do will disrupt
her. But she may not be on the beach yet. So let's be quiet."

We got out of the car, shutting the doors as gently as
possible, and followed Tammy over the dunes. The sand
was so white, the moon gave a surprising amount of light.
Fred reached over and took my hand. It was hard to remember in this setting how mad I was at him.

The dunes along this part of the beach are so high that
the water is not visible. One of them is nicknamed The Mat-
terhorn; fortunately, that wasn't the one we had to climb,
but we were out of breath when we reached the top and
saw the Gulf.

Tammy paused and looked around. "There," she whispered. About forty feet to our right and lower down the
dune, we could see two figures crouching low. We made
our way toward them.

"Anything?" Tammy whispered as we sat down beside
Jack and Sophie.

"She's trying to make up her mind," Jack whispered back.
"She's been out of the water twice and gone back. Skittish."

We settled into the sand to wait. Fred's hand still held

mine, and in a few moments, I was aware of a pulse beating between us. Was it my heart? His? I had cried on the phone, and he had come to rescue me. Wasn't that what I had wanted?

I think during part of the wait that I was half asleep, drifting somewhere between the slightly hazy stars, the distant lightning, and the water that rippled phosphorescent, white on white sand. At one point, a meteor burst across the sky, green, glowing. Fred's hand squeezed mine.

And then someone (Sophie?) touched my shoulder and I was no longer drifting but watching a huge black form materialize from the water. It came slowly, dragging itself across the sand, a creature of the sea ponderous in an alien world.

We were afraid to breathe. In the distance we could hear music and the hum of an airplane. Would the noise frighten her off? She stopped, and against the white sand, we could see her huge head darting this way and that. Was all safe?

She lumbered forward again, dragging herself onto the dry, upper beach, through the first vegetation. Then she stopped. In a moment we heard the rhythmic scoop of sand.

"We can go see her now," Jack Berliner murmured. "She's nesting."

"Wait a minute," Tammy said. "Let her get the nest dug."

So we waited for the sound of digging to stop, and then we followed Jack to the spot where the turtle had disappeared.

"Any of you ever seen a turtle lay eggs?" he asked.

We all shook our heads no, with the exception of Tammy and Sophie.

"Well, they cry."

I remembered that Sophie had told us that.

"I just thought I'd better warn you. They aren't real tears, of course; they wash sand from her eyes and get the salt out of her system."

"So they say," Tammy said.

Sophie was the first to shine a light on the turtle. "Oh, look, Daddy. She's a big one!"

And she was. She had looked huge crossing the beach. Up close, she was immense. Sophie's flashlight, and then Jack's, shone down on a reddish-brown shell that was larger than a table. From this shell a huge reptilian head jutted forth. She paid no attention to us. Tears poured from her eyes and she groaned like any woman in labor.

"Damn," Fred said in awe. But Haley asked if it was all right to touch her.

"Sure," Jack said. "The Rolling Stones could be playing on her back right now and she wouldn't know it."

The turtle groaned loudly. Haley knelt beside her and patted her shell. "It's okay," she said. "Push!" She didn't think it was a damn bit funny when we laughed.

"She's pushing," Tammy said. "Show them, Jack."

"Okay. Come on, Sophie. We forgot to count the eggs." The two of them knelt behind the turtle and shone their flashlights into the surprisingly deep hole the turtle had dug in such a short time.

"I count nine, Daddy. She's just started."

"Y'all look," Jack invited us. "Keep counting, Sophie." He got up and I knelt in his place. Eggs the size of Ping-Pong balls were dropping into the nest.

"Oh, my," I said, pulling Fred down beside me. "Look at this."

"Fifteen, sixteen, seventeen," Sophie counted.

"Let me see." Haley pushed between Fred and me. Frances was right behind her. "Lord have mercy," she said when she saw the size of the eggs and how they were popping out. "Now this is the way to do it."

"Nature trying to beat the odds," Tammy said. "The babies that hatch and find their way to the water still face all kinds of survival problems."

"But we'll be back in two months to see they get to the water," Jack said. "We can do that much." He held up a small strip of metal. "I'm going to clamp her tag on now so we'll know if she comes back." He turned the light on the metal. "She's number 349, Sophie."

Sophie nodded. "Forty-one, forty-two."

"Where do you tag her?" Fred asked, getting up to see.

"Front left flipper. It doesn't hurt her. It's like piercing ears."

Which hurt like hell, I remembered, but I didn't say anything.

"Who keeps up with all this stuff?" Fred asked.

Jack knelt to his job. "The Florida Department of Natural Resources. Millicent was the Okaloosa County volunteer coordinator and she handled the information and gave out tag permits. You've got to have control over the tagging or it won't do any good. I guess I'll have to find out tomorrow who to report Miss 349 to."

Miss 349 had not flinched when Jack put the tag on her flipper. The Ping-Pong-ball-sized eggs were still popping out, forming a white mound in the nest.

"How many?" Haley asked Sophie.

"Seventy-two. Millicent and I counted 153 one night last week." Sophie didn't look up from the nest, but in a moment she brushed the back of her hand across her eyes.

On the horizon, lightning streaked across a cloud, and moments later we heard distant, muffled thunder. I looked at the dark water of the Gulf, at the turtle laying her eggs, at my daughter, her face filled with awe as she knelt in the sand, at all of us caught in a small pool of light on this beach on this primal night. It was something I'll always remember.

"She's through," Sophie said. "A hundred twenty-one."

"Let's move back," Tammy said.

The turtle heaved herself from the nest, turned, and clumsily began to push sand over the egg-filled hole with her front flippers, throwing more sand around after she had finished so the site would be concealed. Then she lumbered home to the Gulf.

"Will she be back next year?" Frances asked.

"She'll be back," Sophie answered.

# Chapter

## 14

The dark shape became one again with the water. Behind her, in the sand, she had left a wide rut that looked like a tractor had been driven across the beach.

"Amazing." Haley voiced what all of us were thinking.

"We mark the nest now," Jack explained. "It won't keep the ghost crabs and raccoons out, but people have learned to respect the nests. Some of them the hard way. This is federal property and they're breaking the Endangered Species Act if they bother them." He took a wooden stake, pushed it deep into the sand, and then tamped it. On the side of the stake was the number sixteen. "This is the sixteenth nest we've marked," he said. "I'm sure there are some we've missed, but sixteen is pretty good. They'll be coming in here until August, even September sometimes, to lay their eggs, and by that time these eggs will be hatching. That's when the volunteers really get busy. The adult turtles

won't go near a light and the hatchlings are just the opposite, heading straight for them, even headlights on the road."

"I want to be here when this nest hatches," Haley said.

"I'm looking forward to it," Tammy said. "Jack's seen the
hatchlings, but Sophie and I haven't."

There was another distant roll of thunder; the clouds were
building in the southwest.

"Looks like we might get that storm," Jack said.

"Do you think more turtles will come in tonight?" Haley
asked him.

"Maybe. I'll stick around until midnight. Joe and Edna
Tarrant are coming then. When there have been sightings,
we try to keep several watchers posted down the beach."

"I had no idea all this went on," I admitted.

Sophie looked up from the notebook she had been writing
in. "I want to stay, too."

"Ask your mother."

"I'll stay with you," Tammy said.

The four of us thanked them, told them good night, and
crossed the dunes without talking, still under the spell of
what we had just witnessed. The sound of our feet scrunch-
ing in the sand was loud in the quiet night. And then from
the pine barrens beyond the road came the most ungodly
scream I've ever heard in my life. Multiply Sophie's Tarzan
yell exponentially and you're getting close.

And then came one of the shining moments of Fred's life.
We three women threw ourselves at him for protection.
Threw ourselves so hard, we literally upended him in the
sand, knocking him on his butt with the three of us on top
of him.

The scream came again, with a protracted moan this time.
Someone was being tortured in the pine barrens. Dismem-
bered in the pine barrens by a sadistic monster.

"My God!" Frances moaned.

"Do something, Papa!" Haley said.

"Get off him!" I pushed my way under the other two. I could feel Fred shaking. "You've hurt him." Fred shook harder. "Get up, sweetheart, if you can."

"It's a screech owl," he said. "Just a plain old screech owl. Y'all let me up." He started snickering.

"Are you sure?" Haley asked.

"I can't believe you city women don't know what a screech owl sounds like." The snicker became a laugh.

The three of us got up and brushed the sand off. "Hush," I told him.

But he laughed like hell all the way to the car. In fact, we were across the bridge and headed east down 98 before his fits of laughter stopped. The last one was accompanied by a pat on my leg and a request to clean off his glasses, which were fogging up.

"I can't believe that turtle," Haley finally said into the silence.

"And the number of eggs!" Frances was trying.

After five more miles of silence, Fred announced that the Berliners were very nice people. We all agreed that they were. But how, he asked, could they work in Atlanta and live in Destin and wasn't Gulf Towers still a "no children under sixteen" facility?

I had forgotten about that. But the moment he said it, I realized that Millicent had bent the rules for the dark-eyed Sophie. It also meant that while there were plenty of children visiting during vacation seasons, much of the time Sophie would live in a world of adults.

We explained to Fred about the Berliners' jobs, that they had wanted to get Sophie away from Atlanta.

"She's very precocious," Haley said. "And I think they

thought the environment would be safer here." She paused. "That's ironic, isn't it. Anyway, Sophie can't spread her wings quite as widely here."

"She still does a pretty good job, though. Wait until you see her black gauze outfit and her bikini," Frances added.

I came to her defense. "But she's also got the turtles and sharing them with her parents. She didn't have anything like that in Atlanta."

"True," the others agreed.

Mary Alice and Berry West were sitting on the sofa drinking wine when we came in.

"Hey, y'all," she said. "Where've you been?"

"To see the turtles."

"It was wonderful."

"You should have been with us."

Berry stood and was introduced to Fred. "There's some beer in the refrigerator, Fred," he said. "Can I get you one?"

"Sure." Fred sat in one of the wicker rockers.

"Ladies?" Berry asked.

We all declined. Fred leaned forward. "I think Mary Alice's glass needs topping off there."

"Of course." Berry headed for the kitchen.

Fred smiled at Sister who scowled back at him. "How you doing, Mary Alice?"

"Fine."

"I heard you did a great reading tonight."

"Thanks."

"You ever heard a screech owl?"

"No. Why?"

"You should have been with us a while ago. They get your attention right off."

"I'll vouch for that," Haley said.

Berry came from the kitchen with Fred's beer and the wine bottle. "How many turtles did you see?"

Frances spoke up. "One huge one. She laid 121 eggs."

"I hope some of them make it," Berry said, pouring more wine into Sister's glass.

Fred opened his beer with such an exaggerated swoosh that we all turned to look at him. "Well," he said, "you never can tell. I have an idea that some of them will."

"I do, too," Haley agreed.

"Where did y'all eat?" I changed the subject.

"At The Boat House," Sister said. "It was great. I had broiled grouper and Berry had scampi. Angel hair pasta. The doggy bags are in the refrigerator."

Berry reached for his jacket, which was across a dining room chair. "And I've got to call it a night. I don't want to wake Jason if he's asleep."

"You're still staying over there?" Frances asked. She realized the question sounded rude and apologized. "That didn't come out the way I meant."

Berry shrugged into his jacket. "It's real uncomfortable, but I'm not sure what I ought to do. Jason is so upset about Emily and Millicent's deaths that I feel like I'm intruding on his grief. On the other hand, if I'm not there, he's by himself. And I've been able to help some by seeing that he eats and by taking some of the phone calls. Somebody needs to be there with him."

"He doesn't have any family?" I asked.

"A son in the navy. He's coming next month on leave."

"It's so sad," Frances said. "Being alone."

"Yes, it is." Berry leaned over and kissed Mary Alice on the forehead. "Thanks for a great evening. I'll see you tomorrow." He turned to Fred and held out his hand. "Fred, nice meeting you."

"Yes," Fred agreed. I gave him a sharp look. He had fallen into his king-of-the-mountain mode.

Mary Alice walked Berry to the door and they stood there for a moment whispering.

"The two of you seem to be hitting it off fine," I told her when she came back into the room.

"He still counting dimples?" Fred asked.

Sister surprised me. She smiled and said that, as a matter of fact, he was, and that it was amazing how many he had discovered. Then she picked up her wine glass, told us good night, disappeared into her room, and shut the door.

"What's the matter with you?" I asked Fred.

"I'm hungry. I'm going to go find the doggy bag. Any takers?"

"I want some," Haley said.

Frances sat on the sofa examining her fingernails carefully.

"Penny for your thoughts," I said.

"Just thinking about Jason Marley over there by himself in that beautiful pink house. That's not a bachelor's house, Patricia Anne. That's a Hansel and Gretel house." I had no idea what a Hansel and Gretel house was, but I knew where this was headed.

"You can check on him tomorrow," I said. "See if he needs comforting."

"I'm sure he does," Frances smiled.

Before we went to bed, I knocked on Sister's door. Her departure had been too sudden, too agreeable.

"You okay?" I asked. She was lying on the bed wearing the peignoir that had nearly blinded Fairchild and reading *Beach Music*.

"Sure. I had a good time tonight."

"You did a great job at the reading. I was proud of you."

She patted the bed and I sat down beside her. "Tell me about the turtles."

I did, describing the eggs and the way the turtle cried and groaned. The way Haley had said, "Push!" "Maybe we can all go back tomorrow night," I added.

Sister shook her head no. "Berry and I are going to The Slipper dancing. He's a great dancer, Mouse."

"He can dip you?"

"You got it."

"Fairchild wanted to make sure you were coming to the funeral tomorrow. Fred asked what he could do for him and he said bring Mary Alice."

"That's sweet."

Was Sister half crocked? God forbid that she was falling in love.

"Fairchild also told us that Eddie Stamps is in the early stages of Alzheimer's."

That got her attention. "Really? I haven't noticed anything."

"He says Laura's done a good job of covering up for Eddie. Fairchild is convinced the police think he killed Millicent and Emily. Fairchild, that is, not Eddie."

"Fairchild wouldn't hurt a flea." Sister yawned and then smiled.

Lord, let her be half crocked!

"Sister's being too nice," I complained to Fred as I crawled into bed a half hour later. "She's acting like somebody's hit her over the head with a two-by-four. Last time she acted like this was when she fell for that ancient guy that nearly croaked in her hot tub."

"How's he doing?" Fred asked. "I haven't heard about him in a while."

"His daughter gave him a big birthday party at the Birmingham Country Club a couple of weeks ago. The pictures were in the paper, and he looked pretty good for ninety-something. Plaid jacket.''

''So the skin grafts must have worked.''

''Dummy.'' I leaned over and gave Fred a very satisfactory kiss in spite of the fact that he now tasted like Scope and Crest masking recent garlic butter that had been added to the earlier onions from Porky Pete's.

''I think she's really falling for Berry West,'' I added. ''I think he's real nice. You were short with him, though.''

''I'm sure he's fine. He just looked like he was taking over.''

''A macho thing.''

''Hush,'' Fred said, ''or I'll throw you to the screech owls.''

So I hushed.

The small town of De Funiak Springs is about forty miles from Destin. It's a beautiful old Chatauqua town built around a large lake, supposedly one of only two perfectly circular lakes in the world. Victorian and ranch houses exist harmoniously side by side beneath live oaks older by far than the oldest of the homes. A few palm trees, planted by the city or a garden club, struggle to survive in the city park.

It's a good town with good people and sidewalks and a library with large windows on the lake. It's where Fred and I were when we heard Kennedy had been shot. We were sitting at the soda fountain at the drugstore eating grilled cheese sandwiches. We sat there until Walter Cronkite wiped his eyes and said Kennedy had been pronounced dead. The pharmacist said, ''God rest his soul.''

We have not been back to the drugstore since, but it's still there. We passed it on the way to Millicent's funeral.

The thunderstorm of the night before had proved to be the forerunner of a low pressure system that had moved in over the coast. Rain had fallen most of the night, and now a fine mist was enveloping us in fog. We were driving on a dark, dismal day to the funeral of a friend who had been murdered; we were both lost in our own thoughts.

I closed my eyes and saw once more the photographs of Millicent and Emily at the picnic. They had looked so happy. What on God's earth had happened to bring them to such violent deaths? Greed? Was Blue Bay Ranch and its potential millions the motive? Or something as simple as an insurance policy? Or jealousy?

"There's a crowd here," Fred said as we neared the chapel. Cars were parked on both sides of the road.

"Everybody loved Millicent," I said. And then I realized not everybody. Somebody had definitely not loved Millicent.

Mary Alice and Fred had both insisted on driving so we had ended up taking both cars, Sister and Haley in one, Fred and I in the other.

"This is dumb," Haley muttered to me while they were arguing.

"Don't tell me," I said. "Tell them."

So as Fred pulled in behind a pickup with a Confederate flag decal on the rear window, the Jaguar pulled in behind us.

"We beat Mary Alice here," Fred gloated.

Inside the chapel was as dark as the day. As we stood at the door looking for seats, Berry appeared. "We've got you places up front."

"Up front" turned out to be the second row. In front of us were Fairchild and several people we didn't know, Millicent's brother and sister, I assumed, and their families. Beside us were Jason Marley, Laura and Eddie Stamps, and a pale woman who looked so much like Emily Peacock that she had to be her daughter Barbara. The Berliners sat behind us; Tammy leaned forward and patted my shoulder. Mary Alice leaned forward and patted Fairchild's shoulder. He looked back, saw who it was, and covered her hand with his.

"Quit that!" I hissed in Sister's ear.

"Quit what?" But Miss Innocent removed her hand.

The setting, I realized, was eerily like the movie Sister and I had seen a few days earlier. The gray, closed casket, covered with spring flowers, loomed large before us. I looked around, half expecting the villain with slicked-back hair and a bow tie to come sneaking in. Jack Berliner, holding Sophie's hand, was the only one who wore a bow tie. But as the services began, it occurred to me that if Millicent's death was not the act of a serial killer, which seemed highly improbable to me, then the killer was someone who knew her; someone who was sitting here in this chapel. I shivered.

"You cold?" Fred whispered. I shook my head no. Before me, Fairchild bent his handsome white head in prayer. Is it you, Fairchild? Rich Fairchild, the nude swimmer, already flirting with other women? Did Millicent make a cuckold of you? Was it more than you could take?

Or Eddie? Is it you? Are you raging at the world as your mind clouds? Or Laura? Are you so hungry for financial security? Or Jason? You had the most to gain, Jason Marley. Did you kill Millicent and then Emily to get their property? Who are you, Jason? What kind of person are you? What are you capable of?

Behind us someone was crying quietly; I knew it was Sophie. Millicent, I thought, you made a difference; you're going to be missed.

The funeral was short, a Bible verse, the minister's philosophy that there was no such thing as death, a few nice words about Millicent, and another prayer. Then we were invited to the cemetery for the conclusion of the service. There we stood under umbrellas for another prayer, and then it was over.

"Bummer," Haley said as we sloshed back to the cars. The drizzle had become a heavy rain again.

"Y'all wait up," Jason Marley called. When he caught up to us, I saw he looked sick. He was pale, and the flesh around his eyes looked bruised. Add to that the fact that his toupee seemed to be shrinking in the rain, and you had a sight that, as Sister declared later, would twang your heart strings.

"Come by the house," he said. "I've had a light lunch brought in. And drinks. There'll just be a few of us; Millicent's sister and brother need to get home out of this weather. But Fairchild's coming, and we'll sit around and have a few drinks and talk." He held out his hand to Fred. "I'm Jason Marley."

"Fred Hollowell. Hell of a place to meet, isn't it?"

Jason didn't answer, just looked around as if he were suddenly puzzled to find himself in a cemetery.

"Ladies?" Fred asked. We all nodded. "We'll be there," Fred said.

"Good." Jason headed off through the gravestones to his car.

"Where's Berry?" Haley asked Sister.

"Bringing Fairchild home. There are still a few things Fairchild has to tend to, and Berry said he didn't mind waiting. The Stampses went on. They left right after the church service."

"I wonder if Eddie is okay," I said.

Fred unlocked the car door. "Laura's looking rough."

"She needs some Retin-A something awful," Sister said.

"Or that new one, doesn't make you peel," Haley agreed.

Sister touched her palms lightly to her cheek. "When you get middle-aged like we are, Haley, you can't let yourself go."

Middle-aged? This woman was sloughing years like a snake does skin. Haley, bless her heart, kept a straight face. Fred was doing his shaking number again, though. He climbed into our car, wet, muddy.

"I declare," Sister said, surveying the graveyard, "funerals have just got to be the most depressing things in the world."

"God's truth," came from our car. For once even Fred agreed with her.

## Chapter
### 15

I've been to meals after funerals that were very comforting, feeding not only the body but the emptiness that lies in all of us after a death. Old friends eat, visit, and share stories, reminding each other that the dead live on within us. The lunch at Jason Marley's was not one of those comforting events. One reason was that many of the people didn't know each other; the other was the shadow of violence. Neighbors from Gulf Towers and, I assumed, some of the staff of Blue Bay Ranch crowded around the bar, ignoring the lovely lunch that some caterer had provided. Not me. I took the opportunity to help myself to a couple of small turkey sandwiches, some crab claws, boiled shrimp, and veggie sticks.

"Keeping up your middle-aged strength, I see," Fred said, passing by with a beer in his hand and snitching one of my crab claws.

I ignored him and found a seat that had a view of the

bay. The rain had become mist again, and I saw Eddie
Stamps walk down the pier and enter his boathouse. Then
a black-clad figure appeared on the Stampses' pier. Sophie,
I realized. She walked to the boathouse but didn't go in.
Instead, she leaned against the pier and looked over the
water. Several seagulls, expecting to be fed, circled and
landed near her, but she paid them no attention, just stared
into the distance. I had been that age when our Granny Alice
died, and I could still remember how my sorrow had been
mixed with fear. Death was real. People left and didn't come
back. Ever. I was considering going to see about her when
I saw her father step onto the pier. She turned and ran
toward him and his outstretched arms, ran by him and disappeared from my view. What in the world was that about,
I wondered?

"Where's Frances, Patricia Anne?" It was Jason Marley
asking the question.

I explained that she hadn't gone to the funeral because
she really didn't know Millicent or Fairchild and said she
would feel out of place.

"She shouldn't feel that way. Call her and tell her to come
on over."

To the Hansel and Gretel house? I wondered how many
seconds it would take her to get there.

I took my empty plate into the kitchen where a skinny
woman with greenish-blond hair was rinsing out glasses.
When she looked up, I recognized Lolita of the Blue Bay
sales staff.

"I'm Patricia Anne Hollowell," I said. "My sister and I
met you the other day."

She smiled. "I know. The pot-of-gold lady."

"Sorry about that. Is there a phone in here?"

She pointed down the counter with the dishcloth she was holding.

"Come on over," I told Frances when she answered. "We're at Jason's and he's asking for you."

"You're lying."

"Cross my heart."

"Give me five minutes."

The answer I had expected. I hung up and turned back to Lolita. "How'd you get KP duty?"

She shrugged. "I don't feel much like partying. Might as well make myself useful."

"I'll help you," I offered. "What can I do?"

"You could take these glasses out."

I took a tray of clean glasses out to the bar. Fred was talking to a couple of men I didn't know, and Sister and Haley were standing at the bay window with Jack and Tammy Berliner. "Lot of guzzling going on out there," I said when I came back to the kitchen with dirty glasses.

Lolita startled me by suddenly burying her face in the pink-and-white-checked dishcloth and sobbing.

"Here," I said, taking her arm and leading her to a chair. "Are you sick? Can I get you something? Some water? Aspirin?"

"Oh, God," she said. She leaned her green head on the table and cried. "They were both such wonderful women."

I assumed she was talking about Millicent and Emily. I pulled out a chair and sat down.

"More ice," Jason Marley said, coming into the kitchen with an empty ice bucket. He scooped ice from the ice maker, wiped the bucket with a paper towel, and left, oblivious of the fact that one of the women at his kitchen table was sobbing with her face buried in a dishtowel. I looked at Lolita's hair. Definitely green. A Chia pet head.

"Tylenol?" I offered.

Lolita shook her head no.

"Did you know you can't give Tylenol to cats?"

"I don't have a cat," Lolita mumbled.

"I don't either, but my sister does. She has a huge, lazy cat named Bubba that sleeps on a heating pad on her kitchen counter. Terrible fire hazard."

Lolita lifted her head, but the dishtowel was still pressed against her eyes.

"Probably shouldn't give them aspirin, either." I was rambling.

Lolita blew her nose loudly into the dishtowel, which I would personally see went straight to the washing machine, and looked up. Eye makeup was coming off in rivulets, not a pretty sight.

"Blue Bay is the best job I've ever had," she said. "The lots are selling like hotcakes; all we have to do is show them." She quit talking but I could tell she wasn't through.

"But?" I encouraged.

"But I think I may have been responsible for Millicent's death." Back to the dishtowel. "And she was so good to me."

"I don't understand," I said. "How were you responsible for her death?"

"I was late getting to work." The words were muffled, but understandable. "Millicent and Emily gave me a birthday party the night before at The Redneck and I overslept. I didn't get to the office until 9:30, an hour after I was supposed to open up."

"I still don't understand."

"Millicent had been there. That man, I know it was the serial killer, caught her by herself, probably saw her unlocking the door. You can see it from 98, you know."

"Wait a minute, Lolita. You're telling me you're blaming yourself for Millicent's death because you weren't at the office? That's pretty farfetched. And even if there were some truth to it, how does Emily's death fit in? Hers was a murder, too, you know. And it makes sense that they're connected some way."

Lolita looked up. "I've thought about that. Emily came up as the man was abducting Millicent and saw him. He knew she would eventually realize what she had seen. So he had to come back for her."

"And he waited for her over at her condo, killed her, and tried to make it look like suicide? Unh uh, Lolita. I don't know much about serial killers, thank God, but I don't think one would go to that much trouble. I think they want people to know they've struck again."

"Well, maybe not. But Millicent was at the office the morning she was killed, and I think she was forced to leave."

"What makes you say that?"

Lolita wiped her face generously on the dishcloth. "God, Mrs. Hollowell, I'm so scared."

Her nervousness was contagious. "Is this something you should have told the Marine Patrol and haven't?"

"I've got two kids, Mrs. Hollowell. I can't afford to get involved in anything."

The schoolteacher in me wanted to tell her that she couldn't afford not to. But I kept my mouth shut. Fortunately, she decided for herself. She got up, went to the counter where her purse was, and brought it back to the table.

"Here," she said, unzipping the side compartment and taking out a large gold earring shaped like a turtle. I recognized it instantly as one of the pair Millicent had had on the night we saw her at The Redneck.

The kitchen door opened and Fred stuck his head in. "Just wondered where you were."

"I'm here."

"So I see." The door closed. Lolita had clamped the turtle between her palms and her skin color was fast approaching that of her hair.

"It's okay," I assured her. "I know what it is. We saw Millicent wearing them."

Lolita put the earring back in her purse. "It was in the office by the door. The door was unlocked and a chair was turned over." She grabbed the dishcloth again. "It's my fault. If I'd gotten to work on time, it wouldn't have happened."

The sight of the earring had shocked me. For a moment, I had seen it dangling again against Millicent's shoulders. And now I was suddenly angry at the woman sitting before me for withholding this important evidence. Highway 98 is heavily traveled. If Millicent were forced from the office, surely someone would have noticed something amiss, something they might have passed off as inconsequential unless they knew what had happened.

"What should I do?" she asked the towel.

"You know what you have to do," I said calmly, pushing back my chair. I started toward the door, but anger got the better of me. I turned. "Call Major Bissell at the Florida Marine Patrol right now, Lolita! If you don't, I will!"

So there!

I nearly ran over a woman who was coming into the kitchen with some dirty plates.

It was easy to spot the supernovas. Sister was bending

over brushing at her shoe with a paper napkin. I grabbed her by the arm. "You're not going to believe this."

"Believe what?" She didn't look up.

"We've got to find a bathroom or somewhere we can talk."

"What about?"

"Just follow me."

"Why? Berry and Fairchild have just come in."

"Okay, suit yourself. But I just found out something very important about Millicent's murder."

"There's a bathroom right down the hall." Sister led the way.

"Okay," I said, perched on the side of the tub, "you remember Lolita? The saleswoman in the Blue Bay Ranch office?"

"Sure. She has green hair." Sister looked in the mirror. "Lord, I hope it's the fluorescent light making me look like this."

"Well, listen," I said, and told her what had happened in the kitchen.

"She's got the earring in her purse now?" Sister sat down on the toilet and frowned. "How come she told you?"

"Because she was desperate to tell someone. Maybe I look like the type of person who would know what to do."

"Hmmm. And you told her to call Major Bissell?"

"I told her if she didn't, I would."

"Do you think she will?"

Somebody knocked on the door. "Just a minute!" Sister called.

"She has to," I said. "If Millicent was abducted from the Blue Bay office, there could be fingerprints. Or somebody could have seen them leaving."

Sister gazed up at the ceiling, which was papered in a

Laura Ashley print, small pink flowers that coordinated with
bouquets of the same flower on the wall. Definitely not a
bachelor's choice. Whose? Emily's? Millicent's?

"What are you doing?" I asked finally.

"Thinking." She propped her feet on the tub. "Millicent
didn't go to the grocery for tomato juice. She came here to
Blue Bay to meet her lover."

"You don't meet your lover early in the morning. God
forbid."

Sister continued as if I hadn't said a word. "She met her
lover in the office and they had a quarrel."

"A lover's quarrel."

"Exactly. She was giving him money, and she was getting
suspicious that that was all he was interested in. So she told
him farewell."

"Farewell."

"Isn't that what I said? Quit repeating what I say, Mouse.
Anyway, Millicent said no more money, lover, and
goodbye."

I nodded, caught up in the story.

"He grabs her." Sister jumped up so suddenly, I nearly
toppled over into the tub. "He's furious. Cuts her throat and
drags her to the water." Sister acted this out. "Throws her
in." She turned to me. "How about that?"

"Drags her a half mile to the water? Lord, Sister. He has
to take her from the office to a boat. They go out by the
jetties where he kills her and throws her in the water. I
believe your words concerning the blood were something
like spouting and spurting."

"Those were Major Bissell's words."

"Well, there wasn't any spouting in the office. I'll bet you
there's a boat somewhere with a hell of a lot of blood on
it, though."

"Every fishing boat in Destin."

True. "Okay, let's say that Millicent's lover, if she had one, killed her. Then who killed Emily?"

"Someone in her condo who knew she owned a lot of rare signed first editions worth a fortune."

"I didn't know Emily collected first editions," I said, confused.

"I need a pencil and paper," Sister said, opening the medicine cabinet as if she expected to find some there.

"To write all this down."

"You forget it if you don't."

"Shit!" I opened the door and stomped out. A tall, thin man was waiting in the hall, doing the stiff-legged dance of one who is badly in need of a bathroom. "Go ahead," I told him. "Don't mind her."

"Well, it could have been that way," Sister said as we went down the hall.

I stopped. "Listen," I said, "that girl in the kitchen confided something to me that doesn't need to go anywhere but to the police. She's scared to death that the murderer will find out she has the earring and come after her. Don't make me sorry I told you, Mary Alice."

"Have I ever?"

Lolita and I were in deep doo-doo. I looked in the kitchen, but she was gone. I hoped she was on her way to the Florida Marine Patrol office.

"Hey, pretty lady." Fred sidled up to me. "Come home with me and I'll show you my CD-ROM."

"Okay, if you'll twiddle with my VCR. It's flashing 12:00 again."

"Be still, my heart."

I looked at the glass in his hand. He had switched from beer. "Better go get something to eat before you need CPR."

"God, I love this dirty talk!"

"Want me to get you some food?"

"Crab claws." Fred smiled happily.

"Wait right here for me."

Haley was at the table fixing a plate. "Your papa's getting smashed," I told her. "That's not like him."

"I think he's more upset about his business than you realize, Mama. Papa can't cope with change."

"True." I realized guiltily that I hadn't talked to Fred about the details of the Metal Fab merger. I put some crab claws on a plate and added some cocktail sauce. I considered telling Haley about Lolita and the turtle earring but decided against it. Instead, I told her that Frances was on her way over.

"She's not going to want to go home tomorrow," Haley said. "And I've got to be at work Monday morning."

"If she doesn't, your papa and I will take you to Mobile. You can get a direct flight." It saddened me to think of Haley leaving. "It hasn't been much of a vacation, has it? How about we all go to The Flamingo tonight? Eat high on the hog."

Haley grinned. "Thanks, Mama, but I've got a date."

"Major Bissell? How come I thought you weren't interested?"

"He's a nice man."

I certainly hoped so.

I took the food to Fred and ordered him to eat it. Sister had Berry West cornered, Frances had come in, waved, and was already talking to Jason Marley, and Fairchild was surrounded by women. So much for the departed Millicent and Emily.

But not as departed as I had thought. Jason Marley went over to Fairchild and they talked for a moment. Then Jason

We watched him walk down the pier.

"Damn," Sister said.

"Damn," I echoed. We stood looking at the water, neither of us mentioning what was foremost in our thoughts, that the man on the video dipping a glowing Millicent had been Jack Berliner.

Finally Sister said, "You're making a mountain out of a molehill, Mouse."

There's no telling what I would have been accused of if I had said anything.

# Chapter
## 16

The sun came out during the afternoon and the trek over the stile began for the beach lovers. Fred had gone down for a long summer's nap when we got back to the condo, and was still asleep. Haley and Frances were at the outlet mall, and Sister was coloring her hair Summer Marigold ("A New You In Twenty Minutes!").

"You ought to try this, Mouse," she said, coming into the living room with her hair plastered against her head. "I was looking at your hair this morning at the cemetery and thinking it would look okay if it weren't so gray. Here," she handed me a plastic bottle, "there's plenty left."

"Gee, thanks for your kind thoughts. But it might turn out like Lolita's."

"Don't be silly. She's ruined her hair with chlorine. This will just make your gray look a little blonder. It'll shine more, too."

"I like my gray."

"You're lying." Sister sat down and checked her watch. "Twenty minutes."

I was reading *The Destin Log*, the biweekly newspaper that keeps everyone abreast of the local news. In this issue, pictures of Millicent and Emily were on the front page. I laid it on the coffee table so Sister could see the story. "Says right here that Lieutenant Major Bissell says progress is being made in the murder investigations of the two women."

"Hah. He still thinks he's going to blame it on that sweet Fairchild." She picked up the paper and looked at the story.

"Well, he sure had a motive. A million dollars and maybe a Jack Berliner."

"Nonsense. Fairchild wouldn't lay a finger on Millicent or anybody else." She folded the paper. "You know what I wonder? Who are the Berliners, anyway? I mean, face it, Mouse, commuting to Atlanta doesn't make sense. And, for that matter, who is Jason Marley? We don't know a hill of beans about him either, except he has money and likes pink."

"I'm sure the police know."

"I'm not sure the police know diddly." Mary Alice pulled a strand of hair out, dried it on the towel and asked how it looked. It looked great, a nice golden blonde.

"There's plenty left for you. It'll do wonders."

God forbid! In sixty years how is it that I haven't learned a damn thing? The new me turned out as redheaded as Lucille Ball.

"Look at this!" I moaned. "I'm ruined."

Sister looked over my shoulder into the bathroom mirror. "I don't understand. It didn't do my hair that way. Maybe you should have done the patch test."

A knock on the door prevented a third murder.

"Don't let anybody in!" I screeched. "Not until I can get to a beauty parlor and get this stuff out."

"A beauty parlor won't do any good. It says on the box it won't come out for twenty-four shampoos." Mary Alice opened the door for Major Bissell.

"Mrs. Crane, is it okay if I talk to you a few minutes?" he asked. "I've just left Mr. Weatherby, and you could save me a trip."

"Sure," Sister said. "Come on in."

I pulled a towel over my head.

"Mrs. Hollowell," he greeted me. "You okay this afternoon?"

"She's trying to decide whether or not she likes the color of her hair," Sister said. "It's supposed to be Summer Marigold, the same thing I have on mine, but it's slightly redder."

Major Bissell looked at me sympathetically. "That happened to my mother. If you decide you don't like it, she went to a beauty parlor in Shalimar called Curl Up and Dye. They could probably help you."

"That's good to know, isn't it, Patricia Anne? They sound like specialists." Sister smiled. I might kill her yet. "Sit down, Lieutenant. What can we do for you?"

"Mrs. Brown called. Lolita Brown? She said she had talked to you, Mrs. Hollowell."

"She did. She showed me the earring."

"Patricia Anne told me about it," Sister said.

"Well, I know the morning she was killed, Mrs. Weatherby came over to tell you she was okay."

We both nodded.

"Do you by any chance remember if she was wearing those earrings that morning? I've asked Mr. Weatherby and he can't remember."

Sister and I looked at each other.

"She had on the same outfit she was wearing the night before at the Redneck," Sister said. "The same one she had on when she was killed. An off-white jumpsuit." She turned to me. "Did she have on earrings?"

"I'm trying to think." I closed my eyes and tried to picture Millicent. "Her makeup was messed up. Mascara smeared. I remember thinking she looked a mess." I opened my eyes and looked at the lieutenant. "No earrings. I'm sure. At least not those turtles. You couldn't miss them."

"Mr. Weatherby said they were a gift from Mrs. Peacock."

"They were both involved in the turtle watch program," I said. "The earrings would have been a nice memento of that."

Lieutenant Bissell got out his notebook and jotted something down. "I know you saw Mrs. Weatherby at the Redneck Riviera the night before her death," he said. "Can you tell me about the meeting?"

"We've already told you," I said. I didn't have time for this.

But Sister was cooperative. "We were surprised when we saw her," Sister said. "She'd lost about fifty pounds and had her hair streaked a nice blonde. And she may have had a face-lift. Anyway, she looked great."

"She said she was meeting someone for a drink and then the Blue Bay folks were having a birthday party. Mrs. Brown told me it was for her," I added. "And she had the earrings on. I noticed them."

"Do you know by any chance who she was meeting?"

"We didn't see who it was. We were leaving when we saw her," Sister said.

"Had either of you met Jason Marley before this visit?"

"I may have met him," Sister said. "But, to tell you the truth, I haven't paid that much attention to Blue Bay Ranch. It's like kudzu. It wasn't there and then it was."

"I hadn't met him," I said.

"How well did you know Emily Peacock?"

"Just as a friend of a friend. We weren't close, but I knew her and liked her." Sister ran her hand through her hair.

"And Mr. Weatherby asked you to go check on her and that's when you found her body?"

Mary Alice said testily, "My sister's right. We've already answered these questions."

The lieutenant held up his pen. "I'm almost through. What about the Berliners? How long have you known them?"

"We just met them," I said. "We went to watch turtles with them last night."

"Did you know that Sophie had Mrs. Weatherby's other earring?"

"Sophie? Where did she get it?" I asked.

"She says Mrs. Weatherby gave it to her the morning she was killed."

Something in his tone made me say, "But you don't believe her."

"No. I think she found it somewhere. Her father recognized it as Mrs. Weatherby's earring and gave it back to Fairchild."

That explained why Sophie was so mad at her father. Millicent's turtle would have been precious to her.

"She's sticking to her story, though," the lieutenant said.

"She's fourteen. You're not so old you've forgotten fourteen."

"I guess not."

"So," Sister said, "you have a pair of earrings."

"And a pair of unsolved murders," I added, slightly angry at Major Bissell for his indictment of Sophie.

"We'll find out what happened," he said, closing his notebook and getting up. "Thanks, ladies, for your time. Tell

Haley I'll pick her up around seven. And, by the way, Mrs. Crane, the phone call that you and Mrs. Stamps believed was a threatening one?"

"Believed? It was."

"Well, a trace showed it was made from the pay phone in front of Delchamps Super Market." He started out, paused, and turned around as if something had just occured to him. "And, by the way, Mrs. Stamps didn't receive the same call."

"Sure she did," I exclaimed. "She came running in here scared to death."

"There's no record of her getting a call at that time or from that phone."

"But that doesn't make sense," I said. "She came in here white as a sheet." I realized "white as a sheet" would never describe Laura. "Well, you know what I mean."

"So scared she said she was leaving town and I should, too," Sister added. "Maybe she got the call somewhere else, like in her car."

Major Bissell shrugged. "We're checking it out."

The bedroom door opened and Fred came out looking like the wrath of God. "Hey," he said.

The towel had slipped from my head. He looked at me, rubbed his eyes, and looked again. "Good God, Mary Alice. What have you done to Patricia Anne?"

"She did it to herself, you old fool."

Somewhere in the ensuing scene, Major Bissell let himself out and I went into the bathroom to assess the damage. Actually, I decided, my hair wasn't too bad. No color known to man, but as it dried, it was slipping back into its natural curls. I scrunched it up and a new me, as promised, looked back from the mirror.

"I'll go to the drugstore for you, honey," Fred said, looking in the door. "Just tell me what to get."

"Get me a dark brown eyebrow pencil."

"What?"

"Mauve eyebrows won't do with this red hair."

"You've got to be kidding. You're not going to keep that
hair color."

"Just through twenty-four shampoos."

Mary Alice looked over Fred's shoulder. "Maybe, Mouse,
you ought to let Fred get you some drabber. That'll tone the
color down some."

"I don't think so," I said. I looked in the mirror and
grinned. "And don't call me Mouse." There was power in
that hair.


"Yo! Mama!" Haley said when they came in. "Come out
here, Frances. You've got to see this."

"What?" Frances stuck her head out the balcony door.
"Wow, Patricia Anne! Is that a wig?"

"It's Summer Marigold." I turned so they could get the
whole effect.

Haley came over and looked at my hair closely. "What
did Papa say?"

"He offered to go to the drugstore for me."

Frances leaned over for a closer look. "It'll tone down
when the dye wears off your scalp. Especially around your
hairline. That's kind of red."

"I sort of like it," I said.

"It gives you a rakish look." Haley grinned. "Papa blamed
Aunt Sister for it, didn't he?"

"Like I never had a thought of my own."

"Where are they? Papa and Aunt Sister?"

"Your Papa is walking down the beach trying to get over the shock, and Aunt Sister is over at Fairchild's."

"Is he okay?" Frances asked.

"Far as I know. Major Bissell was here asking some more questions."

"What about?"

I told them about the earrings, how Lolita had found one and been afraid to get involved, and that Sophie had had the other one, claiming Millicent had given it to her.

"I remember those earrings," Haley said. "I remember wondering if they were real gold and how heavy they were."

"He wanted to know if Millicent had them on the morning she stopped by here. The morning she was killed. I told him she didn't."

"She could have pulled them off because they were bothering her and put them in her purse," Frances suggested.

"Or her pocket." Haley leaned forward in her chair. "They could have fallen out of her pocket easily if someone attacked her."

"But it wouldn't make sense for her to give one to Sophie. Maybe both of them, but not one. And when would she have done it?"

"Nope," Frances agreed. "Sophie found that earring."

I thought about it for a moment. "Maybe she's scared to tell where. Maybe she was somewhere she wasn't supposed to be, sneaking around smoking or something. You remember Laura told us that Sophie popped out from behind the dryer in the laundry room and scared her to death."

"Or maybe she saw something she wasn't supposed to see." Haley turned and looked at the beach, but there was no black-clad figure down there.

"That's scary," Frances said.

"I'm sure Major has thought of that possibility."

"I wonder if her parents have," I added.

"Y'all look mighty serious," Sister said, coming out on the balcony. "How was your shopping trip?"

"I got a bathing suit at the Adrienne Vittadini outlet," Haley said. "Bright red."

"It looks great on her. I got a couple of wedding presents at the Lenox place."

"How's Fairchild?" I asked.

Sister sat down beside Haley. "He's doing okay. Some insurance man is already over there with him. Lord, I remember when Will Alec and Philip and Roger died, what a mess the insurance was. And especially with Philip dying on that plane while we were on vacation."

"It was Roger," I said.

"Whichever. They both just went *thump*, right over. Nice men."

We thought about this for a moment. Then Sister asked Frances if I had told her that Major Bissell didn't think Laura had gotten the threatening call.

"Really? What makes him think that?"

"It came from the pay phone in front of Delchamps. It showed up on our phone, but not on Laura's. There was no call made to Laura's from that phone or any other at that specific time."

"Well, if she didn't get a phone call, she deserves an Academy Award," Haley said. "That woman was shaking like a leaf. I thought for sure she was going to keel over."

"I agree," I said. "She didn't say she had just come from her apartment, did she? We all just assumed she had."

"They could even have a phone on the boat," Sister said. "Probably do." She rubbed the frown line between her eyes.

"There could be all kinds of explanations," Haley assured her, and then changed the subject by asking Sister if Fairchild had said what he was going to do with the land over on the bay.

"It reverted to the Blue Bay Corporation, Haley. You looked it up."

"Not all of it. Wait a minute." Haley disappeared inside for a moment, and came back with the brochure for Blue Bay Ranch that Lolita had given us and the photocopied papers she had gotten at the court house.

"Here," she said, spreading them out on the glass-topped table. "The brochure says Blue Bay Ranch is nestled on 650 acres of prime woodland fronting Choctawhatchee Bay and bordered by Sellers Magee Bayou and Indian Paint Bayou.

"But look here." She pointed to the top sheet of the photocopied stack. "Tod Abernathy bought 942 acres over there. Let's see. Subtract 650 from 942. You've got roughly three hundred acres over there that Millicent didn't put into Blue Bay. Two hundred ninety-two." She looked up. "That will go to Fairchild, won't it?"

"I'll be damned," Sister said. "I totally missed that."

"So did I." I took the paper and brochure and studied the figures again. "Reckon there's a chance that acreage has already been sold?"

"Maybe," Haley said. "We could ask Fairchild."

"The insurance people are with him. He's been talking about his property on the bay, but I just assumed he still felt like part of Blue Bay Ranch." Sister took the papers from me. "Sellers Magee Bayou. That's toward the Mid-Bay Bridge. I'll bet you money this land goes from the bayou toward the bridge."

"Maybe Laura would know," I said. "We've got a couple of questions to ask Miss Laura, anyway."

"I'll call and see if she's home." Sister got up.

"Not many dull moments around here," Frances said.

*     *     *

"Lord have mercy," Laura said when she opened the door. "I almost didn't recognize you, Patricia Anne."

"It's Summer Marigold," I said. "It's the same thing Sister has on her hair."

"Sure looks different. I remember one time I put some coloring on my hair called Tahitian Night and, believe you me, it gets black in Tahiti at night. I like to have died." She stepped back. "Y'all come on in. Just don't look at the mess the apartment's in. I'm getting ready to go to my sister's, you know." Laura was barefooted, had on snug knit shorts that appeared corrugated, topped by what must have been Eddie's shirt. Since it was tie-dyed, it was either twenty years out of style or a year ahead. My bet was on the former.

"We just want to ask you something," Sister said.

"Sure. Come on in. You want a Coke? I'm ready for a break."

"Thanks." Sister and I sat on the sofa while Laura clunked ice into glasses and brought in a tray with three Cokes. "I swear I can't believe all this."

"Is Eddie okay?" I asked.

"Pretty good. Somebody's taking him over to the driving range. Fairchild said he told you. About the Alzheimer's."

"We're so sorry." Sister said.

"Well, so far so good. Eddie's always been a gentle man." She grinned. "Always having to calm me down. And, in a way, he's just getting gentler. And some days he's still sharp as a tack."

"And the prognosis?" I asked.

Laura shrugged and handed us our Cokes. "Who knows? But I'll tell you what I told Fairchild. Eddie'll have the best care money can provide. That's about all you can hope for with that awful disease."

No. You can hope for someone who remembers what you once were and who still loves you.

Mary Alice held up her glass. "To Eddie."

"To Eddie," Laura and I echoed.

"Now," Laura ran her palm across her cheek. "What was it you wanted to ask me?"

"A couple of questions," Sister said. "For starters, Major Bissell told us there was no record of you getting a threatening phone call."

"That's because I got it in my car. That was one of the scariest things about it, that whoever was calling knew where I was." Laura shivered. "Why would I lie about it?"

"True," Sister said. "We were just checking."

"Well, there's no need. I got the call just like you did, and Eddie and I are getting the hell out of town. I suggest you do the same." She set her glass of Coke down with a thump on the coffee table.

"We knew there was some explanation," Sister said.

"We told Major Bissell that," I lied.

Laura seemed appeased. "What else did you want to ask me?"

"Did Millicent have several hundred acres of land over on the bay that didn't belong to Blue Bay Ranch?"

"All I know about's Blue Bay Ranch." Laura picked her Coke up and took a sip. "And getting Jason Marley to develop it to suit her was like pulling teeth. You can ask Jason. He said Millicent and Emily were both so hung up on those damn turtles it was driving him crazy. When they made us put a special kind of light on the end of our boathouses, one that doesn't shine very far, he said, 'Hell, that sort of defeats the purpose of a light on the boathouse. Somebody hits it, we're in trouble.' We did it, though." Laura drank some of her Coke. "What do you want to know for?"

"Patricia Anne and I were having an argument," Sister lied. "I told her Millicent said she still owned some land by the bridge and Patricia Anne said it was Blue Bay she was talking about."

"It was Blue Bay."

"Why did she give in and let it be developed, Laura?" I asked.

"Her family. You saw them today at the funeral. Millicent couldn't let them want for anything."

"She looked happy the other night at the Redneck," Sister said.

"I think she was pleased at the way the development's going."

"No, I mean she was glowing. You know that look women get when they're in love."

"Or pregnant," I added. Sister frowned at me.

"Or have had too much to drink." Laura leaned over and put her Coke on the coffee table. "Let's change the subject. I've been down in the dumps all day and that damn Florida Marine officer with all his questions hasn't helped."

"How long will you be at your sister's?" I asked.

"A week. Maybe two. I'll have to get back to see about the stuff over at Blue Bay." Laura looked around the apartment. "You know, I've been thinking I might sell this place. You know anybody who might be interested?"

"Fred and I might be," I said.

Laura and Mary Alice both looked at me, surprised.

"Well, we might. We've been talking about it. A little."

"Bring Fred over," Laura said.

"She was lying," Sister said a few minutes later as we walked down the hall.

"What?" I had no idea what she was talking about.

"About the land. Laura knows Millicent owned more

land." She opened the door to her apartment and we walked into the smell of popcorn. Haley was stretched out on the living room floor and Frances was on the sofa. They were watching *Somewhere in Time* and both were already sniffling. We each got a handful of popcorn, stepped over Haley, refusing her invitation for a good cry, and went to the balcony.

"How do you know she was lying?"

"Her big toe, Patricia Anne. Didn't you see it? It was wiggling up and down like a worm on a hook."

"A worm on a hook?"

"You know. The part that's left over to attract the fish. That's the way Laura's big toe was doing. Up, down. Up, down. I don't see how you missed it, especially with that red toenail polish and the big callus."

"I saw the toe," I said. "Laura needs to wear shoes at all times."

"Well, she was lying. That big toe was a dead giveaway."

"Don't tell me. You learned this in that body language class you took."

"Right."

"But why would Laura lie about Millicent owning the land?"

"She didn't. She was lying about knowing about it."

"Or maybe her callus hurt." I saw Fred coming down the beach and stood up to wave at him. He deliberately turned and looked out over the water, not returning my wave.

"Mouse, you better go get the drabber," Sister said.

I made a gesture with my finger. "Did they teach you in body language class what this means?"

Sister laughed. "I invented it."

# Chapter

# 17

Ten minutes later, there I was with bright red hair haul-assing to the drugstore for drabber. That good, sweet man walking down the beach was obviously not prepared to deal with my Day-Glo curls, and I wasn't so sure I was, either, in spite of my bravado. So when the elevator stopped on the third floor and a teenage boy and girl stood there waiting to get on, I hardly paid them any attention. My mind was already on the hair-coloring aisle at the Big B.

"Get in the elevator," the girl said, giving the boy a shove.

"What's wrong with you? Ladies first." And the boy pushed her into the elevator.

"Stupid!" she grabbed at him. The door began to close, touched the boy, and sprang open. They both smiled at me sheepishly. When we reached the lobby, they sprinted for the beach. But I walked slowly toward our car. There was something I should be remembering, something that sat

there at the edge of my consciousness and that the kids' tussle at the elevator had touched.

Maybe if I had remembered and put two and two together, I could have prevented some of the things that happened later. But the sun was shining, and I was on an urgent mission. No time for introspection. Maybe that's why I paid so little attention to the cyclist turning out of our gate toward Highway 98. In spite of her helmet, I saw it was Sophie when we both stopped at the traffic light at the highway. In fact, we waved to each other. And then she turned down 98 in the direction of Blue Bay Ranch, and I went straight across to the shopping center. But people ride bicycles down 98 all the time. It's a four-lane road with wide shoulders and even sidewalks through Destin. That she might be doing anything other than going for a ride never occured to me.

"You know this stuff's temporary," the tall, tan girl at the checkout counter said as she rang up my purchase. "You have to put it on every time. It'll make your hair darker, too."

"You got any other suggestions? I'm desperate."

"Bernice at the Curl Up and Dye is your best bet. You should see some of the messes she's straightened out. You want me to call her?"

I wasn't sure I appreciated my hair being referred to as a mess, but then I remembered Fred turning his back on me.

"Call. You're the second person who's recommended her. But it's Saturday. You think there's any chance she can take me without an appointment?"

"Bernice loves challenges," the girl said.

Which is how a ten-minute trip to the drugstore turned out to be two hours well spent at the Curl Up and Dye.

Bernice was a plump, grandmotherly woman in her six-

ties. Her own hair was gray and healthy looking ("Wouldn't put that junk on my hair!") and in spite of the fact that it was June and the temperature was hovering in the high eighties, she wore brown corduroy pants and red Tote socks, the heavy ones with traction on the bottom.

"Do, Jesus!" she said when she saw my hair. "Terri Lee said it was an emergency."

"I think it looks kind of rakish," I said. "My husband hates it, though."

"What did you do to it?"

I explained about the Summer Marigold.

"That's pretty good stuff. Shouldn't have done this." Bernice rubbed some of my hair through her fingers. "Most gray hair's hard to color, but I think we've got the exception to the rule here. What did the patch test do?"

"Didn't do one."

Bernice clicked her tongue. "Most people don't. Makes it good for my business. Here." She led me to a row of chairs before a long mirror. She and I were the only ones in the shop.

"Where is everybody?" I asked.

"I give my girls a couple of weeks off in the summer. Just close the whole damn place." She flipped a plastic cape around me. "I still run the emergency room, though."

"Well, I appreciate it." I watched Bernice in the mirror as she examined my hair, picking up strands and looking at it.

"Okay," she said finally, "do you want dark blond with a few gold streaks like Cindy Crawford or do you want to go whole hog like Christy Brinkley?"

My mouth fell open. "You can do that?"

"Of course not. I just wondered. I like Christy's look, myself. You're not allergic to anything, are you?"

"No."

"Then hold your nose and let's get going."

"Shouldn't we do a patch test?" I asked nervously as Bernice led me to a shampoo chair.

"You've already done it," she said. "Flunked."

God's truth.

Over the course of the next hour and a half, I learned that Bernice's blood pressure medicine made her cold, that the beauty shop was paid for lock, stock, and barrel, and that her husband had been addicted to the Weather Channel ever since he decided to ride out Hurricane Opal in their trailer. She, Bernice, had hightailed it to Montgomery with the cat.

"Three o'clock in the morning, he's up sneaking looks at the radar," she said, pouring something cold and foul smelling over my scalp. "Old fool."

"That's sad!" I said when I could catch my breath.

"Should have gone with me and the cat." Bernice wrapped a plastic turban around my head.

"Did you have much damage to your trailer?"

"What trailer?"

Over the course of that same hour and a half, Bernice learned from me that my sister and I had found two dead bodies and been to a funeral on our vacation.

"Millicent Weatherby and Emily Peacock?"

"You knew them?"

"How big you think this town is, honey? I did Millicent's hair. Emily came in with her sometimes." Bernice set a timer and put it on the counter. "We got twenty minutes. Tell me what all happened."

So I did, starting with the meeting at the Redneck Riviera and how good Millicent had looked.

"The Cindy Crawford look," Bernice agreed.

"My sister said she looked like she was in love."

Bernice picked the timer up, listened to it, and gave it a shake. "I think she was having a fling."

"Who with?" I asked the question as casually as I could.

"Don't know. She never said the name. He was involved in that development some way, though. Helping Millicent save the turtles. Crazy, if you ask me, when she had that handsome Fairchild at home."

Jason Marley? Had he come in with money and sweet talk and put dreams right in Millicent's hands?

"Emily didn't like him, I know that."

Not the way I heard it if it was Jason. "How do you know?"

"Things she said. One time Millicent was talking about this 'friend' of hers and how nice he was, and Emily said, 'Just don't turn your back on him, Millicent.' " Bernice set the timer again. "Gave me the creeps when I heard what happened."

"You think he's the one who killed them?"

"Bet my bottom dollar on it. I get these feelings. You know? I got a feeling about Millicent's death. I even had a dream about it one night." She lifted the edge of the plastic and checked my hair. "This beginning to feel warm?"

I nodded yes.

"Good. Tell me what else y'all saw."

So I did, with Bernice nodding agreement.

"That's all?" she asked as I finished describing the scene at Emerald Towers, how Emily had been looking out at the water. By this time Bernice was drying my hair and I had specific instructions not to look in the mirror yet.

"I guess so. Why?"

"I've already heard all that." She clicked off the dryer. "Okay. You ready?"

I steeled myself for the results.

"Voila!" Bernice said, turning the chair so I could see my-self in the mirror.

"My God!" I squealed. "How did you do it?" My hair was a mass of blond curls with enough gray to look per-fectly natural.

"Practice," Bernice said, obviously pleased with my reac-tion. "It's amazing what women on vacation do to their hair. Sometimes I wonder if it means something. You know, psy-chologically." She removed the plastic cape and brushed me off. "I hope you brought your checkbook. I don't take credit cards."

I had, and I was happily writing out a check when Bernice said, "I'm sure the guy was going bald."

"Who was going bald?"

"The man Millicent was seeing. She asked me one time what I knew about Rogaine, and I told her she'd have to ask a doctor. She sure wasn't asking for Fairchild, was she?"

I thought about Fairchild's beautiful white hair. No, Fair-child had no need for Rogaine. But a lot of the men Millicent knew did.

"He was bald in my dream. That's for sure." Bernice stuck my check in her pocket. "You come back, now."

As I headed back toward the condo, I mulled over what Bernice had told me about the Rogaine and considered who might use it.

First, obviously, was Jason Marley. He was bald as a bil-liard ball and the hairpieces proved he was self-conscious about it. He was involved in the development and was try-ing not to harm the turtle habitat any more than necessary.

Eddie Stamps was also involved in the development. He and Millicent had known each other for years, true, but maybe one of the first signs of his illness was an increased libido with Millicent as the recipient. That would have infuriated Laura. Okay, possibilities here.

Berry West was losing his hair but he was not involved in the development or interested in the turtle rescue program. Besides, he lived in Birmingham. Very vague possibility that he was the "fling."

Jack Berliner, though, the man in whose arms Millicent was glowing on New Year's, was still a very good possibility. Home a lot, just down the hall. His wife gone much of the time. Even Sophie, whom Millicent loved, would have brought them closer together. But if he did prove to be the lover, that didn't make him a murderer, in spite of Bernice's "feelings." And there had been two murders. Someone had had a good motive.

The last arc of the sun sank into the Gulf as I crossed the Destin bridge. For a second, the horizon flashed green. I hoped Haley had seen it. I also hoped that Major Bissell and Lisa Andrews would hurry up and solve the murders. Like Bernice, I had a "feeling." I knew there was a cold-blooded killer among us.

Fred was pacing the parking lot when I pulled in. "Where have you been?" he asked, snatching the door open.

"And hello to you, too. I've been to the beauty parlor. See?" I stepped out of the car expecting him to be dazzled.

Instead, I got, "There's such a thing as a phone, you know."

How many times had I said those very words to our kids? Fred had even used the same intonation. I laughed. Big mistake. He turned and marched toward the lobby.

"Wait up, honey," I said, hurrying after him. "I'm sorry." I caught up with him at the elevator. "What's the matter with you?"

"Nothing. You just disappear off the face of the earth for hours and expect me not to worry?"

The light was beginning to dawn. "You had a fuss with Mary Alice, didn't you?" The elevator door opened and we stepped in.

"No, I did not have a fuss with Mary Alice. Philip Nachman is here."

"Really?" I felt a surge of excitement. "When did he come?"

"Right after you left. And I tell you, Patricia Anne, that man is too old for Haley."

I grinned. "They're making a big to-do over him, aren't they?"

"Like he hung the moon."

"Well, just remind yourself he's an ENT specialist and there is a season, turn, turn, turn for all your allergies. Besides, he's not too old and you know it." The elevator opened. "Plus, your daughter loves him."

"Your hair looks good," Fred said. "How long does that smell last?"

"You're pushing your luck."

Dr. Philip Nachman is the nephew of Philip Nachman, Mary Alice's second husband, which can get confusing. Consequently, she has started calling him Nephew which has a sort of old-fashioned charm.

"Look, Patricia Anne," she said as we walked in. "Nephew's here!"

Nephew was sitting in one of the wicker chairs with a beer in one hand and a plate of goodies in his lap.

"Don't get up, Nephew," Mary Alice said, as Philip looked around for a place to put the plate.

"Hello, Philip," I said.

"Hello, Patricia Anne. Your hair looks pretty."

"Who did it?" Frances asked from the sofa.

"A woman named Bernice. Where's Haley?"

"Getting dressed," Philip said. "We're going out to dinner."

"Hmmm. Excuse me a minute." I knocked on Haley's door and went in. She was slipping on a navy sundress with white polka dots and she gave me a big grin.

"Where did that come from?" I motioned toward the dress.

"The outlet mall. I got it for my date with Major Bissell."

I sat on the bed and looked at my watch. "A certain Lieutenant Major Bissell who is due to arrive here in about a half-hour?"

"I called and told him what had happened. I don't think his heart was broken. Here," Haley came over to the bed and turned around. "Zip me, Mama." Her back was young, lovely, and vulnerable.

"What's with Philip?" I asked.

"Don't know." Haley turned and looked at me.

"Don't settle for anything less than what you want."

"I won't, Mama."

But she would. We all do.

Mary Alice stuck her head in the door. "What's going on?" Well, maybe there are exceptions.

"I like your hair, Patricia Anne," she informed me. "Who did it?"

"A woman named Bernice who owns the Curl Up and Dye. She did Millicent's hair. Told me Millicent was having a fling with a bald man."

"Who?" Sister came in the room and shut the door.

"Bernice didn't know his name. just that he was bald or losing his hair. Millicent asked her about Rogaine."

"Well, that narrows it down to about three-fourths of the

men in Destin. Ten thousand men, give or take a few." Sister sat down beside me. "I wish I'd bought some of that Rogaine stock."

"Baldheaded men have more testosterone," Haley stated. She was at the dresser brushing blush along her jawline.

"Oh, I already knew that. Remember, Mouse, how Will Alec hardly had any hair? He was by far the sexiest of my husbands."

"He was the youngest," I said. I got back to my story. "Bernice says she has a 'feeling' that the baldheaded man is the murderer."

"She wouldn't make a very good juror, would she? Haley, don't wear those white sandals with that dark dress."

"I don't have anything else except tennis shoes and flip-flops."

"Well, as long as you know better." Sister got up. "I've got to get ready for Berry."

"Be careful. He's losing his hair," Haley cautioned.

"So are the two men in the living room." Both of them giggled.

"Fools!" I said and stomped out.

Frances had gone out on the balcony and I soon discovered why.

"Deaf as a post in my left ear," Fred was saying to Dr. Nachman. "Couldn't hear it thunder. So I got some of that wax removal stuff at the Big B, but every time I put it in my ear, it gave me a coughing fit. I mean I coughed like I had the whooping cough. The kind that makes you gag stuff up."

I went back to Haley's room. "Better hurry. Your future's at stake." Then I joined Frances on the balcony.

"What time did Philip show up?" I asked.

"About five. Seems like this has been the longest day."

I agreed. A lot had happened: the rainy funeral, the disastrous party at Jason's, my hair debacle and the rescue at the Curl Up and Dye, as well as the appearance of Philip Nachman just to name a few.

"I wonder how Jason's doing in that big pink house all by himself," Frances said wistfully.

Which reminded me of Bernice's feeling about the baldheaded man. I discovered in the retelling that it was becoming more and more farfetched.

But Frances disagreed, saying intuition should not be dispatched lightly. "My grandmother never would go to Kansas," she said. "She always had a feeling that she would die in Kansas. Really believed it."

"Why Kansas?"

"God knows. The farthest the woman ever got from Ramer, Alabama, was Montgomery."

"Maybe she saw *The Wizard of Oz.*"

"Could be." Frances was silent for a moment. "The thing about it, Patricia Anne, is that if she'd ever gone to Kansas, she really would have died. And not from fear, either. There are some things we just know are true."

I thought about the moment on the bridge when I knew the killer was close to us, and I shivered.

"We're gone," Haley said, coming out on the balcony.

"You look beautiful," Frances said. "Turn around and let me see that dress."

Haley swirled and I noticed that Philip Nachman had come to the door and was smiling at her. The look on his face was that of a man deeply in love. Surely, I thought, they could work things out.

In a few minutes, Berry West knocked at the door.

"How's Jason?" was the first thing Frances wanted to know as he came in.

"He seems okay. He and some lady have gone for a ride on his boat."

"Oh." There was no disguising the disappointment in Frances's voice.

"I'm ready," Sister said, sailing into the room.

"And you look very pretty," Berry said admiringly.

Sister bought it. She smiled down at Berry as if she could eat him with a spoon. "You look mighty spiffy yourself."

He looked baldheaded and Bernice's theory of the baldheaded murderer popped right up.

"Sister," I said, "why don't y'all stay here. Berry, don't you like to play poker? We could call Steak 'Em and have dinner delivered."

"We've got reservations, Patricia Anne." Berry looked at Sister. "Unless you'd rather, of course."

"Of course not." She gave me her have-you-lost-your-mind look and stepped out into the hall. "Hold that elevator!" she screeched to someone.

And they were gone.

"What was that about?" Frances asked.

"He's baldheaded. I told you about Bernice's dream."

Frances gave me her version of have-you-lost-your-mind.

"Well, you said to trust your intuition."

"True. But Berry was in Birmingham when Millicent was killed and besides we've already got the motive, Blue Bay, and neither Mary Alice nor Berry has any connection with that."

"Just Jason, Eddie, and Fairchild. And Laura."

"And it absolutely could not have been Jason."

By this time we were back in the living room on the sofa. "Frances," I asked, "have you considered cutting down on your estrogen?"

# Chapter
## 18

After such a busy day, we welcomed a quiet evening. And that was what we had. After Mary Alice left with Berry to go dancing, Frances and I went to Delchamps and picked up salad and sandwich stuff. Fred went next door to see if Fairchild wanted to join us and reported back that Fairchild was surrounded by women who seemed to be hand-feeding him all sorts of delicacies including smoked oysters that had looked delicious. But didn't Fairchild have high blood pressure?

"Not as high as it's going to be," I said.

"When I'm widowed, I want to be living down here," Fred declared. He caught the olive I hand-fed him through the air. "Ahhh, olives!"

We ate, played Scrabble, watched the ten o'clock news. There was no Tarzan yell from the Berliners' balcony to announce turtles coming in, no phone calls. By eleven we were in bed.

"I really do like your hair," Fred said, snuggling against me. "But I liked it red, too. After the initial shock."

"You wouldn't even look at me!"

"When?"

I put my hands flat against his chest. "When you were walking down the beach. I waved at you and you turned your back."

"There was a man too far out on a float. That's what I was looking at. I was wondering if the lifeguard saw him."

Damn! I could have stayed redheaded.

"Honey?" Fred whispered. "You got a shower cap or something? That stuff on your hair's potent."

I shoved him. "Then just get on your side."

Fred went to sleep, but I didn't. I finally got up, slipped on some shorts and went to the balcony. Several people were sitting on the stile, including Fairchild. I could hear the low murmur of their voices; in the shallow water beyond them, flounder fishermen walked with lanterns. It was so peaceful, so serene. The last place in the world for violence, I told Sister when she joined me.

"Tell that to the flounders," she said.

"True. How come you're home early?"

"Berry wasn't feeling well. Stomach bug. How come you're still up?"

"Couldn't sleep. Couldn't get Millicent and Emily off my mind. It has occurred to you, hasn't it, that the killer is probably right in this building, someone we know fairly well?"

"You off on your baldheaded theory again?"

"No, I'm trying to be logical. I don't want anybody else to get hurt."

"That's the police's job."

"I haven't seen Cagney and Lacey wandering around on the beach."

Mary Alice shook her head. "Maybe they're doing a lot that we don't know about."

I thought about this for a moment. "Nah. Major Bissell's been at the writers' conference and running after Haley all week."

"True." Mary Alice leaned forward and looked at the group on the stile. "I hate that Fairchild's still way up on their list. Bless his heart. We should have gotten him cleared by now."

We sat for a moment in silence before I asked Sister if she thought the police had checked Eddie Stamps's boat.

"Well, surely they did, wouldn't you think? And Jason Marley's, too. They're not Cagney and Lacey, but they're perfectly adequate. They found out where the threatening phone call came from right off the bat, didn't they?"

"You think Laura really got one?"

"She had no reason to lie about it."

"She would have if she made the call."

"But it was a man's voice. Besides, why would Laura call me?"

"To get you to leave."

"Why would she want me to leave?"

"She knows you're in danger."

"Good Lord, Mouse. That hair dye's seeped into your brain. Incidentally, your hair looks great," Sister said.

"Thanks." We were both quiet for a moment, thinking.

"I found out Jack Berliner wasn't the boyfriend," Sister added.

"How did you do that?"

"A trip to the third floor to see the Packard sisters while you were at the beauty parlor."

"Good thinking." The Packard sisters, rumored because of their ability to collect information as being retired from the CIA, are also known as the Gulf Towers equivalent of the Internet. "What did they say?"

"All the permanent residents had to vote to let the Berliners in because of Sophie. They wanted to move here because Jack's brother and his family are here. They have a townhouse on the bay. Anyway, the ladies said Jack and Tammy charmed everyone at the New Year's Eve party. Enough to bend the rules for them."

"He and Millicent still looked pretty chummy."

"Nope. He's madly in love with his wife. The Packard sisters say so."

"That's one baldheaded fellow we can scratch off then."

"Maybe. And Berry says Jason Marley's one of the most respected developers in Florida and that he's totally shaken about the deaths."

"Which doesn't mean he's not the murderer. Frances says he's not because he lives in a pink house. That's crazy. And we're convinced Fairchild couldn't be the murderer because he's so nice. Get real, Sister. Remember what Daddy said at his and Mama's fiftieth anniversary when somebody asked him for the secret of their long marriage?"

Mary Alice giggled. "He said the secret was to not keep a gun in the house. But he was teasing."

"Sure he was. He was also stating a universal truth. People usually kill in moments of passion."

"Not Fairchild. He's too nice."

The only thing I had to hit her with was a piece of orange peeling.

A match flared against the dark seawall, went out. Another was lit and flickered against a cigarette. The third one was the charm and also told me who was sitting there.

"Come with me a minute," I told Sister. "I think there's a certain little girl down there who can tell us some things."

The seawall is five feet tall, but on the Gulf side sand has pushed up against it forming a dune and making it easy to climb. We went over the stile, spoke to everyone, and headed out as if we were taking a walk. Then we cut back, climbed the dune as quietly as we could and leaned over the smoker.

"Hi, Sophie," I said.

"Shit!" The rattled child choked. "What are you doing here?" she asked when she finished coughing.

"Just want to ask you something."

"What about?"

"Millicent's turtle earring."

"Millicent gave it to me. I've already told the policeman."

"When she went to buy the tomato juice at seven o'clock in the morning?"

"I don't know what time it was."

"She stopped by your apartment and gave you one earring. Lord, Sophie, you ought to be able to make up a better story than that."

Sister chimed in. "Or you could tell the truth. Like maybe you found it somewhere."

"I didn't find it," Sophie said. "It was given to me. I swear."

I suddenly remembered the way Sophie had walked down the Stampses' pier and a light went on. "Eddie Stamps gave it to you, didn't he?"

"No, Mr. Stamps didn't give me the earring." But there was enough hesitation to tell me I had hit upon the truth.

"And when your daddy gave it back to Fairchild, you wanted to see if you could find the other one."

There was silence from the figure below us.

"Where did Mr. Stamps find the earring, Sophie?" I asked gently.

The child-woman stubbed her cigarette out and sighed. "I don't know. Maybe on his boat. I thought the other one might be there, but I looked all over this afternoon and it wasn't." She stood up and faced us. "Please don't get Mr. Stamps in trouble. He's such a nice old man."

"Yes, he is, Sophie," I agreed. "But somebody isn't. You have to tell the police everything you know so nothing else happens." I sounded patronizing even to myself. So Sophie's reaction didn't surprise me.

"All he did was give me the earring because he knew that Millicent and I did turtle watches together."

"Then tell your parents. They'll take care of it."

"Shit! Leave me alone!" The child turned and fled toward the building.

"Think she'll do it?" Sister asked.

"Of course not."

The two of us slid down the dune.

"Well, damn, Mouse, I'm impressed. How did you know it was Eddie?"

"Part something I saw: part guess. Wait a minute." I stopped and pulled off my sandals. The sand was cool and damp. "I don't think he's the murderer, though. Don't ask me why. Just a feeling."

"I beg your pardon, little sister, but isn't that what you were just fussing at me about?"

True. I tried to get my tail out of the crack. "You just can't let your feelings blind you."

Sister sniffed. "You and your feelings. I remember the day Jimmy Carter got elected President I called you and said 'Let's go to Plains so we can be there for the big celebration.' And you said no, you had a feeling Gerald Ford was going to get it. And I let you talk me out of going to what must have been an incredible party."

"I wonder what an incredible party is like in Plains, Georgia?"

"Fun. All sorts of things happening. I'll bet that night they blew car horns, shot off guns, beat on frying pans."

"And to think we missed it."

"I know you're being sarcastic," Mary Alice said.

When we came to the stile, Fairchild was sitting there alone. "Sit with me a few minutes," he invited us. Mary Alice took him up on it, but I rinsed the sand from my feet, went upstairs, slipped my nightgown back on and crawled into bed. I didn't think I would sleep, but I did. I crashed. About five o'clock, though, I awoke and began to think about the murders, to go over all that had happened. And suddenly, I was sure I knew who the muderer was. Only one piece of the puzzle remained. At six o'clock, I was knocking on Fairchild's door.

Dr. Nachman, Haley informed us, was taking us all to the Sandestin Hilton for brunch before they headed back to Birmingham.

"How did last night go?" I poured her a cup of coffee. I had already had a couple of cups with Fairchild and Major Bissell, but I took another.

"Fine."

I pride myself on being able to read my daughter's moods, but I had no idea what was going on. She seemed happy, but not excited. Or maybe my mind was too much on other matters.

"What your mama wants to know is if Nephew proposed," Mary Alice stated bluntly.

"Not exactly." Haley smiled and turned toward her room. "I've got to get my stuff together."

"Don't forget the cappucino machine," Sister called. And as soon as the door was closed, "How can you not exactly propose?"

"I have no idea, but I'm not going to worry about it." Liar, liar!

The front door opened and Fred came in, his flip-flops in his hand. "Already hot out there. Laura Stamps caught me as I came into the lobby. Had me help her put some stuff in her car."

"She hasn't left yet, has she?" I asked.

"I don't know. She said if we wanted to look at her apartment, she's leaving the key with Fairchild." He took the coffee I held out to him. "Why would we want to look at her apartment?"

"We might buy it."

He grinned at me. "Okay, Miss Money-bags."

"Well, you are going through with the Metal Fab merger, aren't you?"

"I am, but I think we better hold up on Florida condos. Are there any sweetrolls?"

I put one in the microwave for him. When it dinged, I jumped.

"You okay, honey?" he asked.

"Fine." But I wasn't. I wanted the phone to ring; I wanted Major Bissell to tell me if I was right or wrong. I was probably wrong. I hoped I was wrong.

"You were out early this morning."

"Walking on the beach." Okay, Major, so I'm keeping quiet like you asked.

"Don't eat much, Fred," Mary Alice said. "Nephew's taking us to brunch."

He turned toward me. "Our future son-in-law?"

"Your guess is as good as mine."

"Too old."

"But an ENT."

"True." Fred balanced his sweetroll across his coffee cup, gave me a pat on the behind, and went into the living room to turn on "Sunday Morning."

Mary Alice poured a generous amount of milk into her coffee. "I wonder if the police know that Laura's leaving."

"Don't know," I said truthfully.

"Y'all look serious." Frances came into the kitchen, her hair wet from a shower.

"We found out last night that Eddie Stamps gave Sophie the turtle earring," Mary Alice said.

"How did you find out?"

"Sophie told us. Patricia Anne got it out of her."

I jumped to Eddie's defense. "Which may simply mean that Eddie found the earring somewhere."

"Patricia Anne has a feeling." Sister moved so Frances could get to the refrigerator. "But the police sure need to know if he found it on his boat. For all we know, Millicent was leaving earrings as clues."

Frances backed out of the refrigerator with a carton of orange juice. "I read a story like that one time. The woman left licorice jelly beans. They knew it was her because she was the only one who liked them. Traced them right to the murderer." Frances poured a glass of juice and closed the carton. "Maybe the jelly beans lead to Laura. Have you thought about that?"

"I don't want to think about it," I said truthfully.

A knock on the door made us all jump. I opened it to see the subject of our conversation standing there looking worried. For a moment I was spooked.

" 'Morning, Patricia Anne," she said. "Is Fred here?"

"Sure. Come in."

"I just wanted to know if he knows where Eddie is."

"Fred," I called. "Do you know where Eddie is?"

"He was talking to Fairchild in the parking lot when I came up," Fred called back. "Why?"

Laura stepped into the apartment. "Because the car's gone."

"He probably went to get the car gassed up," Fred said.

"I did that yesterday."

"Or maybe to check on the new house," I volunteered.

"I doubt it, but can I use your phone? I'll call Jason Marley and ask him to look out his window and see if he sees the car."

After a short conversation, Laura hung up, smiling. "He's there. Jason says he sees him at the boathouse. I know you think I'm crazy to be so worried, but the first sign we had of anything being wrong with Eddie was that he got lost between here and Blue Bay. It took him four hours to get home."

"We don't think that at all," I said. "Do you want to go over there? I'll take you."

"If you don't mind. I'm not sure he's totally clear about all that's happened and us leaving today."

"I'll go with you," Sister said.

"Me, too." Frances chimed in.

"I'll watch 'Sunday Morning' while you're gone," Fred said. Which is how he missed out on everything that happened.

I slipped into the bedroom and called Major Bissell. He wasn't in, so I left word with the man who answered that I was taking Laura Stamps to Blue Bay Ranch to get her husband.

"Okay," he said. I could hear the Roadrunner's cackle in the background.

"This is important. Call and tell him."

"Yes ma'am." The man chuckled, hopefully at Wiley E. Coyote.

Going down 98, I hoped Major Bissell was already at Blue

Bay Ranch, Sister said she felt like something was going to happen, and Frances admitted she wanted to see the pink house and Jason Marley again. But all of this was discussed later, well after the fact. As we turned into the Blue Bay Ranch gate, none of the three of us had the slightest idea what was going to happen. Except, of course, I knew what possibilities existed.

We came to the bay and to the lavender house. The Stampses' car was parked in the driveway.

"Thank you so much," Laura said, opening the door.

"We'll make sure Eddie's all right before we leave." Mary Alice got out of the car. Frances and I followed her.

"Thanks. He's probably out at the boat."

To this day, I can see little sun-dried Laura walking hurriedly around the house and onto the pier with us following. The sun was shining and there was a sailboat regatta on the bay.

"Look at that!" Frances exclaimed. "Isn't that beautiful?"

"Eddie!" Laura called, striding down the pier. "You on the boat?"

Eddie came from the small cabin and waved. "Hey, honey."

Laura turned to us. "He's fine, y'all. Thanks."

"Come on, I'll take all of you for a ride," Eddie called.

"Some other day," Sister called back.

"Berry's here." Eddie motioned backward to the cabin as Berry appeared on deck.

"Hey, pretty ladies," he called. "What brings you out so early?"

"We just brought Laura over," Mary Alice answered. "How're you feeling?"

"Much better. Sorry about last night."

"Don't be. I had a good time."

Laura was standing on the pier beside the boat. "Come on, Eddie," she said, holding out her hand. "We've got to go."

"I want to go out in the boat," he said. "Berry wants to take a ride."

Laura stepped onto the boat and took her husband's arm. "Come on, sweetheart."

Berry grinned. "You better go, old buddy."

Just at that moment, the Florida Marine Patrol van pulled into Jason Marley's driveway.

"What in the world is this about?" Mary Alice wondered aloud as Major Bissell and two other officers got out of the van.

"Turn around," I whispered to her and Frances. "Go back to the car."

"What are you talking about?" Sister asked.

" 'Morning, Lieutenant Bissell," I called. "We're all over here. Mr. Stamps and Mr. West are on the boat." I grabbed Sister's arm. "Back up, damn it."

The three police officers came striding over to the Stampses' pier.

" 'Morning, ladies," Lieutenant Bissell said. Then, whispering, smiling as if we were having a pleasant conversation, "What on God's earth are you doing here?"

I smiled and whispered back. "We came to get Eddie Stamps. How the hell did I know this would happen? You should have been here an hour ago."

"Hey, Lieutenant Major," Eddie called.

"Hey, Mr. Stamps!"

"Who's the woman?" one of the officers asked.

"It's Laura Stamps," I said.

"What the hell is going on?" Sister asked.

"I think we have our murderer," Major Bissell answered.

"Y'all don't run. It'll spook him. Just turn around slowly. Be prepared to hit the ground."

"Oh, shit!" Frances said.

Laura Stamps was looking at the police officers. She was still standing on the boat, though, holding Eddie's arm.

"Mrs. Stamps?" Major Bissell called. "Could I see you for a minute?"

"What for?"

"It's about the permit to relocate the septic tank."

How in the world had he thought of that on the spur of the moment? I almost forgave him for being so slow getting here.

"You need to talk to Eddie, too," Laura called. She stepped out onto the pier and reached back for Eddie's hand. He pulled away. "Come on, Eddie. We need to see what Major Bissell wants."

We had almost made it off the pier. Laura turned and walked toward us and the three policemen, looking back over her shoulder. "Come on, sweetheart."

"Mr. West and Mr. Stamps, we need to talk to you," Major Bissell called. "If you would please get off the boat."

"Oh, Lord, they've got guns!" Frances said. And, indeed, each of the marine patrol officers was aiming pistols toward the boat.

"I'm just taking Berry for a ride, Laura," Eddie called. "We'll be back after a while."

I didn't see what happened next, but Sister did. She said Eddie turned to the dash and reached down toward the ignition. Berry West screamed, "Oh, shit!" and dived into the water. And then the whole world became hell.

The force of the explosion knocked Frances and me to the pier and Sister into the water. Metal and fiberglass whistled by like bullets. Some gut instinct told me to roll over the edge of the pier, that lying there with my hands over my ears and with my butt in the air wasn't going to go a hell of a long way in contributing to my longevity. Frances credits me with saving her life, but the truth is that she was in my way. I shoved her into the water and went in behind her, which meant that when the second explosion took out the boathouse, we were hanging onto a piling under the pier.

"Sister!" I screamed. "Sister!"

A wall of heat came roaring over us. The world was filled with raining lumber and the smell of molten fiberglass.

Frances grabbed my arm. She was saying something but I couldn't make it out. The thought flitted through my mind that I might never hear again.

"Sister!" I screamed again.

Frances tugged my arm and pointed. I turned and saw Sister hanging onto the piling behind us.

"Are you okay?" I yelled.

I think she said, "That son of a bitch Berry West!"

The rescue squad came over the bridge for us again. By this time we were on a first-name basis with them. Mary Alice, Frances, and I were okay and were simply taken into Jason Marley's house for hot showers and aspirin. Eddie was dead; Laura, badly burned, was transported to the burn center in Tallahassee. The policemen miraculouly suffered only minor burns and injuries, and as for Berry, he had disappeared.

It wasn't until the next day that we found out all the details. And a hectic twenty-four hours it was. The three of us couldn't hear, so everyone was having to shout at us, as well as us shouting at each other. (Dr. Nachman said he thought it was temporary. Thought?) Mary Alice was furious at me because I had figured out Berry West was the murderer and hadn't told her.

"It was simple!" I shouted.

Later on, when we could hear, Major Bissell would fill us in on all the details, many of which were supplied by the critically injured Laura, and many of which we had already figured out. Berry had become Millicent's lover, hoping to get her to sell him the remaining three hundred acres. She refused because of the environmental impact. Then he had enlisted Laura Stamps's help with promises of money. She was in a vulnerable position, faced with Eddie's illness. Laura was with them on the boat the morning Millicent was killed. She swore they didn't intend to kill her, that Berry forced Millicent onto the boat knowing how frightened she was of water and had her sign a bill of sale for the land. Suddenly, furiously, Millicent had turned on Berry with the gaff. They struggled and Millicent was killed. Maybe a jury would believe it.

But the day of the explosion, Sister yelled into my ear, "Laura tried to warn me, didn't she?"

"Berry was going to use your money to buy the land!"

"The hell you say!"

Haley held up her hands for silence. "Why did he kill Emily?" she wrote on a Post-it and handed it to me.

"She knew! She was spending the night at Jason's house and saw them leave. She also saw them come back without Millicent. Laura told Major Bissell Emily walked down to the boat to find out what had happened while Berry was cleaning it."

"Can of worms!" Frances shouted.

Chapter

19

B y the next morning, things had calmed down considerably. In fact, they were almost back to normal, with Sister
mad at me for figuring out what was going on and for talking to Fairchild and Major Bissell without telling her. Also,
according to Sister, it was entirely my fault that we were
almost killed and that we would forever and a day suffer
from deafness.

"They don't call it being deaf any more!" Frances yelled.
"It's audibly challenged!"

Haley and Nephew had left the night before after they
had determined that we were okay.

"I wouldn't go," Haley said, hugging me beside Nephew's
piled-up Porsche. "But Papa's here to take care of y'all."

"You remember *The Grapes of Wrath*?" Sister said as they
pulled out of the parking lot. "How everything they owned
was tied on top of their car?"

"All that Porsche needs is a California Or Bust sign," I agreed. I turned around to find Fred, but he had already gone back into the condo.

"Is Fred okay?" Frances asked.

"What?"

She pointed toward the building. "Fred. Is he okay?"

"He's all right," I said. "He's upset because we had such a close call." Which was true, and which I felt guilty about. I swear marriage is such a peculiar, delicious arrangement.

So I wasn't surprised to wake up by myself the next morning and to see Fred walking down the beach in the distance. I got some coffee and joined Sister and Frances on the balcony. That was when I was informed that our deafness was my fault.

"Lord, Sister!" I said. "Major Bissell was supposed to have arrested Berry an hour or so before we went down there. How was I to know it would take him longer to get some of the information because it was Sunday?"

"What information was he looking for?" Frances asked.

I propped my feet up on the railing. "A couple of things. One was his record as a land developer, and the other was a connection between him and Laura Stamps."

"What did he find?"

"That Berry West was basically a con man. He'd been involved in a couple of developments but both of them had gone bust. A lot of people had invested money in them, bought lots, et cetera and lost all they'd invested. Criminal charges were filed against him, but somehow he'd managed to squeak out from under them. It's why he left Georgia, though. I doubt he could have gotten away with another scam there."

"What about Laura?" Frances asked.

"She's his sister-in-law. His wife was Eddie's sister. That's how he found out about Blue Bay Ranch."

"Tell me his wife died a natural death," Sister said. "I'm sure you know."

"Well, yes, I do, and she did."

Frances sipped her coffee thoughtfully. "I'm glad Jason wasn't involved. What I can't figure out is how you knew it was Berry and Laura."

"Put two and two together," I said. I'm sure Sister said, "bullshit," but my ears were ringing so I could have been wrong. "I woke up at five o'clock in the morning and—remember that dream I told you about? About someone making somebody get on the elevator?"

"I remember."

"Well, I was half awake and suddenly I realized it was Berry's voice I had heard. You know how you get those insights sometimes?"

This time there was no mistaking the "bullshit!"

"Shut up!" I told Sister. "Anyway"—I gave her my schoolteacher look—"I figured it had to be Laura he was having the fight with. She hadn't done something she was supposed to do. And what could that be? I asked myself."

"I'm sure you're going to tell us," Sister said.

"The answer came to me clear as a bell. Laura was to deliver Millicent to the boat."

"God!" Sister moaned. "That man was just after my money and I tongue-kissed him."

"That's understandable," Frances said. "He was kind of cute. I guess he's spread all over the bay now, though."

We thought about that a moment. Then I continued with my story.

"I remembered that we hadn't asked Fairchild about those three hundred acres that weren't part of the Blue Bay Ranch parcel. So I simply got up and went over and asked him if Berry West had approached him about buying the property. He had. Fairchild also knew that Laura was deeply worried about the money she would need for Eddie's illness. Anyway, we called Major Bissell. He said they were already honing in on Berry."

"But why did he blow the boat up and how did he do it?" Frances wanted to know.

"I think I know," Sister said. "No matter how much they washed the boat, some of Millicent's blood would still be on it. Blow it up and the evidence was gone. Berry fixed it where the exhaust fans wouldn't come on. He knew a spark from the ignition would blow it sky high."

"And it could have been anybody who turned it on," I said. "Even little Sophie Berliner who was out there looking around. Which makes me think he'd gone over the edge. He was a two-bit criminal, not a murderer."

"That's crazy, Mouse. Tell Millicent, Emily, and Eddie he wasn't a murderer," Sister said shivering.

A small, black-clad figure approached the stile from the beach. She looked up and waved at us.

"Sophie will be okay," I said. And something told me it was true. But I crossed my fingers anyway.

We heard the front door slam and Fred came out onto the balcony. "Patricia Anne," he said, "you and I are having lunch at the Redneck Riviera."

At least I think that's what he said.

We four women had wished for an adventurous vacation. And we had gotten one, a lot more than we bargained for. It was hard to believe that it had been just a week ago that Mary Alice, Haley, and I had had supper at the Redneck and had run into a radiant Millicent. So much had happened, I